D0342693

ALSO BY SHAUN DAVID HUTCHINSON

HOWL

SHAUN DAVID HUTCHINSON

SIMON & SCHUSTER BFYR

NEW YORK   LONDON   TORONTO   SYDNEY   NEW DELHI

SIMON & SCHUSTER BFYR

An imprint of Simon & Schuster Children's Publishing Division
1230 Avenue of the Americas, New York, New York 10020

SIMON & SCHUSTER BOOKS FOR YOUNG READERS
and related marks are trademarks of Simon & Schuster, Inc.
For information about special discounts for bulk purchases, please contact
Simon & Schuster Special Sales at 1-866-506-1949 or business@simonandschuster.com.
The Simon & Schuster Speakers Bureau can bring authors to your live event. For more
information or to book an event, contact the Simon & Schuster Speakers Bureau
at 1-866-248-3049 or visit our website at www.simonspeakers.com.
Interior design by Tom Daly
The text for this book was set in Adobe Garamond Pro.
Manufactured in the United States of America
First Edition
2   4   6   8   10   9   7   5   3   1
CIP data for this book is available from the Library of Congress.
ISBN 9781534470927
ISBN 9781534470941 (ebook)

For the person who said, "I believe you."

Dear Reader,

Howl contains content that may be triggering. For a full list, please see the bottom of the following page.

Howl contains scenes of self-harm, homophobia, gaslighting, disordered eating, body dysmorphia, assault, and bullying. Additionally, while there are no explicit descriptions of sexual assault, much of the language used throughout is evocative of the trauma associated with sexual assault.

ONE

I DIDN'T SCREAM.

TWO

MAIN STREET WAS DARK. SUNSHINE REALTY, DR. KALUUYA
DDS, Gannon's Hardware, Merritt Books and Café, Birdie
Buchanan's Bridal Shop. Doors locked, shades drawn, the
elaborate displays that invited customers to come on in and
sit a spell during the day went dark at sundown and remained
that way until dawn.

Signs fastened to the decorative lamps that lined the
street—WELCOME TO MERRITT! alternating with MERRITT
LOVES YOU!—swayed in the hot, fetid summer wind that blew
in from the sprawl to the west. Shadows pooled around the
weak streetlamps, herding the light into tight, inescapable
circles. Canopies of Spanish moss hung from the limbs of old
oak trees, choking the illumination from the cloudless night
sky before it could reach the street below. It was so dark that

sometimes strangers on their way to Disney World would get lost and stumble across Merritt after sunset and wonder if the town had been abandoned.

But Merritt wasn't abandoned. There *was* one light that remained on after dark. At the far end of Main Street, past Merritt Baptist Church and the old elementary school, the neon glow of a garish blue-and-pink ice cream cone stood against the backdrop of the night like a beacon.

Every month, during the Merritt town council's open forum, Sudie Kennon, who'd been alive and had lived in Merritt longer than some of the oak trees, spent her allotted three minutes explaining in tedious detail why the Tasty Cones Ice Cream neon sign was a blight on the town she had been born in and would, by the grace of God, die in, though not before she'd made damn sure that sign was torn down.

Mayor Marjorie Hart and most of the members of the town council agreed with Sudie Kennon. The neon sign was garish and bright, and it did detract from Merritt's charm. Yet any motion brought to the council regarding the Tasty Cones Ice Cream sign ultimately failed. Sudie Kennon couldn't sway the mayor or the members of the council to join her holy war.

John McIntyre had endured Sudie Kennon's wrath long before he'd sat on the council. Back then, she'd been a teacher short on patience and he'd been a rambunctious sixth-grader who couldn't sit still.

Patty Ornston had only run for the council after being forced to remove the rainbow flag she'd hung from her veranda in support of her niece after Sudie Kennon had complained that it violated the rules regarding what decorations were allowed to adorn a house.

Brett Sadler didn't know why his mother and Ms. Kennon were bitter enemies, but he'd grown up hearing that Sudie was a spiteful, hateful woman whom his mother hoped would die alone and lonely, and he viewed it as his responsibility to see she got her wish.

Each of the three council members had been, at one time or another, victimized by Sudie Kennon, and so they ignored her complaints about the Tasty Cones Ice Cream sign mostly out of spite.

Sudie Kennon's compulsion to meddle and the council's petty efforts to frustrate her had probably saved my life.

THREE

CLOUDS OF MOSQUITOES STALKED ME AS I LIMPED DOWN
Main Street toward the enormous neon ice cream cone on the
horizon. Gnats clung to the crusted blood around the gashes
on my arms and became mired in the blood still oozing from
the slashes across my back.

The toe of my sole remaining sneaker caught in a pothole, and I stumbled forward, shredding my palms and knees
on the asphalt. My jeans, which hung around my hips with
little more than prayer, were already ruined. I crawled until I
reached a bench I could lean on to help me stand.

Where's my phone?

I patted my pockets. Empty.

I need to call Dad.

I reached for my phone, but my pockets were still empty.

Crickets chirped and trees rustled and bats flew overhead. I jerked my head around, trying to search every shadow, but there were too many.

Where's my phone? And my other shoe? My shirt was gone, too, but I'd left the tattered, blood-soaked rag somewhere back in the sprawl. Sweat soaked my hair and ran down my chest. I shivered in the August heat and limped onward.

The bright neon ice cream cone grew nearer as I slowly put one foot in front of the other. I was close enough to the parking lot that I could hear trucks idling. Big things built for pulling trailers and boats and for tearing through the mud and swamps that surrounded Merritt. Beasts with chrome bumpers decorated with Confederate flags, rubber testicles that dangled from the hitch, or stickers stuck to the back that said things like IF YOU CAN READ THIS THEN YOU'RE IN RANGE.

What time is it? Grandma's gonna be so pissed.

I hesitated. The lights were too bright. The sounds too loud. What if people had gotten bored of the party and had decided to get ice cream? Tasty Cones was the only place open after dark, so it was Merritt's natural hangout. I didn't want anyone to see me. The only thing capable of traveling faster than light was gossip.

But I needed help.

I spotted Pastor Wallace and Mrs. Wallace leaning against the hood of their minivan holding court. Missy Pierce was being fed ice cream by Coach Munford in a display that probably should've been private. The Hunt brood, all eleven of them, were running circles around their mom, who stood staring at a sad cone with a single scoop of vanilla ice cream melting over her fingers. I didn't recognize anyone from Finn's party. There were still people inside the shop I couldn't see, though. It was busy for a Thursday night.

I raked a hand through my hair as I shuffled out of the dark and into the halo of neon light, though the gesture was as futile as trying to put out a fire with a thimble of water. Luca would've said I was silly for caring. He would've been right.

I tried to speak, to call for help, but my throat was as dry as a California summer. No one was looking my way. I was invisible. The frantic strength that had carried me from the sprawl to Main Street and from Main to Tasty Cones evaporated all at once. My knees wobbled. They were on the verge of giving out, and if they did, I was certain I would die at the edge of the parking lot, unnoticed until a Tasty Cones employee eventually found my cold, bloody body on the pavement while taking out the garbage.

Earlier, somewhere between the party and the parking lot, I'd said I wanted to die—I'd spoken the words aloud, and I'd asked nicely. In the moment, I'd meant it. Now I wanted to take it back.

Please let me take it back.

With the last surge of will I could muster, I threw my body forward, stumbling a few steps and then finally collapsing.

One of the Hunt children, Nine of Eleven maybe, shrieked in terror. Every conversation in the parking lot skidded to a halt as the child's sound split the night, accomplishing the one thing I'd failed to do. Mrs. Hunt dropped her uneaten cone. Pastor Wallace shouted, "What in the Yankee Doodle?" Coach Munford said, "That ain't blood, is it?" while Missy Pierce slapped his arm and said, "Call the police, stupid!"

I shut my eyes, invisible no more.

"Is that Virgil Knox?"

A hand touched my shoulder. I would've flinched, but it took all my strength to keep breathing.

"Virgil? Virgil, what happened to you, son?"

"Put your phone away, Tyson. He don't need you recording this."

"Ambulance is on the way."

"Someone call his daddy."

"Virgil? What happened? Did someone do this to you?"

Tears welled in my eyes and rolled across my nose.

"A monster," I managed in a hoarse whisper. "I was attacked by a monster."

FOUR

I SWAM THROUGH A WARM POOL OF PAINKILLERS. THE
serenity was only interrupted by the numb tugging on my
skin as a doctor with more jokes than skill stitched closed the
wounds on my back and arm, and by the two cops at the foot
of my hospital bed, snickering and not bothering to be quiet
about it.

Officer Delerue looked like the kind of man who'd
become a cop because he'd had a taste of power in high school
and had become addicted to it. His hand rarely strayed far
from his holster, and his lip, nearly overshadowed by a bristly
brown mustache, remained frozen in a permanent sneer.

Officer Bruford had almost fooled me into believing he
was on my side, with his friendly smile and sympathetic eyes,
but I saw the wolf hiding in that sheep's clothing. Bruford

was the type who'd learned early on that those with real power didn't need to wield it like a cudgel. Delerue might've taken the lead during the questioning, but Bruford was in charge.

"So, are we talking Bigfoot?" Delerue asked. "What d'you think, Bruford? We got a Sasquatch out in the sprawl?"

Dr. Patterson chortled. "I would imagine the swamp's too hot for a Sasquatch."

Delerue and Bruford had been questioning me for ten minutes that had felt like an hour while the doctor stitched me up. If I could've trusted my legs to support me, I would've hopped out of bed and run.

"I seen a show about windigo," Delerue said.

"Don't they usually eat folks?" Bruford asked.

Delerue motioned at me with his chin. "Guess this one ain't got enough meat on him to bother. Monster got a taste and threw him back."

Bruford held his phone in his hand, but he'd long since given up the pretense of taking notes. "You and your daddy moved here from Seattle, ain't that right?"

"I went to school with Tommy," Delerue said. Something passed between him and Bruford that I couldn't read. A raised eyebrow, a lip twitch.

"Your folks are divorcing, is what I heard," Bruford said to me.

"So? I wasn't attacked by my parents' divorce."

Bruford shrugged. "But I bet you're pretty pissed off about it." He glanced at Delerue. "Remember Michael Miller? Set a couple fires to get his folks' attention?"

"Right. I did this to myself. I was at a party and decided to claw my own back because I was angry at my parents."

"Uh-oh," Delerue said. "Looks like you hit a sore spot." Both men chuckled.

"I don't see what's so funny," my grandpa said as he marched into the room, followed by my grandma.

Roy Knox had lived in Merritt since he was seven years old. He'd become a local hero playing quarterback for the Merritt High Coyotes, and he had only left Merritt twice in his life. The first when he enlisted to fight in the Vietnam War, the second when he went to Gainesville to study veterinary medicine at the University of Florida. He'd survived war, hurricanes, and two tussles with prostate cancer. He was an intimidating man, but he was a puppy compared to my grandma.

"Boys," she said, and both police officers wiped the smirks off their faces and snapped to attention.

Harper Lynn Thurston Knox believed there was no situation good manners couldn't improve. She'd grown up in South Carolina and had met Grandpa while he was in Gainesville. Her unassuming demeanor hid a wealth of strange skills and talents. She could fly a crop duster or field dress a deer carcass as easily as plan an elaborate menu for a local meeting of the Daughters of the American Revolution.

"What happened?" It wasn't clear if Grandpa was talking to me or the cops, but Bruford answered.

"The boy wandered into the Tasty Cones parking lot covered in blood. Lance Munford phoned it in."

Delerue cleared his throat. "He claims he was out in the sprawl when a wild animal attacked him. Maybe a raccoon or something." He shrugged. "We got word of panthers up north, but we ain't seen 'em around here. Doc treated him for rabies just in case."

Grandma moved closer to my bed, edging Dr. Patterson, who was finishing up, out of the way. She looked at the bandages covering my left arm. "Do you honestly expect me to believe a raccoon did this?"

"Could've been a gator," Delerue said. "Or a bear."

Grandpa stood with his arms folded across his chest, staring at Bruford and Delerue without blinking or speaking for so long that it made *me* anxious. Finally, he said, "Why don't we talk outside?"

The officers looked like they were being led to their executions. I struggled to find an ounce of sympathy for them.

"Where's Dad?" My throat was dry. I reached for the cup of ice chips sitting on the table beside me.

"Right where he ought to be," Grandma said. "Working."

"Did you call him?"

It was the middle of the night, and Grandpa and Grandma had almost definitely been sleeping when the call had come from the hospital, but Grandma had still taken the time to put on her face and her pearls and to make her hair presentable.

"What good would that have done, Virgil? You're safe, and it's not like your daddy can do anything for you. What use would it be for him drive two hours back to Merritt so he could sit by your bed and watch you sleep?"

Everything Grandma said made sense—Dad was a fire-fighter and a paramedic, but the only work he could get was in a town two hours south of Merritt. He worked twenty-four-hour shifts and wouldn't be home until the next morning—but that didn't stop me from wishing he was with me.

"What about my mom?"

"You can call Clara when we get home. I'm sure she doesn't need you disturbing her beauty sleep."

Mom was on the West Coast, where it was only a little after ten in the evening. She would've still been awake, lying in bed with a glass of red wine and her laptop. But I didn't want to talk to her while Grandma was around, anyway.

"I wasn't attacked by a raccoon. Or a gator."

Grandma patted my arm. "Hush, now."

"It was a monster—"

"You're safe, Virgil." Her voice was as sharp as a talon. "There's no loitering in the past. All talking about it can do now is keep you from moving forward."

The past. Like it happened a year ago instead of a couple of hours.

Grandpa marched in, his hands in his pockets. "What were you doing in the sprawl, Virgil?"

Wanna see something cool?

"How many times have I told you the sprawl's nothing but swamp and to stay away from it?"

"I thought you were at the Ducketts' house?" Grandma said.

"I was—"

"Boyd Bruford said he smelled alcohol on you." Grandpa's thick, wiry eyebrows underlined the question his statement implied.

Grandma's lips thinned to two sharp wires. "Kitty and Douglas let Finn run wild. I'm playing tennis with Kitty Sunday, and I've half a mind to say something."

"How much were you drinking?" Grandpa asked.

"Not much," I said. "A beer. Maybe two."

"And then you went wandering where I've told you explicitly not to go?" Grandpa shook his head. "You're lucky a couple cuts is all you walked away with."

"Yes, sir."

"And I don't want to hear any more of this monster business," Grandpa said. "Anyone asks, you tell them it was a cougar or a bear."

It wasn't a cougar or a bear.

"Bad enough Missy Pierce heard you talking that nonsense."

Grandma nodded along. "No doubt she's already spreading rumors on those internet sites." There were only two things my grandma refused to do: clean toilets and use the internet.

"I just want to go home," I said. "Can I please go home?"

Grandpa's back was rigid, his face stern. "I suppose there's no reason for you to stay. I'll see about getting you discharged."

Grandma kissed the side of my head. "We'll have you home in no time."

But their home wasn't what I'd meant.

FIVE

HOT BREATH SOAKS MY NECK; A CLAWED HAND PUSHES
my face deeper into the mud. Bristly, wiry hair brushes the back
of my arms. My shoulder burns where its teeth penetrated me,
and I feel its poison in my blood.

It lowers itself onto my back, and I don't scream.

I wonder what Luca and Deja are having for dinner. Deja will
eat anything, but Luca's so damn picky. I wonder if anyone at the
party noticed I left. I wonder if Jarrett found someone else to pin
against a wall in an empty room. I wonder how long it will take
Grandma and Grandpa to realize I haven't come home yet. Dad
told me Grandpa used to wait up for him with a clock and a belt.
If Dad didn't beat one, Grandpa would whoop him with the other.

A whimper escapes my lips as it rakes its claws across my
back. I clench my eyes shut as tightly as I can and try to pretend

I'm sleeping. I go still and hope it kills me quickly.

"Virgil," it whispers in my ear. "Virgil, where are you?"

I blinked the sleep from my eyes and shifted, yelping when I accidentally rolled onto my back.

"Virgil?" Morning light spilled into the closet as my dad opened the door. He loomed over me, his hands on his hips, wearing his blue cargo pants and work shirt. "What the hell are you doing in the closet?"

It took me a moment to realize that's where I was. That I wasn't in the sprawl with a monster crouching on my back, crooning my name.

"They pumped me full of drugs in the hospital," I said, hoping Dad wouldn't press the issue.

Dad frowned and offered me his hand. Where my uncle Franklin had gotten my grandpa's sturdy looks and my grandma's sly smile, my dad had wound up with Grandpa's receding hairline and Grandma's wide hips. Mom used to joke that Dad was lucky she liked men with a lot of trunk space.

I hugged my pillow to my chest and limped toward my bed. Everything hurt. In addition to the injuries from tooth and claw, I was bruised in places I didn't know could be bruised, and every bit of exposed skin was covered in mosquito bites. But the pain went beyond the physical. I felt like a slick of rancid grease was floating on top of my blood as it coursed through my body, tainting every cell.

Dad sat on the edge of my desk, studying me like a paramedic rather than a father, cataloging and assessing each injury. "Your grandma told me what happened."

"I bet," I muttered.

"What were you thinking? Were you just drunk or were you high, too?"

"I wasn't high *or* drunk. I had a couple drinks."

Dad crooked his finger at me. "Let me see." When I was close, he turned me around and lifted the back of my shirt. His hands were cold. I shivered when he peeled back the gauze covering the stitches.

"Jesus Christ, Virgil." Dad smoothed the tape back into place. "What were you even doing in the sprawl?"

"I needed some air."

"There wasn't air at the party?"

Bass-heavy rap shakes the furniture, and the white boys in the living room shout along with the words—all the words—without the slightest hint of self-awareness.

I pull out my phone to see if I've gotten any messages from Luca. Nothing. But he posted some new snaps from kayaking with his dad.

"Hey," Jarrett says, "wanna see something cool?"

"I shouldn't have gone—"

"You're damn right," Dad said.

"—to the party."

Dad's mouth was still open, but he must've forgotten what he was going to say.

"I hate it here, Dad. I want to go home."

"We talked about this, Virgil."

"*You* talked about it. I didn't get a say."

Dad rubbed his eyes. I didn't know how busy work had been for him—some shifts he could manage a few hours of uninterrupted sleep, some he could hardly lie down for twenty minutes before he was called out again—but the bags under his eyes were definitely over the weight limit, and he was going to pay extra for carrying them.

"I can't do this right now, okay?" We'd only been in Merritt for two weeks, but Dad's accent was already reasserting itself.

"Yes, sir."

Dad nodded once. "Now, what was it that attacked you last night? Grandma says it was probably a cougar, but there hasn't been a cougar around here in years."

It was a monster. "I don't know."

Dad fixed me with a half frown. If he hadn't been so exhausted, he probably would've pressed me further. "Well, I'm glad you're all right, but I hope you learned a lesson."

That underage drinking leads to being viciously attacked and left for dead? "Yes, sir."

Dad cracked his jaw, yawning, and stood. "You call your

mother yet? I don't want her accusing me of keeping anything from her."

"Lost my phone."

"Here." Dad tossed me his. "Call your mom. Then get a shower so I can change your bandages before I hit the hay. We'll go out tomorrow and get your stuff for school."

I waited for him to leave before calling my mom. It went straight to voicemail, as I'd assumed it would, being that it was only a little after six in the morning there.

"Hey, Mom. I got attacked by a monster last night. I'm alive, but I wound up with something like sixty stitches and had to be treated for rabies. I hate it here, and I want to come home, but you already know that. If you loved me, you never would've sent me away in the first place."

I didn't say that.

The message I actually left was, "It's me calling from Dad's phone because I lost mine. Nothing major. Just call me when you can."

After hanging up, I logged in to my messages to check what I missed. I'd sent my boyfriend Luca a selfie of me hiding in one of the upstairs bathrooms at Finn Duckett's house during the party. Across it, I'd scrawled: **save me lol**.

Luca had opened it at 10:53 p.m., but he still hadn't replied.

SIX

THE WI-FI AT MY GRANDPARENTS' HOUSE WAS SO SLOW
that using it was barely faster than sending a message by
winging it into the air on a paper airplane, the foundation
creaked at night, and the air-conditioning struggled to keep
the house cool. But the house had the best water pressure and
a hot water tank that seemed endless.

The nurse who'd discharged me had said I should keep
my stitches covered and dry for forty-eight hours, but Dad
told me that was nonsense, so I turned the water as hot as
I could stand it and scrubbed my skin until I felt as raw
on the outside as I did on the inside. I washed my hair
and rinsed it. I washed it again and rinsed it again. By the
third time, I was worried it might fall out, but I washed it
a fourth time anyway. I used a file to dig the dirt and mud

from under my nails, scraping until the beds bled.

I envied lizards their ability to shed their skin. I wished I could scrape off the entire top layer of mine and leave it behind so I didn't have to keep living in the skin the monster had touched. Eventually, my skin would flake off, a little at a time every day, but that would take a couple of weeks, and I wanted it gone now.

I shut off the water and stepped out of the shower. I didn't recognize the person in the mirror. A bird chest and a round belly. Weak, flabby arms barely bigger around than a pool cue. I didn't think it was possible to look skinny and fat at the same time.

I wiped the steam that had fogged the mirror and tried to find what it was about me that had looked so tasty to the thing in the woods, but I didn't see it. Puberty seemed to have mostly passed me by with a shrug, which meant that I rarely had trouble with zits but that I also looked twelve instead of nearly sixteen.

"Hey," Jarrett says, "wanna see something cool?"

"Not really." I barely glance up from my phone. I'm trying to figure out which lake Luca and his dad are at, which is tough, seeing as most of the pictures are of Luca's feet. He got new Jordans. Gold and black. No one in our group could pull them off but him.

"Don't be lame," Jarrett says.

"Shouldn't use that word." Annoyed that Luca took the time to post his kayaking pictures but not to say hi to his boyfriend, I shove my phone in my pocket to avoid writing something I might regret.

Jarrett Hart has a charming smile. One eyebrow is slightly raised so that he always looks like he's on the verge of asking an embarrassing question. He's handsome in an effortless way that annoys me.

"Words are just words. They don't mean nothing."

"That's not . . ." I shake my head. "Of course words mean things. That's literally their purpose." I snatch the beer from Jarrett that he offered me earlier. One beer shouldn't do much. Grandma wouldn't let me leave without eating dinner, so I've got a stomach full of chicken and collard greens.

Jarrett motions with his head toward the stairs. "Come on. You'll like it."

Jarrett Hart didn't look sixteen. He looked eighteen at least. I'd overheard him bragging he could buy beer at the Sunoco by the interstate and that he didn't even need a fake ID. Maybe it was because he was handsome or looked older than his age or because his mom had been mayor of Merritt for ten years, so everyone let Jarrett get away with everything.

Why hadn't the monster attacked him instead of me?

I pulled on my underwear and a pair of basketball shorts, leaving my shirt off so Dad could put fresh gauze on.

Grandpa's voice echoed down the hall when I opened the door.

"You're too soft on the boy, Tommy. He needs discipline."

"Our ideas of discipline are very different, Dad."

"Which is the reason Virgil's running around in the middle of the night getting drunk and making up stories about monsters."

"So, what? You think I should whip him with the belt? After he spent the night in the hospital?"

"He'd think twice about his decisions next time."

"Leave Virgil to me," Dad said. "I can take care of him."

Grandpa didn't need a belt to whip Dad. "You can hardly take care of yourself, Tommy. You fled Merritt as fast as you could after high school. You wouldn't have returned if you had anywhere else to go."

"That doesn't mean I need lessons on how to raise my boy from you two."

Grandma chimed in. "You and Franklin turned out all right."

"Frankie's an alcoholic, Mom."

"Don't take that tone with your mother." Anger crept into Grandpa's voice. "I know you don't want to hear it, but Virgil's weak. Living with Clara out West has turned him into one of those—"

"What, Dad? One of those what?"

"What your father means is that Merritt will be good for Virgil. We just want to help you, Tommy. Both of you."

Dad kept arguing, though not as forcefully as before, but maybe Grandpa was right. After all, predators hunted the weakest prey, didn't they?

SEVEN

NO MATTER WHICH WAY I SAT, THE PATIO BENCH SWING
was uncomfortable. The cushions pushed into the gashes on
my back. The summer heat made the wounds itch, too. But it
was still better than being inside with Grandma and Grandpa.

I'd been hiding outside for an hour. I played the conversation I'd overheard on a loop, trying to find the flaws
in Grandma and Grandpa's logic. I couldn't. Instead, I distracted myself trading messages with Luca. He was in a
chatty mood, and I hadn't wanted to ruin it by telling him
what had happened yet. I felt bad keeping it from him, but
it's not like he could do anything about it from the other side
of the country.

"Hey, Virgil."

I didn't scream.

Jarrett Hart stood at the bottom of the steps of the patio with his hands in his pockets.

"Hey," I said.

He reached for the door and opened it without asking. "I heard about . . ." His voice trailed off as his eyes roved over the places where the gauze peeked out from under my clothes. "Damn, dude. I thought Finn was joking."

"Nope."

Jarrett pulled a plastic stool over and sat across from me. His long legs bent like a grasshopper's. He was still pretty in the light of day, but he seemed somewhat more timid than he had the night before.

Don't tell no one about this, all right?

"What happened?" Jarrett's sincerity felt real. I hadn't expected that from him.

I shrugged.

"Finn heard you got attacked by a possum out in the sprawl, but he was pretty hungover and he's usually full of shit, so . . ."

"Wasn't a possum." If Finn had told Jarrett about the attack, then someone must have told Finn, which meant the story had already made its way around Merritt.

"I can see that." Jarrett's eyes wandered over me, lingering on the places where I'd been hurt worst, as if he could see the wounds through my clothes.

Teeth dig into my shoulder. It worries me like a dog with a chew toy and then flings me aside.

"How'd you even get out to the sprawl?"

I shook my head. "Don't remember."

"You must've been wasted."

"I wasn't." Dad's phone vibrated. I would've ignored it if it'd been my phone because it was probably just Luca responding to my last message. But it could've been Dad's work, so I took a peek. Luca had sent me a picture of his dog, Willow, an enormous, cuddly wheaton terrier.

Jarrett was watching me. "Boyfriend?"

I nodded.

"Bet he's worried sick about you."

"He doesn't know."

Jarrett raised his eyebrows but didn't comment. "So if it wasn't a possum that got you, what was it?"

"It was a monster." I don't know why I said it. Maybe because it felt good to speak the truth or maybe just to see Jarrett's reaction. I should've kept quiet.

Jarrett's mouth twisted into a laugh before he realized I wasn't joking. "There're no monsters in the sprawl. Gators, sure, but monsters?"

He didn't believe me. Just like Officers Delerue and Bruford. Just like Grandma and Grandpa. Just like Dad.

"What do you want, Jarrett? Did you come over to make

sure I wouldn't tell anyone about what happened at the party?"

Hey, wanna see something cool?

"I said I wouldn't tell anyone, and I won't."

Jarrett waved me off. "I ain't worried about that."

"Then what? Why're you here?"

"Just came to see if you're okay."

"Well, I'm fine."

"Sure you are." Jarrett stood, looming over me for a moment before moving toward the screen door. "See you in school Monday, Virgil."

EIGHT

DAD PULLED THE TRUCK INTO THE PARKING LOT AT TARGET, but he didn't shut off the engine. The cab still reeked of cigarette smoke from the previous owner, and no amount of cleaning could exorcise it.

"Can't we do this tomorrow?" I asked.

"Church tomorrow." Dad sat with his hands on the wheel. "And supper at Frankie's after."

"No thanks."

"If I have to go, so do you."

"Who says you have to go?"

Dad finally shut off the engine. "We're living at your grandparents' house; we have to abide by their rules."

There hadn't been many rules back home in Seattle because having rules meant having to enforce them, and neither of my parents had been that invested. So long as I did well in school, didn't burn anything down, and kept out of jail, my parents left me alone. Grandma and Grandpa, on the other hand, loved their rules, and Dad had fallen right back into following them the moment we'd arrived in Merritt.

"What do I need from here, anyway?" I changed the subject, figuring I wasn't going to make any headway with him on the church issue.

Dad tapped his phone's screen and handed it to me. There was an email with a list of school supplies I was expected to have for the first day, which was on Monday.

"I've got a backpack, and when have you ever seen me highlight anything?"

"You need clothes, too," Dad said.

"There's nothing wrong with the clothes I've got."

Dad shut his eyes and took a deep breath. "I'm really trying here, Virgil, so can you please not argue with everything I say?"

"I just—"

"Do you think I want to be in this town? Do you think I want to be living with my parents again? Having to see the people I grew up with snickering about how I came crawling back? You think I want to hear them whispering about you? About the way you dress and the way you talk, and now about this monster nonsense?"

It lowers itself onto my back.

I didn't scream.

"Merritt will chew you up if you let it, and I wouldn't have brought you here if I'd had any other options. The least I can do is help you avoid the worst of it." Dad's hands were clenched into fists. "I know you're hurting, which is why I left you alone yesterday, but it's time to suck it up and move on. So we're going to get your damn school supplies and we're going to find you some new clothes that you'll probably hate, and all I want to hear out of your mouth is 'Yes, sir' or 'No, sir.' Okay? Can you do that?"

I opened the truck, got out, and walked toward the store.

Dad caught up to me at the entrance. He pulled out a red cart and passed it to me. "Start getting what you need. I'll find you in a few minutes."

"Yes, sir." The moment he was out of sight, I leaned on the cart. I'd been holding the pain at bay, ignoring the aches in my muscles and the way the stitches itched as sweat from the hot, sticky Florida air soaked the bandages. Being outside for two minutes was enough to make me need a shower.

As I pushed the cart up and down the aisles, looking at the products on the shelves without really seeing them, I thought I must be dreaming.

I lie on my stomach, my arms askew, and try not to breathe. I can hear it panting. Feel it moving.

There was no way I'd been shoved onto my stomach by a monster the day before yesterday. There was no way I'd caught the reflection of a two-thirds-full moon in a stagnant puddle where mosquitoes had laid their eggs.

Maybe if I stay perfectly still, it'll think I'm dead and will lose interest and leave.

There was no way I'd been *there* and now I was here. Inside a Super Target.

A whimper escapes my lips as it rakes its claws across my back. I clench my eyes shut as tightly as I can and try to pretend I'm sleeping. I pray for it to kill me quickly.

"Virgil Knox?"

I turned around and elbowed a display of shampoo, sending a couple bottles skittering across the floor. The woman standing behind me was a short pear with a PE teacher's no-nonsense ponytail and a gold cross nestled between the flaps of her plaid shirt.

The woman shoved the shampoo back on the shelf, managing to knock a couple more down. Finally, she rolled her eyes and left them. "Jodie Duran." She stuck out a stubby-fingered hand. "Merritt's chief of police."

"Oh." My manners took over, and I shook her hand.

"Heard you had some trouble out in the sprawl." Chief Duran frowned like she smelled something rotten.

"Yeah."

"Sorry I didn't come talk to you in the hospital, but my momma was having a bit of a crisis herself."

"I hope she's okay."

Chief Duran didn't look optimistic. "Diabetes is probably

going to take her leg this time. I told her to stop eating those damn Reese's Peanut Butter Cups, but they're more addictive than fentanyl."

"I'm sorry to hear that."

"She might wind up saving me some money if I can find a shoe store that'll sell me shoes one foot at a time."

"Sure."

Duran shook her head. "You got your sense of humor from your granddaddy, didn't you? Roy Knox wouldn't know a joke if it crawled up his pants leg and—"

"Jodie?" My dad stopped at the end of the aisle, confused by the scene in front of him. I'd been standing there longer, and I didn't understand what was going on either.

"Tommy Knox, you got old." Jodie Duran eyed my dad up and down. "Where the hell'd your hair go?"

"My back," Dad said. "Where'd your waist go?"

"My ass."

Dad and Jodie Duran cracked up and fell toward each other like old friends. We'd visited Merritt a dozen times over the years, but I still forgot sometimes that Dad had grown up here. He probably went to high school with three-quarters of the town.

"Frankie told me you'd moved back with your boy, but I thought he was pulling my leg until I saw the report Delerue filed about some animal attack."

Dad blushed and glanced toward the floor. "Sorry Virgil

wasted your time with that. He shouldn't have been out there in the first place."

Chief Duran leaned in conspiratorially. "Anything that keeps Delerue from doing real police work is fine by me. Don't get me wrong; he was something else when he was playing for the Coyotes in high school, but I think he took a few too many hits to the head." She turned to me. "You doing all right, Virgil? You don't look too chewed up, but that don't necessarily mean much."

"I'm fine."

"Report said it was a bear?"

It was a monster. "Could've been. I didn't get a good look at it."

A clawed hand pushes my face deeper into the mud.

"Mom and Dad told him to stay away from the sprawl."

Chief Duran laughed. "When'd you ever let anything your folks said stop *you*? If I recall correctly—"

"Let's not go telling tales out of school, Jodie."

"All I'm saying is Finn Duckett's parties are more dangerous than the sprawl," she said. "I wouldn't go wandering around neither after dark."

Dad looked chagrined. "I told him the party was fine. I hoped he'd make some friends before school starts up."

"How'd that work out for you, Virgil?"

Hey, wanna see something cool?

Dad and Chief Duran were looking at me like I had spiders crawling out of my ears.

I don't know where I am. I pull out my phone to call for help, but I don't know who to call. Everyone I love is on the other side of the world.

"You okay?" Dad asked.

"I'm going to look at phones." I turned to leave, but Duran stopped me.

"You ever need anything, you call me, all right?" She handed me an actual business card. I didn't know people still used them. I shoved it in my wallet and took off.

Dad caught up to me a few minutes later. I was browsing the rows of cell phones, each one more expensive than the last.

"We should get you some clothes," he said.

"I need a phone."

"Then you shouldn't have lost yours."

Something crashes into me and I hit the moist ground. My phone slips out of my hand and spins off into the dark.

I kept my eyes on the screens, still hoping to see a reflection that looked like me. "It's not like I did it on purpose."

"You're not getting a new phone, Virgil." Dad's voice softened. "But tomorrow you can ask Frankie if he's got a spare you can use. He never throws anything out."

I rolled my eyes and tried to walk away. Dad grabbed my shoulder, and I screamed as his fingers dug into the bite marks. The red-shirted Target employees stopped and stared. The other customers slowed down and pretended not to stare.

I feel its poison in my blood.

"I'm sorry!" Dad yelled. "I forgot about the stitches! I forgot!"

I scowled and shook him off. "It's fine." It wasn't fine. Nausea lurked around the edges of my consciousness, and it was only my anger that kept it at bay. I'd hoped I'd be able to wear Dad down about the phone issue, but I gave up and headed toward the clothing aisles to escape the gawkers.

Dad and I spent an hour collecting the supplies on the school's list, even though I had no use for any of it. I got new jeans, a couple shirts, and some underwear and socks. Dad picked most of it out because I kept saying I didn't care. The faster we left the store, the better.

When we were finally standing in line at the cash register, a guy who was older than me but younger than my dad jogged over to us.

"Mr. Knox, glad I caught you." The guy's name tag read TODD. He was kind of doughy and bland, like a loaf of white bread. "Any chance we could do that interview Tuesday at three instead of one?"

"Sure. Three's fine."

"Good. I'll see you then." Todd ambled away.

I waited for Dad to explain, but it didn't seem like he was going to. Finally, I said, "Interview?"

"Yeah, Virgil."

"But you already have a job."

"And soon, hopefully, I'll have two." He glanced at me. "Raising you isn't cheap."

NINE

I STARED AT THE PHONE UNCLE FRANK HAD GIVEN ME AND forced myself to smile. The thing was a brick at least a decade old, and it took a whole minute to start up when I turned it on.

"Thanks, Uncle Frank."

"Don't worry about it, kiddo." Uncle Frank had an easy, mischievous smile that had made him my favorite relative when I was younger. It wasn't until I was older that I realized his smile was simple misdirection. That he used it to prevent anyone from digging beneath the surface. "We're All Just Fine" could've been the Knox family motto.

Before supper, I snuck off to find a quiet room where I could plug in my new old phone, set it up, and transfer my number. The first thing I did when I finished was call Luca.

"Hey, Virgil!" The voice on the other end of the phone

didn't belong to Luca, and I had to check the screen to make sure I'd dialed the correct number.

"Deja?"

"Duh. Who were you expecting?"

"Uh, Luca?"

Deja Lewis's manic laughter filled my ear, and I couldn't help smiling as I pictured her face and her cheeks and her unbridled joy. Deja was Luca's best friend, and mine. We'd been a tight group since eighth grade, but Deja and Luca had a special bond that I sometimes envied.

"He's swimming in the lake," she said. "I saw your number come up, and since you never call *me* . . ."

I shouldn't have been surprised they were at Green Lake. Luca was practically half fish. He'd joined the swim team just so he'd have an excuse to use the heated pool during the winter. I imagined Luca standing on the diving platform in the middle of Green Lake, waiting to jump into the water until he was sure enough people were watching. My boy loved an audience.

"I was gonna call you—"

"Sure." Deja drew out the word dramatically and laughed. "How've you been?"

It looms over me, framed by the night and the stars and moss-choked oak trees. The smell hits me first. Like a decomposing corpse. Sweet in a way that fools my brain for a

fraction of a second before I realize it's rotting flesh.

"All right, I guess."

"How's Merritt? As bad as you feared?"

Finding a comfortable position to sit was impossible because of the stitches, and the sounds of my cousins chasing each other through the house kept intruding. I had to plug my finger into my free ear to shut them out. "I went to a party Thursday night that you would've hated."

"No cute boys?"

"Everyone here acts like Wes Krenik-Scott."

Deja made a sound that was a mix of gagging and groaning. "So a bunch of entitled white boys who think their shit don't stink?"

"Who like to shoot things."

"Entitled white boys with guns. Sounds like paradise."

"Hardly."

Someone hollered Deja's name in the background. I strained to listen for Luca's easy, husky voice.

"You're busy," I said. "It's cool."

"When're you coming home, Virgil? We miss you."

Never. "Soon. I hope."

"Did Luca show you his tattoo?"

"Luca got a tattoo?!"

Deja's laugh made the phone's cheap speaker crackle. "I can't even. You just have to see it."

"Seriously, Deja, what'd he get?" My eyes had roved over every square centimeter of Luca's perfect skin, and I was having trouble imagining a tattoo marring the landscape. The skin I'd left him in wasn't the same as he was wearing now. I guess we had that in common.

"No way. He'll kill me if I don't let him tell you the story."

"Then put him on."

"He's—" Whatever else Deja said came through muffled. "Sorry, Virgil, gotta run. Watch out for hurricanes or gators or whatever."

"Tell Luca to call me."

Deja ended the call before I finished.

I immediately sent Luca a message: You got a tattoo???

I couldn't believe Luca had gotten a tattoo without talking to me. We used to talk about everything. We used to share everything.

The door to the den flung open. Ciara charged in and launched herself at me. I caught her but kept her at arm's length to protect my stitches. She was four with red hair from her mom and had enough energy to power the state of Texas.

"Come play!" Ciara grabbed my hand and tugged me toward the hall. "Jimmy and RJ won't let me play with them, and I'm *bored*."

I glanced at my phone to see if Luca had responded. He hadn't. "Yeah, all right. What're we playing?"

* * *

After chasing and being chased by my cousins for twenty minutes, I grabbed a soda and sat at one of the picnic benches in the yard. The sun was burning my neck and arms as surely as Uncle Frank was burning the burgers on the grill. Dad hovered behind him, his shoulders tense, dying to take over. Grandma and Grandpa had stolen the only seats in the shade, and nothing was moving them. Aunt Kelly, Frank's wife, sat with her sister near my grandparents, but not too near.

"Were you really attacked by a bear?" Astrid asked.

Astrid was Uncle Frank's stepdaughter, though he'd been her father for so long that no one made the distinction. She looked more related to the Addams Family than ours, but she was one of us, regardless. Her razor-cut hair was streaked black and purple, and she wore more makeup than a drag queen. She didn't dress like most of the teenage girls in Merritt, either. She wore lots of corduroy pants and baggy T-shirts. We'd hung out when I'd visited before, but I didn't actually know much about her. I got the impression she preferred it that way.

I lifted my arm and peeled back the edge of the bandage so Astrid could see the stitches. The skin around the wounds was bruised and purple, and it itched constantly.

Teeth dig into my shoulder. It worries me like a dog with a chew toy and then flings me aside.

Astrid didn't grimace or flinch. She examined the gashes and then nodded that she'd seen enough. "Did you fight back? Everyone thinks you're supposed to play dead if you're attacked by a bear, but that's only brown bears, and they're not native to Florida. We have black bears. You have to fight those. Punch them right in the snout. Did you punch the bear?"

I lie on my stomach, my arms askew, and try not to breathe.

"It probably wasn't a bear," I said.

"You looked pretty messed up when you stumbled into the Tasty Cones parking lot."

I was smoothing the bandage back into place. I looked up sharply. "You were there?"

Astrid shook her head. "Saw the video, though. Pictures, too." She fished her phone out of her pocket and tapped the screen before handing it over. There I was, bloody and shirtless in the parking lot, just like she'd said.

"Don't read the comments."

Too late.

Eat a sandwich, dude.

I would've fought it off. No way that would've happened to me.

WTF was he doing in the sprawl at night for anyway? Did he hang a steak around his neck too???

yikes! Was he that ugly before the leopard ate his face?

Job 37:8

you know he probably faked it for the attention

what a wuss. I've seen people hurt way worse than that

Astrid took her phone back before I could read more, but I'd burned every word into my memory. "Well, at least you won't be the new kid at school tomorrow, seeing as everyone already knows who you are."

"Is that supposed to make me feel better?"

"Sure."

"How?"

Astrid shrugged and motioned at her phone. "Video like that's usually the bottom for most folks. So, for you, there's nowhere to go but up."

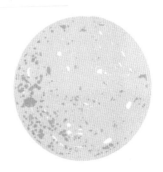

TEN

MY MOM FINALLY ANSWERED MY CALL, BUT SHE DIDN'T
sound happy about it. "Sorry, Virgil. I'm about to hop onto a
video call for a meeting."

I was exhausted from spending the day at Uncle Frank's,
and my temper snapped. "I'm fine, by the way. It only took
sixty-three stitches to close the wounds on my arm and back."

Mom fell silent.

I didn't scream.

"I talked to your dad," she finally said. "He told me it
wasn't serious."

"Sure."

She went quiet again. I checked the phone's screen to
make sure she was still connected.

"Do you want me to fly to Florida, Virgil? Is that what
you want?"

"I *want* to come home."

Mom sighed. I could see her tucking a loose strand of hair behind her ear and rolling her eyes. "I'm not the one who decided to move to that backward town. Your father could have stayed in Seattle."

"Why can't I live with you?"

"You know why. I have to work, Virgil. And I can't leave you home alone that much."

"I'm almost sixteen, Mom. I can take care of myself."

"You've certainly proven that," she snapped. "Do you know how much that hospital bill is going to cost?"

A whimper escapes my lips as it rakes its claws across my back.

"Forget it. I have to go."

"Virgil, wait."

"What?"

"I'm sorry. It's been a long day, and it's still not over. Can we discuss this tomorrow?"

"Sure."

"Damn. Not tomorrow. Wednesday would be best."

"Wednesday's fine."

"You can tell me how you managed to get attacked by a bear in a swamp in the middle of the night."

"It wasn't a bear."

An alert dinged. "Damn, that's Glenn. Love you, Virgil!" The line went dead.

I checked my messages. Still no reply from Luca. I knew a long-distance relationship was going to be hard, but I hadn't anticipated this. Always waiting around for Luca to remember I existed. Constantly wondering if he'd already moved on.

Someone knocked on my door and then came in without waiting for me to answer. I was expecting Grandma, but it was Dad carrying a plate covered with tinfoil. "I noticed you didn't eat much at Frankie's."

"I wasn't hungry."

Dad set the plate on my desk. I wondered how he'd snuck it past Grandma and Grandpa, who had strict rules about not eating anywhere but in the kitchen or dining room.

"I'm at the station tomorrow, so I won't be here when you leave for school in the morning."

"Okay."

"The bus will pick you up at six forty-eight at the end of the road."

I wrinkled my nose at the idea of riding a school bus.

"You're welcome to use one of the bicycles in the shed," Dad added.

"All right." The smell of the food turned my stomach. Everything had looked good—baked beans, potato salad, corn on the cob; Uncle Frank had even managed to not burn a few of the burgers—but my appetite had fled the moment I'd tried to eat.

Dad pursed his lips and furrowed his brow. "Merritt

High's going to be different from school in Seattle."

"I figured."

"Just give it a chance, though, okay?"

"Wasn't that why I went to that stupid party?"

Dad cocked his head and pursed his lips. "Did something happen while you were there? Did you get into a fight?"

Jarrett shuts the door and flings himself at me.

"No."

Dad patted my leg as he stood. "Look, Virgil, folks here are different than you're used to, and you're gonna need a thicker skin to be a Coyote." He left and shut the door behind him.

Maybe he was right. Maybe if I'd had thicker skin, I wouldn't have needed so many stitches.

ELEVEN

The top of the head of the bronze Merritt High School Coyote that stood guard in the courtyard watching the buses unload was shiny from the hands that had rubbed it reflexively as they'd passed. The animal was curved like a mountain road, with its nose at the peak. I wondered if it had a name or if it was just "Coyote."

"Outta the way." A tall girl pushed me aside so she could exit the bus and was gone before I could apologize for taking up space.

Merritt High School was a sprawl of buildings connected by covered walkways with doors thrown open in welcome. No security guards, no gates surrounding the campus to keep students in or out. Just kids streaming into the buildings from every direction like ants returning to their nest.

I hadn't been nervous about meeting people on my first day of high school at Lincoln because I'd had Luca. I hadn't worried about getting lost trying to find my classes because Deja had an older sister who'd already told her where to find everything we'd need. I'd actually felt sorry for the kids who'd come from private middle schools or who'd recently moved to the area as I watched them wander like ships without a compass and no shore in sight. Now I was the one lost and alone.

But Merritt High wasn't just a different school. It was a totally unfamiliar planet. I was surrounded by cowboy boots and sun-kissed skin and so much swagger. They looked like aliens to me, except *I* was the alien. I was the weird new kid who wore hoodies even though it was eighty degrees at seven in the morning. I was the freak who'd been attacked by a monster. Someone had doxxed me, leaking my phone number and email address. I'd woken up that morning to texts on my phone and messages across different social media accounts calling me a liar, saying the monster should've finished the job, commenting on my ugly clothes and hideous face. People who didn't know me, people who had only seen me in church or passed me in the grocery store, had already made up their minds that I was worthless and unworthy and worse things I can't bear to repeat.

I wanted to turn around and run, but I couldn't. Instead, I adjusted my backpack on my shoulder, careful to keep it from hitting my back, and headed for the entrance. As I walked inside, I felt like I was being swallowed.

I had geometry first period with Mr. Gardner, which seemed a terrible way to start my day. Not that anyone had asked my opinion. Second period was world history with Mrs. Sanchez, followed by world lit, biology, and gym.

The classes were boring. My teachers took roll, introduced themselves, and laid out what they expected of us—show up on time, turn in homework, study hard . . . the usual. I tuned most of it out. Coach Munford gave me a reprieve in gym, telling me I didn't have to dress out until my doctor said it was okay to participate.

Astrid had gotten it right when she'd said everyone had seen the video and would know who I was. I hadn't made any friends—most of the other students gaped at me in the hall-way or whispered comments under their breath as I passed—but nothing truly disastrous had happened, either.

Then the bell for lunch rang.

At my old school in Seattle, we'd been allowed to leave for lunch. We'd swarm through the neighborhood like locusts. Sometimes we'd walk down the hill to Dick's for a burger; when the weather was good, we'd grab tacos from a truck and sit outside; if no one had money, we'd gather at my apart-ment, raid the fridge, and hang out on the roof. We had the option of eating in the cafeteria, and sometimes we did, but no one forced us to stay.

At Merritt High, students weren't allowed to leave. Everyone was expected to eat in the cafeteria, even seniors, though they were allowed to use the patio on spirit days. It was too bright and too loud and there were too many people fighting for one another's attention. I waited in line to buy a drink and wished I could expand like a puffer fish to warn others to keep their distance. Each time someone jostled my arm or pushed my backpack against my stitches, it sent a hot surge of nausea through me.

Finally, I grabbed a bottled water and a cookie, paid for them, and stood near the wall, scanning the room for an empty table. I couldn't discern a pattern to the way the students organized themselves. There were no signs that said COOL KIDS SIT HERE! or THIS TABLE RESERVED FOR OUTSIDERS WHO WIND UP IN DEEPLY EMBARRASSING VIRAL VIDEOS. I spotted a table where Finn Duckett and Jarrett Hart were sitting with a few people I recognized from my classes. I took a step toward their table, rethought my decision, and found a table by the restroom with a couple empty seats instead.

The acoustics in the cafeteria amplified the conversations so that it sounded like everyone was simultaneously shouting at me. The noise was unbearable. So were the seats. They were little more than backless, plastic pucks attached to a table by a metal rod.

I pulled out the lunch Grandma had packed me. The peanut butter and jelly sandwich had gotten warm and moist sitting in my locker. And Grandma hadn't spread peanut butter on both sides of the bread, so the jelly had turned that piece to mush. Adding insult to injury, she'd used apricot jelly. The only place I expected to find apricot jelly was in the cupboard in hell.

I didn't scream.

I don't know where I am. Everyone I love is on the other side of the world.

My wounds pulsed with every heartbeat. They felt infected and hot. Grandma had changed the bandages that morning and said they looked fine, but I felt like they must've been bloated with foul, putrid pus.

"Not gonna eat your cookie?" Astrid sat down across from me, ignoring the ninth-grade boys nearby who were leering at her. She was dressed like she was on her way to audition for the role of a comic-book villain. Striped leggings covered her arms, her black skirt was decorated with safety pins, and she'd pulled her hair into two ponytails on the sides of her head. She looked as out of place as I felt.

I pushed the cookie across the table. "I don't trust the food here."

Astrid grabbed the cookie, and broke half off before eating it. "Smart. The food here is awful."

"Then why does anyone stay? It's not like there's a gate around the parking lot."

"School doesn't have to be a prison when the whole town is one."

"Oh."

"Exactly. You could leave and go grab a sandwich at the Dill Hole, but Katy would call Vice Principal Kline, and he'd have a detention slip waiting for you by the time you got back."

"This place is the worst," I muttered.

"Yup."

If Astrid hadn't shown up, I probably would've tried to call Luca so I could hear the reassuring voice of someone who loved me, but it felt rude to pull out my phone with Astrid sitting right there watching me like she was waiting for me to perform a magic trick. "Did your mom tell you to sit with me?"

"Nope."

"I'm sure you have friends of your own."

"Yup."

"Then why—"

"I really wanted a cookie," she said. "And you looked like you had a cookie you weren't planning on eating."

"Oh."

Astrid ate the other half of the cookie. "How're you feeling, by the way?" She motioned at my arm.

I'm terrified every second of every day. I hear it breathing when I close my eyes. I feel the poison it left inside me. I was sitting in world literature listening to Mrs. Kepple extol the virtues of exploring the literature of other cultures, working hard to keep students from falling asleep, and I couldn't breathe. The monster was still standing on my back, pressing my chest into the mud, and I couldn't catch my breath. I needed to get out of class, I wanted desperately to ask for a bathroom pass, but I couldn't even draw enough breath to speak.

"I'm fine," I said. "It was my fault for wandering around the sprawl in the first place."

Astrid frowned; her eyebrows dipped to form a V. "Sure, but—"

"Rawr!" Something fur-covered and huge rushed at me with its arms raised. It roared. I fell out of my chair and hit the floor.

I didn't scream.

I scramble backward as it looms over me, framed by the night and the stars and moss-choked oak trees. The smell hits me first. Like a decomposing corpse. Sweet in a way that fools my brain for a fraction of a second before I realize it's rotting flesh.

Teeth dig into my shoulder. It worries me like a dog with a chew toy and laughter erupted.

Astrid shoved the thing back. "What the hell are you doing?" She ripped off its head and threw it on the floor.

I blinked and breathed.

I didn't scream.

It was only the mascot. The Merritt High Coyote. The kid inside the suit had a shaved head, a mouthful of braces, and he looked terrified of Astrid.

But everyone was laughing.

"Don't hurt me!" the Coyote was saying. "It was only a joke!"

Astrid probably would've ripped the kid's actual head off if a teacher hadn't thrown herself between them.

I scrambled to my feet, grabbed my backpack, and walked toward the doors, keeping my eyes forward and my back straight.

TWELVE

I DIDN'T RUN OUT OF THE CAFETERIA. I REFUSED TO RUN.

I refused to let them make me run.

I did, however, spend the last ten minutes of the lunch period in a bathroom stall. The porcelain was shiny and white; the walls were freshly painted. Of course, it was only a matter of time before they'd get dirty. Nothing stayed clean for long.

My arm itched under the gauze. I peeled back the tape. The skin around the wound was red and tight. The stitches looked like a zipper. If only I could pull it down and slide out of this soiled meat suit. Emerge as someone different. Something better.

The bell rang.

My sixth-period class was theater. It was one of the few

classes I was genuinely excited about. My theater instructor in Seattle had been a teacher who'd insisted we call her Kris. She was a semi-manic cat lady who'd seen one too many inspirational movies about teachers who motivated apathetic students with the power of the creative arts, she wore lots of pastel cardigans, thought she was hip because she knew a few Eminem songs, and had a tattoo of a butterfly on the underside of her wrist.

Despite those things, I liked her, and I enjoyed acting. I loved stepping into a role and inhabiting someone else's life for a while.

I realized as soon as I stepped into Mr. Hilliker's classroom that he was nothing like Kris. He looked like one of the dwarves from *The Hobbit*—short and round, with a frazzled gray perm, a frizzled gray beard, and glasses perched on the end of his nose. He was standing behind his desk with his hairy arms folded across his chest. I was the first to arrive.

In my other classes, the desks had been arranged in neat rows—except for world history, where the desks had been arranged in an orderly circle—and we'd been assigned seats alphabetically. There were no desks in Mr. Hilliker's classroom. Instead, there were a couple beanbags, a few yoga mats, one weird legless rocking chair, and a lot of pillows.

Where the hell am I supposed to sit? I glanced at Mr. Hilliker, the question unspoken but not unstated. He smiled, and his smile seemed to shrug in reply.

Three more students arrived, and they each stopped at the doorway, peeking around me to see why I was loitering there. The crowd behind me grew as we waited for someone else to go in first.

"What's up, Hilly?" A tall, lanky boy strolled past us and threw Mr. Hilliker an unironic high five. His long auburn hair was nearly shoulder length and curled at the ends, and he walked like he'd grown up on a sailing ship.

"Tripp," Mr. Hilliker said. "Nice to see you. Again."

"Second time's the charm."

"Third."

"No way, sir," the boy Hilliker had called Tripp said. "I'd know if I'd failed this class more than once."

Mr. Hilliker sighed and rubbed his forehead, but his rosy-cheeked smile never slipped.

Tripp hiked his thumb at me and the others gathered behind me. "Which one do you think it'll be?"

"I have a guess, but I've been wrong before." Hilliker leaned closer to Tripp and whispered in his ear. Tripp glanced at us, shook his head, and whispered back.

"We shall see, Mr. Swafford."

The warning bell rang. There were at least ten students standing behind me, and more huddled at the door at the back of the classroom.

Whatever. I finally walked in, dropped my backpack near a green beanbag, and eased myself onto it. The seams bulged but thankfully didn't split, and it smelled vaguely of antiseptic. As soon as I sat, the other students followed, claiming pillows or blankets as their own.

"You lose, Hilly," Tripp said.

"It's good for the soul." Mr. Hilliker winked. "Keeps me humble."

When the final bell rang, Mr. Hilliker moved out from behind his desk and stood in the center of the room. "In this class, we will be studying the glorious craft of—" Hilliker coughed into his fist. "As I was saying. We will be studying . . ." Hilliker gripped his chest. His face was red. He fell to one knee and toppled over.

"Dude," a guy two pillows over said, "is he dead?"

I reached for my phone, but I caught Tripp out of the corner of my eye grinning, and it stayed my hand.

A moment passed, and then Mr. Hilliker sprang to his feet, his arms held wide. "And that, ladies, gentlemen, and nonbinary friends, is *acting.*" He paused as if expecting applause. No one clapped.

The first time I'd met Kris, she'd introduced herself to the class by performing a scene from her favorite classic movie, *Edward Scissorhands.* She'd taped actual scissors to her hands. Theater teachers are a rare species.

"You're going to be spending a lot of time working together in my class." Hilliker spoke rapidly, moving his hands as he did so, and it took me a while to realize he was signing as he spoke. "So I think it's best that we begin today by introducing ourselves."

Most of the people around me groaned.

"Without using words," Hilliker added.

The groaning intensified, but our lack of enthusiasm didn't discourage Mr. Hilliker.

"Since Tripp's done this dance before, he can go first to demonstrate what I expect from the rest of you."

Tripp hopped up from the rocking chair, his arms and legs flailing like an understuffed scarecrow. "Sorry to disappoint, but I won't be dancing this time."

Hilliker pressed a stubby finger to his lips. "No talking."

Tripp Swafford stood in the center of the room, just staring at us for a moment. His jean shorts exposed long legs covered in mosquito bites, and his flip-flops showed off narrow toes that were nearly as long as fingers. He turned around, bent forward, and rested his palms on the carpet. He held that position, teetering a bit, and then, in one swift motion, swung his legs up so that he was standing on his hands. His hair brushed the floor as he walked the length of the room. When he was done, he ambled behind Mr. Hilliker's desk, sat in the man's chair, and put his feet up.

Any other teacher probably would've given him detention or kicked him out of class, but Hilliker filled the room with a belly laugh. "That's accurate, Mr. Swafford. Now, pick who goes next." He began to turn, stopped, and added, "And get your nasty paws off my desk."

Tripp scratched his chin and peered around the room like he was putting serious thought into his decision. "Who looks like they're absolutely going to crap their pants if I pick them?"

Everyone. The answer you're looking for is: Everyone.

"You. Monster Boy." Tripp Swafford didn't need to point for everyone to know he meant me, but he did it anyway.

"My name is—"

Hilliker arched his eyebrow and shushed me.

Behind me, someone let out a quiet howl, which earned them a sharp look from Hilliker.

I didn't scream.

"Do something," Tripp said. "It ain't gotta be like what I did. Just something that makes you *you.*"

I lie on my stomach, my arms askew, and try not to breathe. I can hear it panting. Feel it moving. Maybe if I stay perfectly still, it'll think I'm dead and will lose interest and leave.

Tripp huffed. "Come on, do something. *Anything.*"

Mr. Hilliker smiled. "The actions a person takes, Mr.

Swafford, can tell us as much about who they are as the actions they don't." He motioned at me. "Very interesting, Mr. Knox. However, going forward, be aware that while not participating is a choice, it's a choice that'll earn you an F in my class. Understood?"

I hung my head. "Yes, sir."

"Excellent. Who's next?"

THIRTEEN

FOLKS IN MERRITT LOVED TWO THINGS: HIGH SCHOOL football and gossip. Their appetite for the first was whetted at the end of the first week of school when the football players showed up wearing their jerseys—students and teachers both treated them like royalty. Their thirst for the second was slaked by swapping stories about and harassing the boy who claimed he'd been attacked by a monster in the sprawl.

That first Friday, I sat on the sidelines of the PE field while the rest of the boys played flag football. I was supposed to be doing homework, but none of my teachers had given me any yet. Instead, I was texting Luca. The phone Uncle Frank had given me was barely functional. The battery only lasted an hour on a full charge, it got so hot when I used it that I was afraid it was going to explode, and I had to restart it at least ten times a day. But it was my only link to the world outside Merritt, which made it the most precious thing I owned.

This was my first real-time conversation with Luca in a week. We never seemed to be on the same schedule anymore, and it felt like we were separated by three thousand light-years instead of three thousand miles.

PE sucks. I sent the message along with a picture of the guys on the field.

Looks okay to me, Luca wrote back. Which is the one who hit on you?

I'd told Luca about Jarrett trying to kiss me at the party. Luca wasn't the jealous type, and he'd laughed it off. Besides, I'd been in PE with Jarrett all week and he hadn't so much as acknowledged I existed.

I hadn't told Luca about the monster, though; it never felt like the right time.

How's your first week? I sent.

Literally the worst.

Yeah.

What's wrong??? Luca sent. You never let me get away with misusing "literally."

Before leaving Seattle, Luca and I had been able to get lost talking to each other, but now I was just lost.

You around tonight? There's something I need to tell you.

Dad hadn't believed me, Astrid hadn't believed me, Grandma and Grandpa hadn't believed me. I guess I'd been afraid of telling Luca about being attacked because I couldn't bear it if he didn't believe me either. But I had to tell him.

...

Those dots were torture. They'd appear and then disappear. I pictured Luca typing a reply, staring at it, deleting it, trying again.

...

A shadow fell over me, and I looked up as Jarrett Hart stood dripping sweat perilously close. His legs were smeared with grass stains, and his PE uniform—green polyester shorts and a gold shirt with a coyote silkscreened on the front—was dirty and damp. He dropped down on the grass beside me, near enough that I had to breathe through my mouth.

My phone buzzed. Tonight's no good, Luca wrote. Saturday maybe?

I didn't scream.

"Sorry about Kelvin," Jarrett said.

"Am I supposed to know who that is?"

"The Coyote?" Jarrett combed his hand through his hair. "The kid in the costume."

"Oh."

"We put him up to it. Me and Finn."

The casual way Jarrett admitted his involvement left

me speechless. Jarrett didn't share my affliction.

"It was a dick thing to do, but I didn't think it through, you know?" He laughed. He actually laughed. "My mom says it's a recurring theme with me."

Wanna see something cool?

Jarrett motioned at the bandage on my arm. "Can I look?"

I peeled back the bandage. Jarrett grabbed my wrist and pulled the wound closer to his face like he was going to sniff it.

He pushes his lips to mine and grabs me harder. His tongue slips into my mouth, and then he backs away, laughing.

"It hurt?"

I twisted my arm free and gently pressed the bandage back into place. "All the time."

"What were you even doing in the sprawl in the first place?"

"Don't know. I was inside, and then I was outside. I only had one beer. Maybe two." The memories of that night felt like I'd run them through a blender.

"You weren't drunk when we talked."

Don't tell no one about this, all right? I ain't no homo.

"Anyway," Jarrett said, "it's probably my fault you were there in the first place."

I was going to tell him it wasn't his fault, the reply on my tongue before I'd fully processed what he'd said, but I stopped. "Wait, what? How was it your fault?"

Jarrett's cheeks, already flushed from the heat, burned even brighter. "I was at the store with my mom, and we ran into your grandma. She was going on about how you'd just moved to town with your dad and didn't have no friends, so I told her about the party. Said you should come."

When Grandma had told me she'd run into Marjorie Hart and her son Jarrett and that he'd invited me to a party at Finn Duckett's house, I hadn't thought much of it. Merritt was a small town. Everyone knew everyone else.

"You invited me because my grandma spun you a story about how pathetic I was?"

Jarrett shrugged. "I didn't think you were pathetic. It was, just . . . I know how it feels, is all."

"Sure."

"You ain't the first person this town's talked about. Folks here got nothing better to do." He knocked his knee against mine. "They'll move on eventually."

Jarrett sounded like he was speaking from experience, which I doubted. Everyone in Merritt seemed to adore him, and he wasn't even on the football team.

"Obviously you've never had people send you messages saying they hoped you hadn't given the animal that attacked you food poisoning or that you deserved worse than stitches for being in the sprawl."

Jarrett waved me off. "Don't listen to none of that. **Words are just words. They don't mean nothing.**"

One of the boys on the field called Jarrett's name, and he stood to head back out.

"Why are you being nice to me?" I asked. "Is it so I won't tell anyone you tried to kiss me at the party?"

Jarrett loomed over me again, and he smiled. "Nah. You just seemed like you could use a friend. Besides, you can tell anyone you want about that night. No one'd believe you anyway."

FOURTEEN

SOMETIMES ASTRID ATE LUNCH WITH ME; SOMETIMES she didn't. I had no idea where she sat when she wasn't at my table. She said she had friends, but I never saw her with anyone. Friday, she decided to join me. Lunch was another peanut butter and apricot jelly sandwich that I threw in the trash unopened. My stomach growled, but I ignored it.

"What do you know about Jarrett Hart?" I asked.

Even when Astrid sat with me, we didn't talk much. I was pretty sure it was pity that kept her coming back. That or Uncle Frank was paying her to be my friend. Either way, she seemed surprised by my question.

"He's cute, if you like that kind of thing."

"What kind of thing?"

"Future frat boy voted most likely to ghost the first girl he gets pregnant."

"So you don't like him?"

Astrid shrugged. "Only slightly more than I dislike most people."

I didn't know what to make of Jarrett admitting he and Finn had put Kelvin up to scaring me while wearing the mascot costume. Kelvin hadn't gotten in trouble for it, so there'd been nothing for Jarrett to gain by apologizing.

"You don't want to be friends with him, though," Astrid said. "Or the people he hangs out with."

She'd caught me looking in the direction of Jarrett's table, where he was sitting with Finn Duckett and some people I recognized from the party. Finn was wearing a football jersey and had his arm around a girl with short black hair. They were all laughing and smiling. They looked happy.

"Why not?"

Whatever Astrid was going to say was lost in the noise of the bell ringing, releasing us to our next classes. I didn't know where her sixth period was, but she quickly disappeared into the mass of students funneling toward the doors.

Mr. Hilliker's room wasn't far from the cafeteria, but I had to stop at my locker first. People were gathered around the wall where my locker was, making it difficult to reach without being jostled. It wasn't until I cleared the crowd that I understood the cause of the commotion.

The door of my locker was papered with pictures of

werewolves and Swamp Thing and some pretty graphic yiff that would've given Grandma a heart attack. When people realized who I was, they faded away. It was easier to mock me from behind the shield of anonymity. Folks in Merritt were happy talking about others, so long as they didn't have to actually talk *to* them.

"Where the hell would you even go about finding a drawing of a wolf-man packing that kind of meat?" Tripp Swafford had sidled up beside me and threw his arm around my shoulders. "Talk about unrealistic beauty standards."

I shoved Tripp's arm off and started tearing down the pictures, ignoring the snickers of students passing in the hallway. Tripp helped, picking up the papers I dropped.

"If I find out who's decorating my locker, you can ask them yourself."

"Any guesses?" Tripp asked. "About who's doing it, not about the wolf-man porn."

I grabbed my Spanish book out of my locker and headed to Mr. Hilliker's room. Tripp walked with me but didn't ask any more questions. He dumped the pictures he'd collected in Hilliker's recycling bin.

Mr. Hilliker caught a glimpse of one of the drawings and raised an eyebrow.

"New hobby," Tripp said.

"I suppose it's better than your last hobby."

"Shyriiwook's a tough language."

Mr. Hilliker's belly shook when he laughed. "I age five years for every year you're in my class, Mr. Swafford."

Hilliker was a strange teacher by Merritt standards. He didn't care if we cussed in class, but he had a no-tolerance policy regarding words that denigrated people or groups. He didn't mind if we argued with him; he practically encouraged it. On the third day of class, we'd gotten into a discussion about words like "crazy" and "stupid."

"Context is key," Hilliker had said. "If you call a person in this class one of those words, you're out. But an idea? An object? They don't have feelings. They can't be offended. However, you should get into the habit of being specific. Rather than calling an idea crazy, describe what about it you find challenging."

A couple students had argued that calling an idea crazy was, by extension, calling the person who'd come up with the idea crazy. Hilliker had listened to their arguments and told them he'd give them serious consideration. Most of my other teachers would've hung Confederate flags on the walls if they could've gotten away with it, so Mr. Hilliker's open-mindedness made me feel more at home in his class than anywhere else in Merritt. He would've been my favorite teacher if it wasn't for his bad habit of calling on me so frequently.

Acting required becoming someone else, and I enjoyed that aspect of it. However, to succeed, the people watching also needed to believe I could make that transformation.

But if I couldn't convince them of the truth—that I'd been attacked by a monster—I didn't stand a chance of persuading them I could become anything other than an attention-seeking boy who cried wolf.

"I've got a dog named Titus," Mr. Hilliker said, after the final bell rang and we'd all settled into our seats and beanbags. "A boxer. Goofiest dog I've ever had. Smart, too, though. He steals food and hides the evidence where he thinks I won't find it. When I *do* catch him, Titus moves very, very slowly, thinking I won't be able to see him."

Hilliker's eyes roamed the classroom until they finally came to a stop. "But I see him, and I see you, too, Mr. Knox. Get on up here."

I didn't scream.

There was no excuse I could use to avoid the inevitable—I'd already tried them all. I dragged my bones to the front of the room to stand beside Mr. Hilliker.

"I call this game The Liar's Academy," Hilliker said. "What I want you to do is make up the most elaborate lie you possibly can, and then sell it to us."

I'd played something similar in Kris's class, only she'd called it Imaginarium.

"The lie can't just be in the story, it has to live in your voice and your body language and your choice of words." Mr. Hilliker wasn't talking solely to me; he was instructing the rest of the class. "It's not enough to say you're a pirate." He leaned more heavily on one leg, and his shoulders stooped. "Ye got ta be a pirate from yer beak to yer rudder."

My mind raced. Deja was quicker on her feet than I was, but I could usually come up with a good lie fast. Like the time me, Deja, and Luca skipped school and got caught coming home and I said there'd been an outbreak of lice so they'd released us early. I'd had to endure Dad picking through my hair with a metal comb, but it'd been better than getting grounded.

Standing at the front of the room, with everyone watching me, however, I froze.

I clench my eyes shut as tightly as I can and try to pretend I'm sleeping.

"This is only a forty-seven minute class, Mr. Knox," Hilliker said.

Tripp caught my eye from where he was sitting in the legless rocking chair he'd claimed, and smiled. I think he probably meant it to be encouraging, but it distracted me more.

I wonder if anyone at the party noticed I left. I wonder if Jarrett found someone else to pin against a wall in an empty room.

Mr. Hilliker was sitting on the edge of his desk. "The lie doesn't have to be elaborate or showy. Sometimes the best lies are the ones that are closest to the truth."

Jarrett's free hand brushes across my crotch and stops.

"Hasn't Knox already told a big-enough lie for one week?"

I couldn't see who'd said it, but the students laughed. Even Tripp.

"Enough of that," Hilliker snapped.

I thought you said you weren't into it.

"You can sit down, Virgil." There was a note of pity in Hilliker's voice. "I'll torture someone else today. How about—"

"I was born and raised in Merritt." Slowly, my back bowed forward. I let my jaw go a bit slack, doing an exaggerated imitation of Merritt's Southern drawl. "Folks figure I ain't real bright on account of how my family tree's practically a wreath, but that ain't it at all. It's because my ma dropped me on my noggin when I was a little baby.

"My favorite foods are mayonnaise and white bread, and my whole life revolves around a high school football team who ain't won a game in years 'cause I got nothing else worth a damn to give my pitiful life meaning.

"I'm probably gonna die here, unaccomplished, unknown, and unloved, because Merritt ain't nothing but a hungry beast that devours your soul a little at a time 'til there ain't nothing left but an empty husk."

The room was quiet after I finished. No one laughed. No one snickered.

Mr. Hilliker coughed, breaking the silence. "Right. You can sit down, Virgil. I think that's enough for today."

FIFTEEN

THE TREES ARE SCREAMING. THEIR THICK, GNARLED

limbs grasp at me, try to ensnare me with nets of moss.

"... watch me go, go, go, go ..."

My phone vibrates as I run. I answer it.

"Hey, Virgil," Luca says. "Got time to talk?"

"Now? You want to talk now?!" A root bursts through the moist earth and catches my toe. I stumble and fall forward. My phone sails through the air and lands in a puddle.

"Virgil?"

The monster is heaving somewhere behind me. The shadows distort the echoes. It could be anywhere.

It could be everywhere.

"Virgil? Answer me right this second."

I stand. It knocks me down. Its teeth penetrate me—

I don't scream.

—and its poison is in my blood now.

"I'm coming in, Virgil."

The dream tried to claw me back in as I jerked awake and accidentally smacked myself in the face.

"I'm coming in, Virgil." I wasn't sure what scared me more: Grandma's voice on the other side of my bedroom door or the rattle of the handle as she turned it.

"Don't come in! I'm naked!"

Either she didn't hear me or she didn't care. I was crawling out of the closet as Grandma opened the door. "Were you sleeping in the closet again?"

"Didn't you hear me say I was naked?"

Grandma's lips thinned. "You don't look naked."

"Why was that a chance you were willing to take?" I stood and brushed my hand through my hair. "What do you want?"

Grandma gave me that narrow-eyed look that said I was close to crossing the line. "You've got chores to do today. Hurry up and shower. We'll get started after breakfast."

"Chores? Are you serious?"

"Yes."

"But it's Saturday. Can't I do them later?"

"No." Grandma turned and left.

There was no point arguing, so I showered, brushed my

teeth, and threw on some clothes I didn't mind getting dirty. Doing chores for Grandma inevitably involved getting dirty. I checked my phone to see if Luca had tried to reach me, but my only notifications were linked to comments about what a liar or loser I was and how I should go home to Seattle or back to the sprawl so the monster that attacked me could finish the job. I told myself they didn't matter, but I was a liar, right?

Waiting for me at the table was a plate of scrambled eggs, two sausage links, two strips of bacon, and toast. Beside it was a bowl of grits drowning in butter, and a glass of orange juice. The sight of that gluttonous array of food made bile rise in my throat.

"Where's Grandpa?"

Grandma was sitting in front of an empty plate, reading a battered paperback. She read more than any person I knew, easily breezing through a book a day. Romance, science fiction, history, biographies. When it came to books, Grandma wasn't choosy.

"Went to the Schumachers' to take a look at Seymour." Grandma must've seen my confusion because she added, "Their horse."

"Oh." Grandpa had retired from being a vet over a decade ago, but he still made house calls for some of the folks in town.

"Eat up before it gets cold."

I eyed the eggs, trying to imagine putting the runny yellow or squishy white in my mouth. "I'm not hungry."

Grandma lowered her book and arched an eyebrow. "In all my life, I have never known a fifteen-year-old boy who wasn't perpetually hungry. Roy and I nearly went broke trying to keep Tommy and Frankie fed."

Once Grandma got an idea in her head, there was no fighting her. I ate a couple bites while she was watching, and then shoved the food around the plate when she went back to reading. I could feel every morsel I'd swallowed swimming through me until it reached my stomach, where it formed a soft, gelatinous ring around my belly.

"How was your first week of school, Virgil?"

Well, before I even set foot on campus, everyone had seen a video of me sprawled on the asphalt in front of Tasty Cones claiming I was attacked by a monster. The ones who don't think I'm a pathological liar think I'm a few players short of a team. Someone plasters monster porn on my locker every day during lunch, people harass me online, and students think it's funny to howl in my direction in the hallways between classes. "It was fine."

"Make any friends?"

Hey, wanna see something cool?

"Not really. There's a kid in my theater class who follows

me around, but I'm not sure if he's friendly or bored."

"Who?"

"Tripp Swafford?"

Grandma turned up her nose. "You can find better friends than that one. Even the Duckett boy would be an improvement, though only marginally."

Clearly, she knew something about Tripp or his family that I didn't, but I also knew that Grandma had opinions about everyone in Merritt. Most of them unkind.

"Enough dawdling," Grandma said. "I want you to wash up the dishes. After that, there's some weeding in the backyard I haven't been able to get to in a while. Once you're finished out there, I'll have more for you to do."

There was a curtness to Grandma's voice that confused me. It wasn't that she was giving me chores—Grandma could *always* find work to keep idle hands busy—but the way she was speaking to me made me feel like I was being punished.

"Did I do something wrong?"

Grandma folded the page of her book, shut it, and set it down. "Do you know how much the bill was for your little trip to the emergency room?"

Every mouthful I'd managed to swallow threatened to come back up.

"Dad's got insurance."

"Not yet, he doesn't. And your mother forgot to put you

on hers after your father quit his job in Seattle."

I knew I'd been on Dad's policy back home because every year he gave me a new card to keep in my wallet. But I hadn't thought about the repercussions of him quitting before we'd moved to Merritt.

"Your ambulance ride alone cost over three thousand dollars." Grandma tapped her finger on the table to punctuate her words. "And that isn't even a quarter of the total amount."

"What about Mom—"

"Oh, your father, in all his pride, told her he would take care of it." Grandma was an expert at hiding her feelings about most anything behind rosy cheeks and a sweet Southern smile, except when it came to my mom.

"Is that why Dad got a second job?" He'd gone in for the interview at Target, and they'd hired him as a security guard.

Grandma shook her head. "He was hoping to save enough to put a down payment on a house, but since he doesn't have any savings yet, your grandfather and I paid the hospital bill. After talking it down from that ludicrous amount they were trying to collect, of course."

Mom could've paid the bill. I knew she earned a lot of money because I'd overheard her and Dad arguing about it frequently before the divorce. But now Grandma and Grandpa were going to hold it over Dad's head. We were never going to get out of their house.

"Your actions have consequences, Virgil," she said. "You might not be able to pay the bill, but you should still have to pay."

"So I *am* being punished."

"Think of it as a lesson you're in dire need of learning."

"I was attacked by—" I stopped myself before I finished. "I was attacked, and you're blaming me for it? Do you think I wanted to get chewed on by whatever the hell it was that jumped me?"

"Watch your tone with me, Virgil."

It was hard reining in my temper, but I refused to be the kind of person who yelled at his grandma. "It wasn't my fault, but you're treating me like it was."

"You didn't make that animal attack you, but you went to that party. You drank alcohol and you left the house to go traipsing through the sprawl in the middle of the night."

I chug the beer he gave me to wash away the vinegar taste of him.

"If you had stayed at the house or abstained from drinking, you might have been more aware of your surroundings."

"That's not fair! You're the one who guilted Jarrett Hart into inviting me. If you'd stayed out of my business, I wouldn't have been there in the first place. So you—"

Grandma's eyes narrowed, the lines around them tightening. "I want you to think very carefully about the next words that come out of your mouth, Virgil Knox."

"It's just . . ."

"Yes?"

I'd never get through to her. No matter what I said, she'd already decided it was my fault. "Nothing."

"I thought so." Grandma picked up her book. "Now get moving. You're wasting daylight."

"Yes, ma'am."

SIXTEEN

I WEEDED THE BACKYARD, CLEANED OUT THE SHED, AND helped Grandpa fix the porch swing at the front of the house after he got back from tending to the sick horse before Grandma cut me loose for the rest of the day. By then I was too exhausted to do anything but sit on the swing and stew in my sweaty, filthy clothes. Which is, of course, when Luca decided it was a good time to video chat me.

"What happened to you?" was the first thing he said when he saw me. Luca was many things, but a romantic wasn't one of them.

"It's been a long couple weeks. You're going to have to be more specific."

"Deja found this video and she sent it to me, and you were cut up and bloody, and people were standing around staring at you." He ran out of breath before he ran out of words. "What kind of backward-ass place did you move to?"

Bass-heavy rap shakes the furniture, and the white boys in the living room shout along with the words—all the words—without the slightest hint of self-awareness.

"I should've told you."

"Told me what, Virgil?!" Luca's nostrils flared wide and his eyes were wild. "What the hell happened?"

I didn't scream.

"It was last Thursday—"

"Didn't you go to a party that night?"

ride ride ride ride.

"Yeah—"

"Did someone beat you up?" It infuriated Deja when she was trying to tell a story and Luca interrupted her, but he was cute so I let it slide.

"There was a party, and I had a couple drinks. I went outside—I think."

My legs feel like jelly. I sit down on the couch and it's dark outside. My skin's prickling from the heat and I'm stumbling around. I thought I was sitting.

I don't know where I am. I pull out my phone to call for help, but I don't know who to call.

Something crashes into me and I hit the moist ground. My phone slips out of my hand and spins off into the dark.

It looms over me, framed by the night and the stars and moss-choked oak trees.

"Something attacked me."

I waited for Luca to respond, unsure how he was going to react. After a couple moments, he let out a sigh of relief. "Jesus, Virgil. Here I am thinking a bunch of rednecks jumped you for being gay. I already told Mom if that happened you were coming to live with us no matter what anyone said."

I ain't no homo.

"Lots of rednecks. Probably some that don't like gays, but that's not what happened."

"You had me so worried, Virgil." I could see his face. I could see his concern and that little mole on his earlobe. I wanted to touch him. I wanted to feel his hand in mine.

"I got sixty-three stitches."

Luca pursed his lips. "Yeah, but it was just an animal, right? Like a big cat or a crocodile or something?"

"Gator."

"It was a gator?"

I shook my head. "No, but crocodiles don't come this far north. There are only gators up here."

"Fine, it wasn't a crocodile *or* a gator." Luca's nostrils flared when he was annoyed. "What was it, then?"

It lowers itself onto my back.

"Probably a bear." I picked at the stitches on my arm. The

skin itched and felt hot and infected even though Dad said the wounds were looking good when he'd cleaned them last. I kept expecting warm pus to ooze from between the threads.

"When're you coming to visit?" I asked because I didn't want to talk about the attack anymore. "Thanksgiving? Maybe sooner?"

Luca chewed his bottom lip. "Mom said no to Thanksgiving and a lukewarm 'maybe' to Christmas."

Everyone I love is on the other side of the world.

"Oh."

Sympathy painted Luca's face, and that made it even worse. "I want to see you, Virgil. I really do."

"Sure."

"You know how my mom gets." Luca's voice rose nearly to a whine. "If I push her too hard, she'll never let me go."

When it came to being stubborn, Mrs. Costa could've given Grandma some competition.

"Is there any chance you can come home?" Luca asked.

Before spending the day doing chores for Grandma as punishment for winding up in the hospital, I would've said "hell, yes," and bugged Dad until he gave in. But I couldn't ask for money now that I knew he was working two jobs to pay off my hospital bill.

"I can't." I was near tears. My bottom lip wobbled.

"We're all right." Luca pressed his fingertips to the screen.

"We're gonna be fine. We can talk, and I can see your handsome face."

"It's not the same." I knew I was being unfair. Luca was making an effort, and I should've tried harder, but I wanted him there beside me.

"If I have to steal the money to get there for Christmas, I'll do it."

"What about your mom?"

"She'll get over it."

I laughed, because the last thing Luca's mom would do was get over it, and Luca was either lying or delusional.

"Right," Luca said. "So maybe she won't. I don't care."

The knot in my chest loosened slightly. It might be another 117 days before I saw Luca, but I could make it until then. I had to make it.

I was going to cry, and I didn't want that, so I said, "Tell me what you've been doing. How's school? Has Deja found her nemesis yet? I want to hear everything."

I did *not* want to hear everything—it hurt knowing Luca and Deja's lives were going on without me—I just wanted to hear Luca's voice.

Sometimes to get the things we want, we've got to endure things we don't.

SEVENTEEN

SATURDAY HAD JUST BEEN A WARMUP FOR GRANDMA. THE
real work began on Sunday after we got home from church.
She showed me her list, and it contained enough projects to
keep me busy every weekend until I graduated high school.
I tried appealing to Dad, but he muttered something cryptic
about the need to pick our battles and left me to fend for
myself.

I forgot that Monday was a holiday and woke up at my
normal time for school, excited that I wouldn't have to do
more chores and gutted when I realized my mistake. Grandma
assumed since I was up that I was eager to get on the roof and
clean the gutters before it got too hot, and I didn't bother to
correct her.

I woke up Tuesday morning soaked in sweat. The closet

was already warm because it didn't have an air vent, but most of the sweat was a result of my nightmares. In the nightmares, I was always hungry and I was always scared. I woke from them feeling filthy and in desperate need of a shower.

I stood in front of the mirror while I waited for the water to heat up and stared at my body. I looked like a doll some child Frankenstein had assembled from the parts of other dolls. Mismatched and grotesque. I was too thick around the middle, too thin in the arms and legs. I angled Grandma's makeup mirror so I could see the injuries on my back. Three raggedy slashes between my shoulder blades.

The bite was worse.

I peered closer. There was something poking out of the wound. At first, I thought it was the end of one of the stitches, but it was too thick.

A coarse brown hair was growing out from between the sutured flesh.

I gagged. When the revulsion passed, I grabbed Grandma's tweezers and pinched the hair. I yanked it out, and it felt like pulling a weed with deep, twisted roots from the ground.

I didn't scream.

The follicle was thick with gore, and it spasmed once like the final beat of a dead heart. I dropped it in the toilet and threw the tweezers in the trash.

I was shaking all over. That hadn't been one of my hairs.

My hair wasn't that color brown, the hair on my head was thin and soft, and what little body hair I had didn't look like what I'd pulled from the wound.

The water was cold when I finally stepped into the shower. Grandpa insinuated I'd spent so long in there because I was doing something other than washing up and asked that I not run up their water bill. I was too exhausted to argue. Grandma watched me eat, and wouldn't let me leave the house until I'd cleaned my plate. There was no way I could handle school with a stomach full of hash, so I took care of it behind the house before I walked to the bus stop.

I snapped a selfie and sent it to Luca while I waited for the bus. Since he was three hours behind me, I knew he'd be asleep, but I couldn't help checking for a reply. To distract myself, I tried searching for what the strange hair growing out of my wound could've been. It only took a minute on one of those medical diagnosis sites to convince me I had cancer.

The bus wasn't due to arrive for a while yet, so I didn't look up when a truck drove by. Everyone in Merritt, it seemed, drove a truck.

"Hey, Virgil. Need a ride?" Jarrett Hart sat in his truck with one arm flung over the steering wheel, wearing the kind of smile that opened doors for him that would've been shut to me.

"I'm okay. Bus is coming."

Jarrett grimaced. "Yeah, I don't think so. I seen it back a ways on the side of the road coughing smoke like you wouldn't believe."

"Then I'll walk."

"Up to you. But it don't seem smart turning down a perfectly good ride when it's offered."

Wanna see something cool?

It wasn't a far walk to school, but the thought of doing it made every muscle in my body ache. "Fine." I went around to the other side of the truck and tossed my backpack on the floor before climbing into the seat and buckling my belt.

Jarrett's truck looked older than he was—it even had a CD player—but the air-conditioning blew cold, the inside was clean, and it smelled like vanilla from one of those scented trees hanging from the rearview mirror.

"Thanks for the ride," I said.

"Figured I owed you."

"For what?"

Jarrett shrugged. "Look, I'm sorry, okay? I was drunk and horny that night. I didn't mean to be so aggressive with you. I really thought you'd be into it."

"It's fine."

"Liar."

"Okay, then, it's not fine. I don't like being groped by a stranger after I've said no."

"I get that, and I'm sorry." Jarrett's bottom lip stuck out. He actually seemed contrite.

"Just forget about it."

"So, we're good?"

Words are just words. They don't mean nothing.

I couldn't figure out why it mattered to him. I was nobody at Merritt High. Worse, actually. I would've been happy being nobody if it meant not having to be the guy everyone thought was a liar. Jarrett had no reason to care what I thought or to want my friendship. Yet he'd gone out of his way twice now to be nice to me.

"We're good."

Jarrett broke out a killer smile and slapped the steering wheel. "Hey, you should come to the first football game with me and Reba and a couple of her friends. The team's awful—don't tell Finn I said so—but they're fun to watch. The whole town comes out."

The only thing I wanted to do less than sit on hard bleachers and watch a bad high school football team get their asses kicked was spend another night in the sprawl. "Aren't you afraid hanging out with the town liar will hurt your reputation?"

Jarrett glanced at me, his eyes off the road for a moment longer than made me comfortable, but there weren't any other cars around. "You're getting it real bad, huh?"

I'd locked down most of my social media accounts, and I was considering changing my number to hold back the flood of hate, but even if people couldn't say every vile thing they wanted to, I'd still know they were thinking it. "You have no idea."

"Coming to the game will help," Jarrett said. "Show folks you're one of us. Let 'em see you don't give a shit."

That's easy for you to say seeing as your mom's the mayor. "I'll think about it."

"Bring your cousin, if you want."

I laughed at the idea of Astrid at a game. "I doubt she'd be interested."

"She's kind of different, huh?"

"Kind of, but she's cool."

"Yeah, of course." Jarrett pulled into the student parking lot.

I grabbed my bag and opened the door. "Thanks for the ride."

"You can sit with us at lunch, too. Finn'll probably be a dick about it, but Finn's a dick about everything. You get used to him."

"Thanks."

Maybe I'd been wrong about Jarrett. Maybe judging people by their mistakes alone wasn't the best way to make friends.

*　*　*

Now that we were through the first week of school, the real work began. My teachers piled on the homework and started warning us about exams, giving me little time to worry about anything other than not drowning.

Astrid showed up to lunch, so I sat with her instead of with Jarrett and his friends. He didn't seem to notice. I still wasn't convinced he didn't have an ulterior motive for being nice to me. Like, maybe he couldn't deal with me turning him down the night of the party, so he figured he'd try being charming instead of luring me to an empty bedroom and jamming his tongue in my mouth. I'd texted Luca for his opinion, but he hadn't responded.

After lunch, I hurried to my locker hoping to catch whoever was decorating it in the act, but I was too slow again.

"They're getting creative." Tripp sidled up beside me to examine the pictures taped to my locker door. Whoever was doing it had 'shopped my face onto some of the images, and they'd done a pretty decent job. If I hadn't been so disgusted, I would've been impressed. But every picture on my locker, every howl I heard in the hallway, every name I was called was another wound. They weren't visible to anyone else, but I was bleeding from them all the same, and I wasn't sure how much more blood I could lose.

I didn't want to talk about the pictures, though. "What's

your deal with Mr. Hilliker? He seems like an easy teacher. How'd you fail?"

Tripp shrugged. "It's hard to pass a class you never show up for."

"Oh."

"But you're wrong about him being easy."

"Really?" I swapped out my books after I'd finished tearing down the pictures.

Tripp nodded. "He's the toughest teacher I ever had. You'll see."

There was something odd about Tripp. He was goofy and nice, but for all I knew, he could've been the one decorating my locker.

"Saw you riding in with Hart," Tripp said as we made our way to Hilliker's room.

"Bus broke down. He passed my stop and offered me a lift."

Tripp was looking at me funny, and I didn't understand why.

"What?"

"Nothing." Tripp paused. "Just, Jarrett lives on the other side of Merritt. Ain't no way he was just passing by your place." He shrugged it off and pushed ahead to class.

Mr. Hilliker was giddy, and that scared me. "Today we're going to share embarrassing stories."

"My whole life's an embarrassment," Tripp called out. "How will I know what to choose?"

Everyone laughed, including Mr. Hilliker. "I'm sure you'll figure it out."

I knew Hilliker was going to call me first, and he didn't disappoint. There was no use protesting, so I got up and went to the front of the class.

"Bare your soul, Mr. Knox," Hilliker said. "But keep it PG-13, please."

I wished I'd had more time to think of a good story, but everyone was watching me, so I reached for the first thing I could remember. "Once, I went out on a boat with some friends. I got seasick and puked in my lap."

Mr. Hilliker blew a raspberry. "Unless you vomited *on* your friends . . ."

I shook my head.

"Try again."

A whimper escapes my lips as it rakes its claws across my back.

"I was in the shower—"

"And I'm going to stop you right there," Hilliker said.

My ears burned, and I sucked in a ragged breath. "I was on the bus with some friends, heading downtown—"

Mr. Hilliker nodded. "This sounds promising."

"The driver stopped short, and I fell in the aisle. Everyone was laughing."

"Boring!" called Tripp. Mr. Hilliker threw him a warning look, but Tripp added, "Don't tell me you weren't thinking it."

Sweat rolled down my back. My skin felt hot, and I could feel my heart beating in each and every wound. "Once, I heard my parents having sex."

Mr. Hilliker's shoulders slumped. "How many of you are planning to tell a story about hearing or walking in on your parents having alone time?"

One hand slowly raised into the air, followed by at least ten more.

"No you're not," he said. "Get better stories, people."

I took two steps toward my beanbag before Hilliker stopped me.

"You're not done, Virgil."

I rounded on him. "What do you want from me?"

"An embarrassing story."

"Maybe I don't embarrass easily."

Hilliker made a buzzer sound. "Wrong. Try again."

"What if I'm not comfortable sharing it with you? How do you know my embarrassing moment isn't so traumatic that it'd be harmful to force me to talk about it in front of the entire class?"

"Is it?" Mr. Hilliker asked.

"No."

"Then stop wasting my time and tell the story."

"Fine." I sat on the floor and pulled my knees to my chest. "In sixth grade, I had a crush on Leo Cooper. I'd wanted to tell him so bad, but I could never find the right time.

"We had a carnival to raise money for the school, and I thought that would be the perfect opportunity. I'd tell him on the Ferris wheel and have my own *Love, Simon* moment. It was going to be perfect.

"So I convinced him to go on the ride with me. The attendant locks us in, and the car sails into the air. When we're at the peak, I do it. I tell him I like him.

"Before I even finish, Leo holds out his hand for me to stop, and says, 'No.' Just like that. 'No.'"

A couple students giggled, a few offered sympathetic "awws." I ignored them.

"That wasn't the embarrassing part. I'd been shot down before. The part that crushed me was that Leo snapped a picture of me and posted it online along with what had happened so that everyone at the carnival knew he'd rejected me by the time we got off the Ferris wheel."

Mr. Hilliker was smiling when I finished. "There it is. That feeling of shame. That's the kind of emotion you need to tap into when you're acting."

"What's the point, though?" I asked. "I'm not embarrassed about it anymore. Leo Cooper was a dick."

"Memories have a unique power, Mr. Knox. They're

not just records of our past that we file away. They're living, breathing bits of us that we can revisit whenever we want. Memories fuel the engine of our souls."

"And what if I think memories are better left in the past?"

Hilliker shrugged. "An actor unwilling to tap into their memories is like a car with an empty tank: destined to go nowhere."

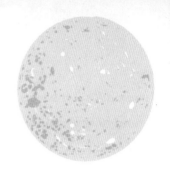

EIGHTEEN

GRANDPA HAD A GREEN-AND-WHITE 1951 FORD TRUCK THAT he'd bought and restored after Dad and Uncle Frank had both graduated from college, and he loved tearing through Merritt's back roads in it. I never saw him smile so much as when he was driving his truck. Unfortunately, he was an awful driver, and I spent every ride with Grandpa gripping the door handle and praying I'd walk away alive.

Grandpa and I didn't talk much as he drove me to the doctor's office to get my stitches removed. Not that we had much to talk about, anyway. Grandpa had a routine, and he stuck to it pretty closely. My life had settled into a tedious routine of its own. Over the last two weeks, my days had begun to blur into one another. I went to school, I went home, I talked to Luca and Deja on the phone, sometimes I hung with Astrid at her house playing video games. On the weekends, I did chores from right after breakfast until suppertime. Grandma hardly gave me a second to rest. The harassment online had eased up because I'd been able to block a lot of it, but I was still waiting for something to happen that would take the attention away from me. Until then, I just continued to bleed.

"Tommy tells me you're taking acting classes at school." Grandpa was a taciturn man, not given to displays of anger or affection. I'd seen pictures of him when he was my age, and he'd looked like the class clown, all big ears and silly smiles. Dad said Grandpa's tour in Vietnam had ground that boyishness out of him.

"Yeah. I did some acting back home, so . . . "

"You should take a weight-training class instead."

"It's too late to change my schedule now."

Grandpa glanced at me. "Your grandmother and I play doubles with your principal and her husband. I could speak to her."

"Please don't."

"I've got nothing against the arts, son—your grandmother and I support the local theater when we can—but you're a man, and you need to start acting like one."

"Is this because I'm gay?"

"Some of the best men I knew were flits. This is about you needing to toughen up. It's good you've stopped telling that story about monsters, but I hear you're sleeping in the closet—"

A whimper escapes my lips as it rakes its claws across my back.

"—just want what's best for you."

"I know you do, Grandpa."

Grandpa nodded as if he'd done his job and could move on. He turned on the radio and spun the dial until he found a Dolly Parton song he liked so that we didn't have to talk anymore.

Dr. Nalick was a young doctor who looked like he wore a beard to hide his age and didn't realize the scraggly, patchy hair only made it more obvious. He also had an easy, reassuring smile that made me want to like him. The nurse who'd shown me and Grandpa to the exam room had instructed me to strip off my shirt so Dr. Nalick was able to get right to work when he came in.

"Everything looks pretty great to me," Dr. Nalick said. "How're you feeling, Virgil?"

I made a noncommittal grunt.

"Answer the man, Virgil."

Dr. Nalick glanced at me, then at Grandpa. "Mr. Knox, would you mind if I have a word alone with your grandson?"

"Well, I—"

"Excellent. Thank you." Dr. Nalick spoke with a crisp confidence that left Grandpa no room to argue. When we were alone, the doctor said, "Now, how're you feeling?"

"Fine."

"Sometimes my younger patients feel more comfortable talking without their parents, or grandparents, in your case, hanging around." Dr. Nalick slowly tugged out the stitches. The feeling was strange. It didn't hurt, but it made me feel vaguely nauseated.

"I said I'm fine."

"It's only that I noticed from your chart that you've lost some weight."

"I've always been skinny. My mom's whole family is that way."

"Of course. And boys your age grow a lot. Just make sure you're eating enough. Protein shakes might help."

Between the pulling of the stitches and the talk of food, I thought I might actually vomit, so I tried to change the subject. "How do the wounds look?"

"They're still tender, and you're going to have some scarring, but they're healing nicely."

I turned toward him. His aftershave had a clean, minty smell. "They're not infected or anything?"

Dr. Nalick paused, and looked at me for a moment before shaking his head. "Not a bit."

"Oh."

"Are you sure there's nothing on your mind, Virgil?"

"Have you ever heard of a hair growing from inside a cut? Not a normal hair, either. Something thick and dark with deep roots."

Dr. Nalick chuckled. "I've seen some strange things, including weird hairs growing where they shouldn't. The human body is kind of extraordinary. My older brother grew three sets of adult teeth when he was your age."

"What about diseases? Could I have gotten some kind of strange disease from whatever attacked me? I was treated for rabies, but I read about rabbit fever, and then there's plague—"

Dr. Nalick stopped working on the stitches and wheeled his stool around so he could see me better. "You don't have plague *or* tularemia."

"You're sure? I just feel **like there's something inside of me. Like the monster left a piece of itself inside me, and it's slowly poisoning me. Devouring me from within. Turning me into something** weird, I guess. It's probably nothing."

Dr. Nalick patted my shoulder. "Living near a place like Merritt, I've seen all kinds of injuries caused by animals. Cat scratches and—"

"I wasn't attacked by a cat."

"Of course not, but I'm telling you your injuries aren't

the worst I've ever seen. You're going to be fine."

Dr. Nalick wheeled around to my back to finish removing the stitches. "In fact, I'm clearing you for regular physical activity. I'll have the nurse write up the release for your gym teacher. How do you feel about that?"

I didn't scream.

NINETEEN

FRIDAY, WE HAD A PEP RALLY AFTER LUNCH TO PSYCH UP the school for the first football game of the season. We were playing the Mustangs, one of our local rivals.

I'd known Merritt was a football town, but I hadn't fully appreciated what that meant until Friday morning on my way to school. Every shop along Main Street seemed to be competing for which could show the most school spirit. Suzie Q's Hair Salon, Pak 'N Ship, Mattress and More, and Excellent Nails For You had draped banners in their windows and painted messages to the players on the glass. Tasty Cones Ice Cream had changed their sign from BEST CONES IN FLORIDA to COYOTES PAY HALF PRICE, MUSTANGS PAY DOUBLE.

"Our boys won one game last year," Tripp was saying as

we got in line to funnel into the gym. "And it was only on account of the other team got food poisoning."

"Then why is everyone in Merritt acting like they're the greatest team that's ever played?"

You should see this place, I texted Luca. These people are ridiculous about football.

Tripp shrugged. "It's like you said. The town's so starved for entertainment that even sitting on uncomfortable bleachers in the heat while getting eaten by mosquitoes to watch a bunch of high school boys get their asses handed to them is better than sitting home and contemplating the mind-numbing uselessness of our lives."

"Oh."

I'm pretty sure Mx. Reinhold is stoned, Luca texted back.

Aren't they always?

Reinhold was an art teacher who believed art was less a skill that could be learned and more of an ethereal talent with which an artist communed.

"It's stupid, though." Tripp was still going off about the football team. It was difficult trying to listen and text with Luca at the same time. "Half the library's flooded 'cause the roof leaks, and they keep saying there's no money to fix it, but they just installed a fancy new scoreboard on the football field, so how's that make sense?"

The conversation had started because I'd idly asked

Tripp if he liked football. He'd gone off about how Merritt was a black hole no one escaped from and on an odd detour through his idea that none of this was real and we were all semiautonomous characters in a vast computer simulation. I didn't understand half of what came out of Tripp's mouth, but he had a weird and wonderful mind, and listening to him ramble was more entertaining than anything else going on.

We finally got into the gym and found seats in the bleachers about halfway up. The air was muggy and warm, and I felt like every person was shouting at the same time. Tripp was still talking, but I was too distracted trying to block out the torrent of noise assailing me from all sides to give him my attention.

"Hey." Jarrett dropped to the empty seat on my other side. **Wanna see something cool?** "Mind if I sit here?"

I looked over at Tripp, who was watching Jarrett with the quiet wariness of a squirrel deciding whether or not to bolt.

"Whatever," I said.

As the rest of the students crowded into the gym, we were squeezed more tightly together. It had to be a fire hazard for sure. Shortly after, Principal Dixon stood at the mic to talk about school spirit. She was an ancient woman who wore a cheap pastel suit she'd probably brought in the 1980s and kept her hair in a long silver braid that hung to her waist. She introduced the coach, who introduced the team. The

Merritt High cheerleaders performed a routine that was cho-reographed well but bordered on obscene.

The students cheered.

"So," Jarrett said while Grant Reed, the Coyotes' team captain, mumbled his way through an inspirational speech, "you coming tonight or what?"

Tripp kept his eyes forward but leaned in to listen.

"Merritt's the worst," Jarrett went on. "If you're gonna survive here, you need friends."

"I have friends." It came out more defensively than I'd intended.

Jarrett laughed. "Your cousin and this guy?" He motioned at Tripp.

"Yeah."

"Then bring 'em along."

I searched Jarrett's face, attempting to peel back his smile. His offer came across as genuine, and I couldn't find any ulte-rior motives lurking behind his eyes, but I still didn't trust him. "I'll think about it."

Jarrett held up his hands. "Whatever, it's cool. If you wanna keep being the butt of everyone's jokes, that's your business."

I glanced at Tripp, but he was pretending not to pay attention to us anymore. I wondered what Luca would've advised me to do. He probably would've told me to go. He would've said that it was only a football game and nothing bad was going to happen. That the best-case scenario was I made some friends and people stopped talking about what happened to me in the sprawl, while the worst-case scenario was I got bored and walked home. Luca would've said I had nothing to lose but a few hours I probably would've spent in my room feeling sorry for myself anyway, and he would've been right.

I turned back to Jarrett. "Yeah, okay. I'll go."

Jarrett picked me up around six, and then we swung by to give a lift to a girl named Reba. She seemed familiar. I figured we'd probably met at Finn's party and I just didn't remember. We got to the field early enough that there were still a few places to park. We met up with more people at the ticket booth, and with Jarrett in the lead, we skipped the line and weren't asked to pay.

Everyone had shown up to watch the Coyotes. I spotted Uncle Frank and Aunt Kelly, Astrid, sitting as far from her parents as possible, Chief Duran, the majority of the students at our school, and even the two deputies who'd questioned me at the hospital, Delerue and Bruford.

Surrounded by Jarrett's friends, no one gave me a second glance. No one called me names or howled. I was part of a group. I belonged.

After the pep rally, I'd asked Tripp to come with me to the game, but he'd turned me down without giving a reason. I'd asked him if he thought I shouldn't go. He'd said I should do what I wanted and had refused to say anything more on the matter.

The game commenced with the Coyotes kicking the ball to the Mustangs. One of their players caught it and ran it down the field for a touchdown.

"That's bad, right?" I asked.

"Pretty bad," Jarrett said. "But it ain't the worst they ever done."

"Why do you always gotta bring that up?" said a guy whose name was Chuck, I think.

Jarrett threw up his hands. "Riley ran the ball the wrong way! How does that even happen?"

Of Jarrett's friends, I liked Reba best. She wasn't from Merritt, either, so we had that in common.

"I'm from Calypso," she said when I asked. "It's down south on the east coast."

It didn't sound familiar.

Reba figured I wouldn't have heard of it. "I thought my town was small, but this place is wild. And these people. I can't wait to get out of here and go to college next year."

"Two more years for me."

Reba grimaced. She had a bushy nest of beautiful brown

hair that framed her face, and an athletic build like she probably played softball or volleyball.

As the Coyotes took possession of the ball, Reba pointed to the field. "Watch. Gio's going to try to pass the ball to Finn, but Finn is the absolute worst."

Jarrett leaned forward to get our attention. "Hey! That's your boyfriend you're talking about."

"Ex," Reba said.

Jarrett laughed and threw a handful of popcorn at us.

Sure enough, the quarterback passed the ball to Finn. It looked like he was going to catch it, but he juggled it from hand to hand before a player from the opposing team snatched it out of the air and ran it halfway down the field.

"The worst," Reba said.

The remainder of the game was one error after another for the Merritt High Coyotes, but I was enjoying myself. It wasn't the same as hanging out with Luca and Deja, but it was the first time I didn't hate living in Merritt.

During a lull in the game, Reba nudged my arm. "I'm sure he probably told you, but Finn's sorry about those pictures he put on your locker."

"What?" I was sure I had misheard her.

"Finn doesn't know what it feels like to be on the other side of a joke like that. He thinks he's just fooling around and doesn't realize he takes things too far. I'm glad there are no hard feelings."

I felt like Reba had punched me in the gut. I stood and shoved people out of the way trying to get to the end of the row. Jarrett called my name, and I heard him asking Reba what happened.

"You didn't tell him?" I heard her say.

My shoulder burns where its teeth penetrated me, and I feel its poison in my blood.

"Virgil Knox?" Chief Duran was holding a tray of hot dogs and nachos, and I nearly ran her down by the concession stand trying to get away.

"Sorry." I tried to sidestep her, but she was quicker than me.

"You all right? Did something happen?"

I shook my head. "I'm fine. Everything is just fine."

"You need me to get you someone? I saw your grandparents sitting with the Gardners."

"I said I'm fine!"

"Buck," she said. "Get over here."

I was confused because she was pointing at Tripp as he came out of the restroom. He frowned and ambled our way.

"Buck?" I said.

Duran gave me a lopsided frown. "That's his name. Third Buckley Swafford to live in Merritt."

"No one calls me that but you, Chief. Buck makes me sound like a redneck."

"You are one."

Tripp nodded at me. "Hey."

"Hey."

Chief Duran shuffled the food she was holding from one hand to the other. "Watch after Virgil, all right?"

"I don't need a babysitter. Anyway, I'm leaving."

"Then Buck will give you a ride."

"Sure." Tripp shoved his hands in his pockets. "Game was boring, anyway."

Duran and Tripp were watching me like I was a stray dog they were trying to keep from running off, and they weren't the only ones. Other folks were staring covertly as they walked to and from the concession stand or restrooms. I imagined them thinking, *There goes that Knox boy causing a scene again.*

"I thought you said you didn't want to come to the game," I said to Tripp.

Tripp shook his head. "Just didn't wanna go with Jarrett."

Chief Duran looked from me to Tripp and back. "We good here?"

"Yeah, Chief," Tripp said. "I'll make sure Virgil gets home."

I was annoyed by the way they were talking about me like I wasn't there. "Then let's go already." I stomped toward the parking lot, leaving Tripp to catch up. I'd barely made it twenty feet when I heard Astrid's voice.

"Hey, where're you guys going? Are you leaving?"

"I'm taking Virgil home," Tripp said.

Astrid jogged toward us. "Can I hitch a ride? I came with my parents, but I've got to get out of this place."

"The more the merrier," I mumbled.

"Any chance we can stop and get some food?" Astrid asked. "I'm starving."

TWENTY

WE SAT IN A MCDONALD'S PARKING LOT, EATING GREASY
food while sprawled in the bed of Tripp's truck. Well, Astrid
and Tripp ate. I picked at my fries and ignored the cheese-
burgers I'd bought.

"So you and Jarrett are friends?" Astrid asked after she'd
demolished a Quarter Pounder.

I grunted. "He asked me if I wanted to go to the game,
and, I don't know. I guess I'm just tired of everyone in this
town talking about me."

"It can't be that bad," Astrid said.

I pulled out my phone, unlocked it, opened my messages,
and tossed it to her.

Astrid's eyes grew wider the longer she read.

"You were welcome to come with me." Tripp was eating his cheeseburger slowly, his eyes downcast.

I took my phone back from Astrid. "I know, it's just—"

"We're not as popular as Jarrett Hart?" Astrid's lip curled. "Jarrett's a dick, though."

"He wasn't always," Tripp said.

Astrid and I both turned to look at him, waiting for him to finish the thought.

"He used to be all right. We were friends in junior high. Finn, too, though he was always a prick."

"What happened?" I asked.

Tripp finished chewing before answering. "High school, I guess. Plus, they looked like them and I looked like me."

Jarrett shuts the door and flings himself at me. His lips hit the side of my nose, his chin grazes my cheek, and his hands are everywhere.

"Well, he apologized for . . ." I almost told them what happened but changed my mind at the last second. "For what happened at the party. The sprawl, I mean. Getting attacked."

"He's still a dick," Astrid mumbled.

I didn't disagree. "One of his friends, Reba—"

Tripp bobbed his head. "Reba Daniels. She's good people."

"Yeah, well, she said Finn was the one putting the monster pictures on my locker. I'd asked Jarrett about it before and he said he didn't know anything."

Astrid snorted. "Which was a lie because Finn can't take a piss without telling Jarrett."

"Gross." I was hoping we could talk about something else, but when I turned to Tripp, he was looking at me with a strange expression that made me uneasy.

"What really happened to you out in the sprawl?"

Astrid slapped his leg.

"What? I'm just curious."

Something crashes into me and I hit the moist ground. My phone slips out of my hand and spins off into the dark.

"Does he look like he wants to talk about it?" Astrid said.

It looms over me, framed by the night and the stars and moss-choked oak trees. The smell hits me first. Like a decomposing corpse. Sweet in a way that fools my brain for a fraction of a second before I realize it's rotting flesh.

"He never said what attacked him, though, and I ain't buying that it was a gator or a bear. Bear would've torn him to shreds."

Teeth dig into my shoulder. It worries me like a dog with a chew toy and then flings me aside.

Astrid and Tripp argued, but their voices bled together into a high-pitched whine. Their words became meaningless noise.

I lie on my stomach, my arms askew, and try not to breathe. I can hear it panting. Feel it moving. Maybe if I stay

perfectly still, it'll think I'm dead and will lose interest and leave.

It doesn't leave.

"I couldn't really see anything," I said. "It was too dark. Whatever it was, I didn't get a good look at it."

It lowers itself onto my back.

"The whole time I was out there, the strangest thoughts kept intruding. Like, I wondered what my friends in Seattle were doing or whether Grandma and Grandpa were waiting up for me. I should've been trying to figure out how to escape, but instead I was annoyed my boyfriend hadn't texted me back."

Astrid's face softened, but I turned away. Pity wasn't a good look on her.

"I got a theory about what it was that attacked you," Tripp said.

I wasn't in the mood to hear it, but there was nowhere for me to go.

"You know anything about the history of Merritt?" Tripp asked. Astrid shook her head, and I did the same.

"Way, way back—though don't ask me for dates 'cause I don't have a head for memorizing crap like that—when Merritt was still part of Mosquito County, the Merritt family consolidated their citrus holdings after the big freeze that happened in the late 1800s. The Merritts bought what they could and stole what they couldn't. The town's named after them, but back then you'd've been hard-pressed to find folks who wouldn't have been happy to see them dead."

Tripp's story had the feel of a bullshit folktale, but he was a natural storyteller, and I found myself mesmerized.

"All you really gotta know about the Merritts is that they kept bad faith with the local tribes and fought on the wrong side of the Civil War."

Astrid fired off a bitter laugh. "Why doesn't that surprise me?"

Tripp went on as if she hadn't interrupted. "Folks who spoke out against the Merritt family went missing or wound up dead. One of the rumors was that Abigail Merritt had made a pact with the devil and given birth to a monster that roamed the sprawl and did her bidding."

"Let me guess," Astrid said. "She didn't have a husband?"

Tripp frowned. "He died of illness."

"Right, so she got pregnant, only no one could believe a woman capable of getting pregnant outside of marriage, so they made up a story about how she was knocked up by a demon." Astrid shook her head. "The knots men will tie themselves into to deny a woman's agency is ridiculous."

Tripp didn't seem bothered by Astrid's anger. "I didn't make up the story. We can talk about something else if you want."

Astrid rolled her eyes. "By all means, finish."

"Ain't much else. There are stories connecting the Merritts to unexplained disappearances and deaths in and around the sprawl right up until the last Merritt died in 1943."

"Maybe the Merritt family just happened to produce a lot of terrible people," Astrid said.

Tripp fixed her with a serious gaze. "Except the stories about the sprawl persisted after they were gone. Lots of folks seem to vanish in Merritt."

"They're the smart ones," Astrid said. "I'd vanish, too, if I could."

I didn't believe Tripp's story, but he was right that it wasn't a bear or alligator that had attacked me. "Do you think there's something out there?"

"Like what? Abigail Merritt's demon baby?" Astrid was laughing so hard she drew attention from a couple walking to their car.

"I was only asking," I muttered.

"And *you*." Astrid pointed at Tripp. "You keep talking like that, and folks are gonna say you're just like your dad."

Tripp stiffened. His entire demeanor changed in an instant, but I didn't understand why. He crumpled the wrapper from his cheeseburger and tossed it aside. "We should get going."

Astrid tried to reach for him. "Come on. I didn't mean it like that."

Tripp climbed over the side and got behind the wheel. I still didn't know what was going on, but I figured whatever had happened, we were done for the night.

Astrid's house was closest, so we dropped her off first. She didn't say another word on the way back and slammed the door when she left.

"Did I miss something at McDonald's?" I asked when we were back on the road.

I didn't think Tripp was going to answer because he didn't speak for a long while. Finally, though, he said, "My dad's got schizophrenia. He's all right when he's taking his medication, but sometimes he goes off it and gets it into his head that government agents are spraying Merritt with chemicals to control our thoughts." Tripp shrugged. "It's the kind of thing folks in Merritt ain't got much tolerance for."

"Shit, I'm sorry."

"It's all right. And Astrid ain't wrong. I set one foot out of line, and people start whispering I'm turning into him. He's a good man, though. I could turn into someone way worse than my dad. Taking care of him's why I flunked Hilly's class last year."

It also explained why Mr. Hilliker was so nice to Tripp about it. I wasn't sure what to say. Mental illness was no joke. I didn't know anyone with schizophrenia, but Luca battled horrible anxiety, and I'd talked to Aunt Kelly about the depression she'd gone through after each of her kids.

"I'm sorry for what Astrid said, anyway."

Tripp turned down my street and parked in front of my grandparents' house. "I know she didn't mean nothing by it."

The night felt over. Tripp had been as animated as a live wire at McDonald's but the power had been cut. There was only one thing keeping me from getting out of the truck.

"Do you really think there's something living in the sprawl?"

"Maybe."

"Like what? Merritt's version of Bigfoot?"

Tripp clenched and unclenched his hands around the steering wheel. "I was thinking more like a werewolf, but not tied to the moon or nothing."

"Oh."

"And I'm not saying it *is* a werewolf, just maybe something like it."

"That sounds—"

"Ridiculous? I know. But do you really believe you got attacked by a gator?"

Hot breath soaks my neck, a clawed hand pushes my face deeper into the mud.

I shook my head.

"Me neither."

"Why do you believe me when half the town thinks I'm

lying and the other half thinks I got what I deserved?"

"Just do."

"But *why*? I'd been drinking and it was dark. Maybe my brain twisted what I saw into a monster."

"You think that's what happened?"

"No, but—"

"Then I believe you."

My mouth moved, but nothing came out. People thought I was lying, they thought I'd imagined it, they thought I was looking for attention. Even Luca and Deja had assumed I'd been attacked by a common animal.

"And, look, you don't gotta talk about it, now or ever, if you don't want to, but I'm here if you *need* to."

Tripp had given me no reason to believe he was anything other than utterly sincere, but that didn't even matter. If he was only pretending to believe me, it was more than I'd gotten from anyone else, including my grandparents, my parents, and my boyfriend, and I didn't realize until that moment how badly I needed it.

"Thank you."

TWENTY-ONE

I WATCHED THE BALL SAIL OVER MY HEAD AND INTO THE
net. My teammates shouted a chorus of profanities at me while
the other team laughed and hooted. I retrieved the ball, threw
it back onto the field, and returned to staring into nothing,
thinking about Luca. Missing him. I'd had a dream about him
the night before, and I'd woken up aching to see him.

It was only my second day having to dress out for PE, and
I already hated it. It was muggy, which meant I was sweaty
before we started playing, and Coach Munford took a hands-
off approach to the kind of casual name-calling and bullying
that often happened between boys.

"You're supposed to try to block the ball." Jarrett Hart
jogged toward me, wearing a half grin. "With your hands or
face or whatever. Just so long as you keep it from going in
the net."

I smacked my forehead. "*Oh!* Is that how the game's played? I thought I was just supposed to stand here and look pretty." I'd managed to avoid Jarrett on Monday, but my luck had apparently run out. "What do you want?"

Jarrett sighed. "I was nominated to stay here and keep you from costing us any more points."

"Lucky you."

Our boys had the ball and were downfield harassing the other goalie—a cement wall named Grady. We'd only scored against him once, compared to the five times I'd let the ball through.

"Reba told me why you ran off Friday night, and I just wanted to say sorry."

"Sure. Whatever."

"I mean it."

"It's fine."

Jarrett leaned against one of the goal frames. "I asked Finn to knock it off, so he shouldn't be putting nothing else on your locker. Sometimes he gets carried away."

"If you're expecting me to be grateful, you're going to be disappointed."

A quick, nimble kid—Alex, I think—broke away and brought the ball down the field toward us. I stood in front of the goal, pretending to try so Coach Munford wouldn't mark me off for not participating. Alex would've gotten through, but Jarrett intercepted him, stealing the ball and passing it back to our team.

When we were alone again, Jarrett said, "I really am trying to be your friend. I figured once Finn got to know you, he'd stop messing with you. And it ain't like it was a big deal, anyhow."

"Of course you wouldn't think so."

"I don't even know where Finn found some of that shit, but it was kind of hilarious." Jarrett was smiling. "Think about it. Someone out there was actually sitting around with a pencil and sketch pad going, 'You know, I bet Wolfman's got a really big dick. I should draw that.'"

I rolled my eyes and tried not to laugh.

"And did you see that one of Swamp Thing? I'm never looking at the eggplant emoji the same way again."

I snorted. "Fine, some of them were funny. And maybe I would've found them funnier if everyone else hadn't been so busy laughing at me and calling me names and spamming my phone with messages telling me to kill myself."

Jarrett's smile disappeared, and he hung his head. "I'm sorry."

We didn't get to talk for a few minutes because the other team brought the ball to our end and a fierce battle ensued to try to score on me. Even if I'd wanted to take my position as goalie seriously, Jarrett made sure I didn't have to. He refused to let the ball within ten feet of the goal.

"You're one of those annoying people who's good at everything, aren't you?" I asked when the boys from our team moved the ball down the field.

"Not everything. Sometimes I'm an awful friend."

"You can make it up to me by getting Finn and everyone else to leave me alone."

"I'll talk to him again, but Finn's got his own mind." Jarrett shook his head. "Can I give you some advice, though?"

I replied with a dead-eyed shrug.

"Sometimes you gotta go along to get along in Merritt."

"Right."

"I'm serious. There's lots that's good about living in Merritt. We look out for each other, and folks are willing to help one another. But Merritt magnifies the petty meanness we all got in us, too. Makes being different tough unless you make yourself so hard nothing can touch you."

It was the kind of insight and honesty I would've expected from Astrid, though she would've delivered the speech with more pessimism and profanity.

Jarrett held up his hands and began to back away. "Look, whatever. I'm just trying to be a friend. If you don't want—"

"Why?" I asked.

"Why am I trying to be your friend?"

"Yeah."

Jarrett bit the bottom corner of his lip. "'Cause there *are* monsters in Merritt, but they don't live in the sprawl."

TWENTY-TWO

I SAT ALONE AT LUNCH AND THOUGHT ABOUT JARRETT HART.
I'd written him off as shallow and entitled. The kind of person who tore through life, unaware of and unconcerned by the destruction he left in his wake. Maybe I'd been wrong.

Don't tell no one about this, all right?

I wondered if I should give him another chance. Reba had been cool. Maybe Jarrett's other friends were all right, too. As much as I wanted to hope my mom would change her mind and tell me I could come home, I had to accept that probably wasn't going to happen. For better or worse, I lived in Merritt now.

After lunch, I dropped by my locker and was surprised there were no monster pictures decorating it.

"Maybe your secret admirer's out sick today?" Tripp had an uncanny and kind of creepy ability to show up without me noticing.

"Maybe." Or Jarrett had actually convinced Finn to quit decorating my locker. Either way, I didn't want to jinx it by questioning why. "Come on. Let's see what Hilliker's got in store for us today."

Improv was the answer. Mr. Hilliker didn't call on me first, thankfully. Instead, he saved me for last.

Tripp clutched his stomach before collapsing to the floor. Minnie Spenser shrugged. "Well, doctor?" she said. "It looks like you're going to have to perform surgery."

"On the moon?!" I looked around, my eyes wide with fright. "How am I supposed to cut him open in a vacuum?"

Minnie pointed toward the wall. "We'll have to carry him to that dome."

"That's too far. We'll never make it."

Tripp lifted his head. "I'd like to remind y'all that I've got these alien eggs in my belly, and I'd really love you to get them out before they hatch."

The bell rang, saving us from ourselves. Mr. Hilliker clapped his hands once and took the floor. "You three are deeply strange. We'll do more improv work tomorrow, focusing on 'yes, and . . .'"

I helped Tripp off the floor and went to grab my backpack.

"Oh!" Hilliker said, "Casting for the drama department's fall play starts next week. We'll be performing *Clue*. As part of your grade, you're all expected to audition."

There were a few groans, but no one protested too loudly.

Mr. Hilliker smiled in my direction. "Great job today, Virgil. I can't wait to see your audition."

"Thanks." I followed Tripp out the door.

Tripp nudged my arm. "Don't worry, it's extracurricular. Even if he offers you a part, you don't have to take it."

"I performed in shows at my school back home." The theater had been a refuge, especially when things between my parents had gotten bad.

"Oh." Tripp sounded surprised. "So you're hoping you get a part?"

"Kinda, yeah."

Tripp nodded appreciatively. "Guess things are looking up for you, then. No monster porn on your locker, and now you got the play to do."

"If Hilliker casts me."

"I got a feeling he will."

For the first time since moving to Merritt, I felt hope peeking out. I didn't like living in Merritt. I missed my friends and my boyfriend. I missed my old school and even the teachers there. I missed everything about Seattle, and I hated almost everything about Merritt. But this was where I lived now, for better or worse, and maybe Jarrett had been right. If I loosened up and learned to go along, I'd eventually find my place.

TWENTY-THREE

DAD WAS HOME FOR DINNER WEDNESDAY NIGHT, THOUGH HE looked like he wished he was anywhere else. When he wasn't at the firehouse, he was usually working at Target, picking up as many hours as they'd give him now that his training was finished. It felt like I hadn't talked to him since school started.

Me, Dad, Grandma, and Grandpa sat around the table eating dinner. Corn bread and beans and chicken. Nothing special, except Grandma's corn bread was the best I'd ever eaten.

"You look like roadkill, Tommy." Grandma could say anything in that sweet Southern accent of hers and make it sound delightful.

Dad finished chewing. "Gotta work. Houses are expensive."

"But there's no need to work yourself ragged," Grandma went on. "We have plenty of room, and you and Virgil are welcome to stay as long as it takes you to get back on your feet."

Plus, if we move out, who will you get to pull the weeds and clean the attic and paint the shed?

"Thank you, Mom, but I'm a grown man. Far too old to be living with my parents."

Grandpa pointed at Dad with his fork. "Don't forget to settle your old obligations before you take on new ones."

"I said I'd pay back the money, and I will."

"Half is Clara's responsibility." Grandma sipped her sweet iced tea. "But that's none of my business."

I smelled a fight brewing, and I tried to head it off. "What do you know about the history of Merritt?" I directed the question at all three of them, but Grandpa was the most deeply rooted in the town, so I thought he was my best shot at finding out if any part of the story Tripp had told us Friday night was true.

Grandpa wiped his mouth with his napkin. "Well, Merritt used to be a vibrant town, flush with money from the citrus industry. These days most of the juice comes from California and South America."

I'd heard Grandpa go off on tangents about the reason for the collapse of Florida's orange groves, and I didn't want to go down that path. "What about the Merritt family? Are there any Merritts still living here?"

Grandma eyed me curiously. "There's still Merritt blood around here. Sudie Kennon's great aunt was a Merritt, the Harts are distantly related through Georgia McKinney, and the Pierce family claim they've got Merritt blood, too." Grandma wrinkled her nose. "But Gregory Pierce also runs around telling everyone one of their descendants was a member of the Seminole Tribe, and there's not an ounce of truth to that tale."

"What about disappearances? Especially connected to the sprawl?" I'd done some research online, which was a pain because of how spotty the Wi-Fi was in the house, but I hadn't found much to back up Tripp's story.

"What's this about?" Dad asked.

"School project."

Grandpa picked up his fork and knife. "People don't disappear from Merritt, and I'd prefer we discuss something else. This isn't appropriate conversation for the supper table."

My phone vibrated in my pocket, and I peeked at the screen. I was half out of my chair before Grandma asked where I was going.

"It's Luca."

"Sit down and finish eating," Grandpa said.

With Luca's schedule and mine, *and* the time difference,

finding a few free minutes to actually talk rather than shoot messages back and forth was difficult. I pleaded with Dad, but he shook his head.

"You can call him back when you're done eating, Virgil." Dad never would've cared before, but he slipped into being a kid again when he was around Grandma and Grandpa, deferring to them and letting them tell him what to do.

I scowled while I shoveled food into my mouth as quickly as I could, but I still had to sit at the table until everyone had finished, and then I had to wash up the dishes. It was almost an hour before I was able to hide in my room and call Luca back.

It wasn't Luca who answered. "Virgil!"

"Hey, Deja. Where's Luca? He called me earlier."

"Nope, that was me. Luca's practicing for his first debate tournament this weekend, and I'm stuck here waiting at school for his sorry ass. He made the mistake of leaving his phone in his backpack and his backpack with me. I've already programmed an alarm to wake him up at three a.m., changed his background to a picture of my smiling face, and fixed his autocorrect so every time he types my name, it changes to 'the Queen of the Universe, Her Royal Highness Deja.'"

"Oh."

"Talk to me, Virgil. I'm *bored*. What're you doing? What's new? Made any friends?"

"I miss Luca."

Deja went quiet on the other end. Finally, she heaved an exasperated sigh. "This is hard on him, too. You get that, right?"

"Of course, but—"

"He barely got any warning you were moving."

"Neither did I!"

"I know." Deja's voice softened. "None of this is your fault, but it's not his either. It's tough having his best friend and boyfriend be on the other side of the country."

I sat on the floor and pulled my knees to my chest. "Is he going to break up with me?"

"No!"

"Did he meet someone?"

"Luca loves you, Virgil. Like, I don't even know if there's a word to describe how much that boy loves you."

You didn't answer the question. I asked if Luca met someone, and you straight up dodged. Which means he definitely met someone and feels like he's stuck because he doesn't want to break up with me while I'm exiled in Merritt, but he doesn't want to cheat on me either.

"I love him too."

"And no matter what happens," Deja said, "I'll always be your friend."

"It sounds like *you're* breaking up with me."

Deja chuckled. "I'm not, so can you please tell me what you've been doing in that hellhole you call home so we don't become the kind of friends who only talk about your boyfriend?"

"Sure. Yeah, of course."

"What's all this Luca told me about you being attacked by a bear? What're you doing messing with a bear? Didn't I teach you better than that?"

I didn't want to talk about it, so I said, "I went to a football game, and it didn't suck."

Deja busted up laughing.

"Fine," I added. "It sucked. Our team is terrible. I don't know much about football, but clearly neither does the football team."

"Who'd you go with? Your cousin—what's her name? Or that kid from your acting class?"

"Astrid and Tripp."

"Yeah. Did you go with them?

I paused. "No, I went with Jarrett."

I could practically hear Deja's mouth drop. "The guy who tried to kiss you at that party?"

"He apologized for that."

"You're not—"

"No!"

"Virgil . . ."

My leg itched, and I tried scratching it through my jeans. "It's nothing, Deja. I swear." I could picture her glaring at me with disapproving eyes, but there really was nothing between me and Jarrett, so I changed the subject. "I'm trying out for the play. We're performing *Clue.*"

"Lucky. Kris has us doing some nonspeaking interpretation of *Romeo and Juliet* where we're all going to be wearing the same costume so no one will know who's who."

I told Deja about Mr. Hilliker and the acting exercises he made us do.

"Your drama teacher sounds like a drama queen."

"You have no idea." The itch on my leg grew more insistent, but it was difficult to get at it through the denim.

Deja sighed. "I wish you were here. Life isn't the same without you around."

"I miss you, too." I made an excuse to get off the phone before the conversation grew too melancholy. As soon as I ended the call, I wriggled out of my jeans to see what was itching on my leg. I figured I'd been bitten by a mosquito or an ant, but it wasn't a bug bite.

A quarter-sized patch of mottled brownish skin marred my pale thigh. The surface of it was rough like a scab, and it had thick hairs growing around the edges like the hair I'd pulled out of my wound. The skin where it met the scab was puckered and red and hot.

I didn't scream.

I picked at the scab and tried to peel it off, but it felt like my leg was on fire. Cold sweat broke out on my forehead, and a wave of nausea hit me so hard I swayed to the side.

I knew better than to mess with it. Picking at the scab could lead to infection and another trip to the hospital, which would put Dad in debt to Grandma and Grandpa forever. But I couldn't help myself. It wasn't a normal wound.

Bristly, wiry hair brushes the back of my arms. My shoulder burns where its teeth penetrated me, and I feel its poison in my blood.

Dr. Nalick had been wrong. The monster *had* given me a disease.

I changed into shorts and snuck across the hallway to the bathroom. I had to get whatever the monster put into me out of my body.

The lesion was fibrous and tough. I found one of Dad's straight shaving razors and sawed through the connective tissue, biting back the pain and working through the nausea. When I finally removed it, the skin underneath was pale pink and gelatinous. It looked like the fatty part of a Sunday ham.

I gagged, but kept my supper down. It wouldn't do for Dad or my grandparents to hear me throwing up. I wrapped the scab and the razor in toilet paper, hid them at the bottom of the trash basket, bandaged the new wound, and went to bed.

When I woke up the next morning and peeled back the gauze, the scab had returned. And it was bigger.

TWENTY-FOUR

I WOKE UP ON A PARK BENCH IN FRONT OF BIRDIE BUCHANAN'S
Bridal Shop. I didn't know what time it was, but it was still
dark. My arms and legs were sore, like I'd run a marathon,
and my bare feet were caked with mud. I tasted blood, but
my hands were clean.

What the hell is wrong with me?

I'd never sleepwalked before. I didn't have my phone,
and I wasn't sure I would've called anyone even if I'd had
it. Instead, I walked home. The sun was peeking over the
horizon by the time I got there, which meant Grandpa was
probably just getting out of bed. He was an early riser who
started every day with a cup of black coffee followed by a
three-mile run.

Since I didn't remember leaving the house, I didn't know

how I'd snuck out. I checked my bedroom window first. The screen was leaning against the side of the house. I slid the window open and crawled in, trying not to track dirt on the floor. I'd fix the screen from the outside before school.

As soon as I was safe in my room, I let myself fall apart. Something was happening to me. The scab on my thigh kept returning no matter how often I cut it off, and a new one had appeared on the side of my chest. I'd tried everything to keep them from growing back—peroxide, Neosporin, antifungal cream, rubbing alcohol. Nothing worked. I knew I should stop cutting them off, but I couldn't. I felt compelled to saw off the scabs despite the pain and the knowledge that I was only making it worse.

And now I was sleepwalking and dreaming of blood. The terror of the nightmare I'd had lingered even if I couldn't remember the details.

I thought about telling my dad, but he had enough to worry about. Grandma and Grandpa would only say I needed to toughen up. Deja might've listened, but I doubted she would've understood, and Luca seemed to be pulling away from me. The distance between us was no longer just physical.

I didn't scream.

My life in Merritt was nothing like it'd been in Seattle. I missed walking Luca's dogs around the park, and going to movies, and hanging out at the bookstore with Deja. The three of us had been a tight unit; we'd done everything together. We were the rulers of all we could see. I had none of that in Merritt. But maybe I could. Maybe I could have friends. Maybe I could make some kind of life in this town. Maybe.

But not if people kept thinking of me as the boy who was attacked by a monster. Not if I kept reminding them of what happened to me. I had to forget it. I had to make *them* forget. Getting caught sleepwalking would do the opposite.

It lowers itself onto my back.

I ate just enough breakfast to keep Grandma from lecturing me, told her I'd be home late because of the audition for the play, and then left to catch the bus to school. Grandma hardly said a word.

I was still thinking about what I might've done while sleepwalking when Jarrett's truck pulled to a stop in front of me. Reba was in the seat beside him.

Jarrett leaned out the window. "Can't deal with school this morning. We're gonna grab breakfast and meet up with Finn. Wanna come?"

Reba waved. "Come on. It'll be fun."

Skipping school was probably a bad idea, but I could only turn down Jarret's offer of friendship so many times before he'd quit offering. And it's not like I had much to lose. "Sure. Why not?"

Reba plugged her phone into the truck's stereo and sang along to some loud country song. She had a singing voice that hurt my teeth to listen to, but she sure was enthusiastic.

Jarrett grinned and rolled his eyes, but he was tapping his hands on the steering wheel to the music and bobbing his head, too. I joined in during the last chorus. I didn't like the music, and I wasn't sure I liked the company I was in, but nothing was ever going to be like it was in Seattle. I had to make the best of what I had.

"Damn, Knox," Jarrett said. "You can actually sing."

Reba smacked his arm. "Hey! I can sing."

"No, you can't." Jarrett laughed, but it was lighthearted and good spirited.

"Asshole."

"I performed in the school musicals back home," I said.

Reba's face lit up. "Oh! Are you trying out for *Clue*?"

I nodded. "You?"

"I want to, but my dance classes are at the same time as rehearsals."

"Not me. I can't act my way through an open door." Jarrett chuckled again. "I don't know what y'all see in it, anyway. Bunch of people pretending to be other people?"

"That's what makes it fun," Reba said. "Getting to try on someone else for a while."

I thought back to the first time I'd walked onto a stage. It was during junior high. We'd put on a musical about the solar system. I'd played Mercury. "It's not about who you become. It's about who you are in that moment. You're onstage, and everyone's watching you. There are no do-overs if you screw up. When something goes wrong—someone misses a line or a cue, a prop breaks, a set change gets messed up—are you the kind of person who freezes? Or are you the kind of person who keeps going even if everything around you is on fire?"

Reba raised her hand. "I'm definitely the first one. Probably best I can't audition."

She launched into a story about a dance recital she'd done the year before, but I stopped paying attention when I caught Jarrett looking at me like he was seeing something he hadn't expected.

When Reba stopped talking long enough to take a breath, Jarrett cut in and said, "So, Virgil? Which one are you? Do you freeze or do you keep going?"

I shrugged. "The show must go on."

TWENTY-FIVE

THE GUNSHOT RANG THROUGH THE TREES. A MOMENT LATER
the bottle sitting atop the railing of a wooden fence shattered.
Lucky threw his hands in the air and hollered, "Told you I never
miss." He spit chewing tobacco into the dirt. I wanted to gag.

"Except on the football field." Finn snatched the rifle
from Lucky and then ducked to avoid the meaty fist that
swung through the air.

After stopping to pick up a box of doughnuts, Jarrett
drove me and Reba to a field near the sprawl where Finn was
waiting with Lucky, Chuck, and a skinny, nameless ninth-
grade boy whose reason for being there seemed to be to fol-
low Finn's every command.

I sat on the tailgate of Jarrett's truck with Reba while the
boys shot bottles.

"Bet this isn't anything like you're used to," Reba said.

"That's an understatement. Back home, I don't think I knew a single person who owned a gun. But here?" Each of the boys had brought their own rifles. Except Lucky, who'd pulled out a revolver. "I feel like an anthropologist observing a strange species."

Reba smiled and drank orange juice straight from the container Finn had brought. "You get used to it. And they're pretty harmless."

"Speak for yourself!" Lucky called.

A look passed between Jarrett and Finn that seemed to contain an entire conversation. Jarrett raised one eyebrow.

Finn huffed. "What more do you want?"

Jarrett shifted his rifle from one shoulder to the other and kept his eyes locked on Finn. I didn't know what was going on between them, and none of the others appeared interested in getting involved.

Finally, Finn scowled and turned to me. "I'm real sorry I posted those monster pictures on your locker."

He didn't sound sorry, but I was too shocked he'd apologized to argue. "It's fine."

Finn hiked his thumb at the ninth grader. "I had Worm do the Photoshop work."

"My name's Dylan," the ninth grader said.

"You're name's Worm because that's what you are, Worm.

Now go set up some new bottles before I use your ass for a target." Finn rolled his eyes like that had been a completely normal conversation.

"It's a football thing," Reba whispered.

"Anyway," Finn went on, "I was just messing with you. I didn't mean nothing by it."

The other boys hadn't said anything about me being there, probably because I'd come with Jarrett, but they hadn't spoken to me much, either. They were like dogs, sniffing around, not sure whether they were going to let me stay or run me off.

Finn's apology was a signal to the others that I was okay.

"What *really* attacked you out there?" Lucky edged in closer. He reminded me of a hyena. "I ain't never heard of a gator biting no one like that."

Chuck, a burly guy with glasses said, "You got scars?"

I nodded.

Lucky motioned at me with his chin. "Well? Prove it."

Jarrett was standing off to the side looking like he was going to be no help, so I finally pulled off my shirt and turned so they could see my back and shoulder. I kept my arm pressed to my side to hide the scabby lesion on my torso.

"Damn!" Finn slapped his thigh. "You got chewed *up*, boy."

"Shit," Reba said in a low voice.

Lucky looked unimpressed. "Whatever. I still say it weren't no gator."

Maybe if I stay perfectly still, it'll think I'm dead and will lose interest and leave.

Reba reached out like she was going to touch my scars. "Did it hurt?"

Jarrett was watching me, waiting for an answer. The others were looking at me too.

I didn't scream.

"What do you think?" I felt the weight of their eyes on me, but I stood firm. I was sure they wanted me to brush it off and say it was nothing, but it hadn't been nothing. I lowered my shirt.

Finn cleared his throat and sighted his rifle down the field. "Hurry up, Worm! I ain't got all day!"

Glad to no longer be the center of attention, I turned to Reba. "He wouldn't really shoot the kid, right?"

"Probably not."

Jarrett said, "Finn's all talk. Chuck, on the other hand . . ."

"All talk, my ass!" Finn scowled. "You know who I'd take out?"

"Mrs. Genaro?" Lucky said.

Finn shook his head. "Kelli MacDonald." He raised the rifle, aimed it down the field, and fired. A bottle less than two feet from where the ninth-grade kid was standing exploded, showering him with glass.

The boys laughed.

"What'd Kelli do to you?" Lucky asked.

"Said no when he asked her to homecoming." Jarrett laughed.

Finn sighted the rifle down the field again. "She shot me down. Gotta return the favor."

"Half the girls at school have shot you down," Reba said. "You didn't."

"And I got the STD to prove it."

"Damn!" Lucky hooted. "She got you there, Finn."

Finn snorted. "Whatever. The dance ain't shit. I'm hooking up with Kim Langston at the party after."

"Does she know?" Reba asked.

A slow, sinister grin spread across Finn's face. "Not yet."

"What about you?" Chuck asked.

I was busy watching Finn, trying to decide how creepy I thought his answer had been, so I didn't realize Chuck had been talking to me.

Jarrett said, "Virgil's into guys."

Being gay wasn't something I thought about much. It wasn't something I worried about. I'd never had to tell anyone back home. No one had asked; no one had cared. When I'd said I had a crush on Benito Alvarez in sixth grade, no one had made a big deal about it.

Like everything else, though, it was different in Merritt.

Lucky and Chuck looked at their shoes, and Finn seemed to think it was funny. Jarrett was watching me, like he was curious to see how I'd respond to being outed. I didn't care if they knew I was gay, but I wasn't sure how they'd react to it, either.

Reba seemed to sense my indecision. "What about James Cochrane?"

Lucky spit. "The senior dude who sang that one Dolly song at the talent show last year?"

"Yeah."

"I didn't know he was a fag," Finn said. "But I seen the way he plays guitar. Good with his hands."

I'd never heard that word outside of a movie in my life, and here they were, tossing it around like it meant nothing. "Yeah, I don't—"

"James ain't gay," Chuck said. "He just acts like a fag." He walked in a straight line, holding his hand, bent at the wrist, out in front of him.

Words are just words. They don't mean nothing.

"You don't act like one." Finn held the rifle out to me. "You know how to shoot?"

You're gonna need a thicker skin to be a Coyote.

I stared at the rifle, my hands still in my lap.

"You don't have to," Reba said.

Come on. You'll like it.

"I suppose it can't hurt to learn." I slid off the truck and accepted the rifle. "You know, in case I get jumped by a monster again."

The boys cheered and crowded around me, each excited to offer their advice.

I didn't scream.

TWENTY-SIX

JARRETT GOT ME BACK TO SCHOOL IN TIME FOR LUNCH. HE
and the others had planned on skipping the rest of the day,
but I couldn't miss Mr. Hilliker's class if I wanted to audition
for the play after last period.

Tripp was sitting at my usual table when I walked into the
cafeteria. "Hey, what're you reading for the audition today?
I was thinking of doing something from Shakespeare, but I
don't know if it's appropriate."

I cracked open the bottled water I'd bought and chugged
it. Spending the morning outside had left me dehydrated. "I
hadn't thought about it. Isn't Hilliker going to have us read
from the *Clue* scripts?"

Tripp shook his head. "He likes us to have audition
pieces. Didn't you know that?"

"How would I?"

"Yeah, guess you're right."

"It's fine. I'll think of something."

Tripp dug into his backpack and pulled out a bag lunch. Inside was a sad sandwich and some Cheetos. He motioned at me. "Where'd you get the sunburn?"

I touched my nose absently. "Skipped my morning classes and went shooting with Jarrett Hart and Finn Duckett and some of their friends."

"That's . . . unexpected."

"Tell me about it."

"How'd you wind up with them?"

I shrugged. "Jarrett and Reba stopped by my bus stop before school and asked if I wanted to skip. I think Jarrett was trying to make up for Finn harassing me with the monster pictures. He was having a kid on the JV football team do it. Finn even apologized, if you can believe it."

Tripp frowned. "After all they put you through—the stuff online and the prank calls and texts—you just shrugged it off and went shooting with them?"

Hey, wanna see something cool?

"Sometimes you have to go along to get along," I said. "Besides, Reba was there, so it wasn't too bad."

Tripp kept looking at me like he couldn't believe what I was saying. And the more he stared, the more I kept talking.

"I'd never shot a gun before. Hell, I'd never even seen a gun up close until this morning." My mind wandered back to earlier that day. "I was scared I was going to shoot my foot off. But at the same time, I kept thinking if I'd had a gun that night in the sprawl, maybe—"

"Maybe you would've shot your foot off *and* been attacked by a monster?"

"Yeah, probably. I couldn't even hold onto my phone **slips out of my hand and spins off into the dark.** I'd likely have dropped a gun, too."

Tripp cocked his head to the side. "Be careful, all right?"

"I'll try not to shoot my foot off."

"Not that. I mean, yeah, don't shoot your foot off, but also Hart and Duckett and those boys? You can't trust them."

I'm stuck in Merritt with the taste of Jarrett Hart still in my mouth.

"What do you have against them?"

Tripp bit his bottom lip, worrying at a piece of dry skin. "A water moccasin'll bite you if you try handling it. It ain't personal; it's just in their nature. I got nothing against them snakes, but I know enough to steer clear."

"You think Jarrett's a snake?"

"I think the whole lot of 'em are a nest of vipers, and you keep sticking your hand in even though you already been bit once." Tripp shrugged. "But that ain't none of my business."

Don't tell no one about this, all right?

"Isn't there a kind of snake that looks like a different snake that's really poisonous?"

Tripp nodded. "Scarlet king snakes look like coral snakes, but scarlets are harmless."

"Well, what if Jarrett and Finn are like that? They look dangerous but they're really not?"

"Just 'cause something don't kill you don't mean it ain't dangerous. And the best thing as far as I can see is to avoid getting bit at all."

Tripp meant well, and it was good advice, but it was too late. I'd already been bitten; I had its poison in my blood. I didn't see how any potential danger Jarrett or Finn posed could be worse than what I'd already been through.

TWENTY-SEVEN

THE MERRITT HIGH SCHOOL AUDITORIUM WAS A DUMP. THE air-conditioning barely functioned, most of the seats were threadbare and broken, and the upholstered walls looked straight out of the 1990s. It might've been quaint except it also smelled like mold.

Over the last hour I'd witnessed some truly heinous audition pieces and a couple that didn't suck. Tripp's fell somewhere in the middle. He'd finally settled on a monologue from a book about the end of the world, and he'd managed to sell the character pretty well. When Mr. Hilliker finally called my name, I trudged down the aisle and up the steps to stand center stage.

I began sweating under the hot lights almost immediately.

"What've you got for me, Mr. Knox?"

I cleared my throat. "Well, I didn't actually know I was supposed to prepare something—"

Mr. Hilliker scratched his beard. "Do you have anything at all?"

"I did *Dracula* last year at my old school. I played Renfield. I think I remember the monologue from it."

"Good enough." Hilliker nodded at me. "Whenever you're ready."

In the story, Renfield was a thrall of Dracula's, held captive by the promise of eternal life. It wasn't a big part, but there was a monologue in which Renfield described the horrible crimes he'd committed for his master, and the atrocities he remained willing to carry out for the chance to be blessed with Dracula's curse. I'd never managed to get the monologue quite right—there had been some ineffable essence to the character that I'd failed to grasp—but I didn't have another piece prepared, so it would have to be good enough.

I began haltingly as the monologue came back to me. I wasn't exactly nervous, but a current vibrated within me, a mixture of excitement and anxiety from being on an actual stage again. I thought I was doing okay, but Mr. Hilliker stopped me before I'd gotten halfway through.

"Renfield's not just unhinged," Hilliker said. "He's more dangerous than Dracula."

"How do you figure?"

"Dracula drinks blood because it's who he is. He's just—"

"Following his nature?" I thought back to my conversation with Tripp at lunch.

"Exactly. But Renfield has a choice, and he's choosing to be a killer."

I scratched at the scab through my shorts.

"Try it again."

"Yes, sir."

I began to speak, but I wasn't simply reciting lines. I wasn't recalling a monologue. I delved the cavernous depths, the dark places I'd avoided since I was attacked in the sprawl. I searched for Renfield in the shadowed crevices. I'm not sure I found him, but I did find something.

What if *I* was turning into a monster? What if the monster's poison had gotten inside me and was transforming me the way Dracula had changed Renfield? What if the scabs were the initial symptoms of my hideous metamorphosis?

Hilliker was wrong. Renfield hadn't had a choice. He hadn't chosen the monster; the monster had chosen him.

Come on. You'll like it.

Mr. Hilliker cleared his throat when I finished the monologue. His expression was impossible to read behind his bushy beard. "Well, Mr. Knox, that's one interpretation of the material."

I bowed my head. "Sorry."

"Don't be. It was . . . unique." He looked at his clipboard. "Next up—"

I hopped off the stage, grabbed my bag, and left.

TWENTY-EIGHT

JARRETT SLUNG HIS ARM AROUND MY SHOULDERS AS WE
ran off the field to the locker room. "You are *the* worst soccer player I ever seen, Knox."

I shoved Jarrett away and forced a chuckle. "Can't be worse than Finn playing football."

Jarrett busted up laughing. "You're going to the homecoming game, right?"

"Maybe."

"You gotta go. It's a Merritt tradition. The mayor gets shitfaced and makes a speech—"

I turned to him, confused. "Isn't your mom the mayor?"

Jarrett shrugged. "She's a hoot to watch."

It was weird being friends with Jarrett. He was acting like nothing had happened, but since he'd asked Finn to stop harassing me, most everyone else had too. The flood of strangers telling me to drown myself in the swamp had slowed to a trickle, and hardly anyone mentioned the attack anymore. Now folks in Merritt were gossiping about how Mr. Stedman was dating Jillian Zabrano—who'd only graduated high school the year before and had been one of Mr. Stedman's journalism students—and debating *when* their relationship had actually started. I'd see people at the grocery store, and they'd smile and wave like just the week before they hadn't called me a liar and said I deserved what'd happened to me in the sprawl.

"Anyway," Jarrett went on, "even if you don't come to the game, you gotta hit up the party at Finn's after the dance Saturday. It's gonna be epic."

"I'll think about it."

ride ride ride ride.

"You're not actually going, right?" Astrid was looking at me like I had spiders crawling out of my mouth.

"Maybe. Probably not. I don't know." I'd been planning to sit at Jarrett's table during lunch, but when I got to the cafeteria, I spotted Astrid and Tripp waiting for me at our usual spot. Once I was settled, I told them about my conversation with Jarrett and his invitation to the party.

Astrid rolled her eyes. "Christ, I thought you were the

smart one in our family." She'd added a streak of green to her hair, and her makeup palette skewed darker than normal, giving her a Marvel-movie-henchperson vibe.

Tripp seemed to be taking my developing friendship with Jarrett and Finn and the others in stride. "You definitely gotta go to the parade and game. Merritt High homecoming is *wild*."

So far, it had seemed pretty tame. Each day of the week was a different dress-up day—superhero day, favorite decade day. Thursday, we'd been encouraged to dress like our favorite teacher, so obviously Tripp was doing his best Mr. Hilliker impersonation, complete with a ratty beard. I'd opted not to dress up. Of course, students at Merritt High took homecoming way more seriously than at my old school. I'd sent pictures to Luca and Deja to prove I wasn't making it up.

"Homecoming is stupid," Astrid countered.

"It's mayhem. Someone started a fire at the parade last year."

I arched an eyebrow. "A fire? Really?"

Tripp nodded. "The year before, there was a riot."

"Fine." Astrid threw up her hands. "Go to the parade. Go to the game. It *is* kind of fun watching the Coyotes get crushed. But skip the dance, and definitely skip Finn's party."

At first I'd assumed Astrid was an outcast, but the better I got to know her, the more I thought she was exactly who and where she wanted to be. If she didn't have many friends, it wasn't because she couldn't make them, it was because she didn't want them. I wasn't sure if she was happy with the status quo, but she didn't appear unhappy with it either.

"Why don't you two come with me?" I looked from Tripp to Astrid. "The parade, the game, the dance, the party. All of it."

Astrid snorted derisively. "No to the game, no to the parade, hell no to the dance, and I think you know what my answer to the party is."

"So you'll think about it?"

Astrid gave me the finger.

I turned my attention to Tripp. "Come on. It could be fun."

Tripp drummed the table with his fingers. "I'll go to the parade—I got a great place we can watch it from—but I don't know about the rest of it."

Astrid was a lost cause, but I held out hope I could change Tripp's mind. He was the only person I wasn't related to who'd been nice to me after the attack, and I didn't want to leave him behind now that I was making other friends.

"Why won't you come to the party?" I asked Tripp as we walked from the cafeteria to Mr. Hilliker's class. There was an energy in the hallways that I could only attribute to homecoming. It was like the school had spiked the water with caffeine. "Or at least to the dance? If you go, I might be able to convince Astrid to go. It could be fun."

I might've been imagining it, but I thought Tripp blushed when I mentioned Astrid, and I filed that away for later. "My dad's coming back Saturday."

"Back? Where is he now?"

"On the road." Tripp glanced at me and must've seen that I didn't know what that meant, because he added, "He's a long-haul trucker. Gone for days at a time."

"And he leaves you by yourself?" Tripp hadn't ever talked about his mom, so I didn't want to ask in case there was a story there he didn't want to tell.

"Ain't no big deal. I'm used to it."

I hadn't known about Tripp's dad, and I hated the idea of Tripp home alone on a Friday night. "Why don't you come to my house for supper tomorrow after the parade? We'll go to the game together."

"I thought you'd be going with Jarrett?"

"We'll meet him there, and you don't have to sit next to him. I'll make sure there are plenty of people between you." I threw Tripp puppy dog eyes. "Reba will be there too."

Tripp sighed. "Maybe."

Mr. Hilliker was standing in front of his desk when we got to class, bouncing like a kid on Christmas, wearing a grin to his ears. "I posted the cast list for *Clue*."

"Cool." I tried to sound casual about it, like I didn't care, but I missed being part of a cast. There was a unique magic created by belonging to a group like that. Merritt was never going to feel like home, but being part of a show might help me miss home less.

"Hell yeah!" Tripp was reading the cast list.

"What?" I edged nearer to him. "Who'd you get?"

"I'm the maid!"

I laughed, because of course that made perfect sense.

"We do not allow gender roles to define us in my theater," Mr. Hilliker said. "You're going to make a wonderful maid, Mr. Swafford."

I shuffled toward the cast list, unsure what role I was hoping for. After the audition, I'd found the script and read it twice. The show was hilarious. I'd never heard of it, but it was based on a movie from the 1980s. It was probably something Grandma and Grandpa had liked. Either way, most of the characters had potential, especially if Hilliker was ignoring gender when casting.

I scanned the parts until I found my name. "Wadsworth? You gave me Wadsworth?" I read the list twice more to make sure I hadn't imagined seeing my name attached to the lead role.

Mr. Hilliker was beaming. "There's something inside of you, Mr. Knox. And together, I think we can help it break free."

TWENTY-NINE

EACH TIME I TALKED TO LUCA, IT FELT LIKE I HADN'T TALKED to him in forever. Even when I was busy with school or doing chores for Grandma, Luca was on my mind. Of all the things I missed about Seattle, Luca was at the top of the list. When I got home from school Thursday, I wanted to see his face when I told him my good news, so I tried to video chat with him. Luca answered wearing the biggest smile I'd seen on him in a long time.

"Virgil!"

"Luca! God, it's good to see you."

"You too."

"How's your mom," I said at the same time as he said, "How's school?" and we both cracked up.

"You first," I said.

Luca had an olive complexion, like he'd just come back from a cruise to the Caribbean, and a swoop of dark-brown hair that was almost tall enough to call a pompadour. He looked like he should've been a member of a boy band—probably the heartthrob or the funny one. But what I loved most about Luca was his smile.

"I barely get to talk to you, Virgil. I'm not wasting our time blabbering about my mom." Instead, Luca launched into a story about how much he hated his classes, about the boy Deja was crushing on, and about how he was already tired of the rain. While I cared and was interested in everything he had to say, it was the sound of his voice that I sank into. The familiar rhythm was soothing *and* made me ache for home even more.

"What about you?" he asked.

We'd been talking long enough that I was sitting on the floor of my bedroom so I could keep the phone plugged in. "It's Merritt. It sucks."

"Come on, there's gotta be something good happening."

A smile touched my lips. "Well, I got the lead in the play. We're performing *Clue*, and I'm Wadsworth." I still couldn't believe Hilliker had cast me as the lead.

Luca's grin lit up his eyes, growing brighter as I spoke. "Congratulations! That backwoods town has probably never seen anyone as talented as you."

"Whatever."

"I'm glad you're doing the show. Maybe you'll make some friends you're not related to."

"Hey! I have friends!"

"I'm sure you do, baby," Luca said playfully.

"Seriously! I'm going to the homecoming parade with Tripp. I told you about him. He's the one in my drama class. And we're going to meet Jarrett and Reba at the game. I might even go to a party after the dance."

"I guess that means things are better for you, then? Are you still getting harassed?"

I hadn't told Luca the full extent of what I was going through, but I hadn't been able to hide it from him either. "Not so much. I'm kind of friends with Jarrett and Finn. They hang out with this girl, Reba; she's pretty cool. You'd like her. We skipped morning classes to go shooting once."

"Shooting? Like guns?" Luca's lips puckered like he'd eaten a mouthful of sauerkraut.

"Well, yeah, but everyone around here shoots. It's no big deal."

"Huh," Luca said.

"What?"

"Nothing."

"Luca, what?"

Luca bit his lower lip. "It's just I thought you'd hold out longer before becoming one of them."

I groaned. "I'm not one of anything. I'm trying to make friends. You don't know what it's like here. You don't know what it's been like for *me*."

"But you hate guns, Virgil. You did a whole presentation in speech about how you think gun culture in the United States is destroying society."

"That was just a speech, though."

"Sure."

I don't know where I am. I pull out my phone to call for help, but I don't know who to call. Everyone I love is on the other side of the world.

"Are you mad?"

Luca shook his head. "No, it's just . . ."

"I thought you'd be happy for me."

"I am."

"You don't sound happy."

Luca glanced over his shoulder. "Listen, I gotta go."

"Wait, don't—"

"I'm glad you're making friends and doing the play." Luca pursed his lips and flared his nostrils. "I just . . . I'll talk to you later."

"I love—"

Luca ended the call.

I didn't know what had just happened. It was like our worlds had diverged the moment I'd left Seattle for Merritt.

The differences had been small at first, but the longer Luca and I remained apart, the more dissimilar our lives became. I was starting to wonder if we would even recognize each other by the time I got to see him again.

THIRTY

TRIPP AND I WERE SITTING ON THE ROOF OF THE USED-
book store at the end of Main Street, dangling our legs over
the side, talking while we waited for the homecoming parade.
Tripp worked there during the summer and still had the key
to get inside and onto the roof. I was grateful I wasn't stuck
down below, squeezed on all sides by folks trying to jockey for
a better view.

I turned to Tripp. "Have you decided whether you're
coming to the game with me and Jarrett and Reba?"

It wasn't the first time I'd asked, and it wasn't the first
time Tripp had replied with a vague shrug. "You decided if
you're going to the dance?"

"Get this." I chuckled. "Astrid texted me and said we
were going to the dance together and that she'd murder me
if I argued."

"I thought she'd made her feelings pretty clear where the dance was concerned."

"Me too." I hadn't decided one way or the other about the dance until Astrid left me no other choice. "You could still join us."

"Can't. My dad." Tripp turned his head toward the sound of cheering. I craned my neck to look. The parade had finally turned down Main Street. People in Coyote colors crowded the sidewalks waving foam fingers and little purple-and-gold flags as the train of gleaming, rumbling pickup trucks and floats made their way toward us. The trucks at the front bore the homecoming court, and they were followed by the marching band.

"How can they play football in this heat?" I asked.

"Just used to it, I guess."

Hundreds of people had come out to cheer a group of boys for throwing a ball around a field, even though they weren't any good at it. Back home, folks took to the streets to protest homelessness or police brutality or taxes or corporate malfeasance—they didn't need much reason to grab a sign and march—but Merritt's strange pride in its underachieving high school football team made no sense.

Tripp nudged my arm. "Congrats again on snagging the lead in *Clue*."

"Hilliker probably only picked me because I fit the costume or something like that." My enthusiasm for the role had been dampened by my fight with Luca the day before. It hadn't even been a fight, really. I wasn't sure what had happened. I'd sent him a couple text messages, but he hadn't responded.

"Hilly picked you because your audition was bananas," Tripp said. "That's gonna be like the gold standard by which all future auditions are judged."

"It wasn't that good."

Tripp snorted. "Didn't say it was good." He caught my eye and held it for a moment. "Kidding. I wasn't sure you weren't gonna jump into the audience and try to drink *my* blood."

Teeth dig into my shoulder.

"Just don't give Hilliker no reason to regret casting you."

"I won't." I turned my attention back to the parade as the homecoming court passed beneath us. I didn't recognize most of the people waving at the crowd—not even the ones from my class—but Tripp kept a running commentary going about each of them that made me laugh. The parade jerked to a halt, though, when the truck carrying some of the juniors smacked into the back of the truck carrying a couple seniors.

"Oh damn!" Tripp rubbed his hands together. "Here it comes."

"They barely tapped them."

The driver of the truck that got hit hopped down and

tried to drag the driver of the truck behind him out through the window. It took less than a minute for a brawl to erupt and for the orderly parade to descend into anarchy. It wasn't just the students fighting, either. Judy Sloan, who worked at the pharmacy, swung her purse at Mr. Golding's head, and George Ross threw a punch intended for Nick Miner that accidentally clipped the shoulder of a boy from the marching band trying to protect his flute as he fled.

The chaos was appalling and fascinating at the same time.

"You're lucky," Tripp said, breaking the spell I was under.

"How's that?"

"You don't have to stay in Merritt."

"I'm stuck here for now. Isn't that bad enough?"

Tripp shook his head. "Your mom and dad'll get back together—"

"Never gonna happen."

"Or you'll graduate or something. Either way, you'll leave."

"You can leave if you want."

Tripp's chin dipped to his chest. "I was born in Merritt, and I'm gonna die in Merritt. Ain't much I can count on but that."

I spotted Chief Duran with deputies Bruford and Delerue wading into the sea of bodies, but there weren't enough of them to make a difference against that crowd. I turned my attention back to Tripp. "You could leave and go to college."

"Someone's gotta take care of my dad. He's all right so long as he takes his pills, but he has his spells, and I have to be here to make sure he don't hurt himself."

"What about your mom?"

Tripp flinched and seemed to shrink in on himself.

"I didn't mean to pry," I said. "It's none of my business."

"It's nothing." Tripp was quiet for a moment. "She was the smart one. Got outta here when I was young. Picked up one day and took off."

"Oh. I'm sorry, Tripp."

"Don't worry about it. I don't hate her for it or nothing. Don't blame her, neither. She did what she had to do."

Thinking about Tripp's mom brought my own anger bubbling to the surface. "You're a better person than me. I don't think I'll ever stop blaming my parents for splitting up and wrecking my life."

"You will. Eventually."

The fighting below us flickered and faded. Chief Duran had a couple people in handcuffs, but most had slipped back into the crowd like the madness that had possessed them had evaporated into the afternoon air.

"Hey, Virgil?"

"Yeah?"

"I don't think you should go to that party at Finn's tomorrow night."

Something in Tripp's voice pulled my attention away from the carnage on Main Street. "Why not?"

"Call it a hunch." Tripp was looking at me with a furrowed brow. "You should come hang out with me and my dad after the dance. Bring Astrid, too. It'll be more fun than it sounds. I swear."

"I'll think about it."

Tripp nodded. "Answer me one thing, though?"

"Sure."

"Why would you *want* to go after what happened last time?"

It was a question I'd asked myself during the long stretches of night, huddled in my closet, waiting for sleep to claim me. "I'm tired of being scared, Tripp. If I go, if I prove to myself I can face it, maybe I won't be so terrified all the time."

"I get it," Tripp said. "But fear ain't all bad. There are some things you *should* be afraid of. Just . . . don't forget that, okay?"

The homecoming dance was held in the gym. It was worse than I'd dared to dream it could be, and I took tons of pictures to show Deja.

Paper streamers were hung from the walls, and other homemade decorations dangled from the ceiling. Vice Principal Kline played DJ, and he was armed with a laptop loaded with an unfortunate mix of twangy country music and whitewashed hip-hop. Students line danced to some of the songs, and when Kline played a song they couldn't find the rhythm to, they flung themselves at one another like salmon trying to swim upstream.

Maybe this was how dances were supposed to be. I hadn't gone to my school's homecoming dance in Seattle in ninth grade. Luca had said dances were a waste of time. I checked my phone to see if he'd messaged me, but he hadn't. I'd finally called Deja and talked to her about him, but her advice had been to give Luca some space to breathe, so that's what I was doing.

Astrid heaved a sigh. "I'm already bored."

"Well, you look nice." I nodded at the outfit she was wearing—black slacks with a short-sleeve white button-up blouse and a bow tie. It was Astrid's kind of weird, and it worked for her.

"Yeah, yeah. You clean up pretty okay yourself."

I plucked at the sleeves. "Eh, it's a little small. I wore it to a wedding a few months ago." I'd almost changed my mind about going while I was getting ready. The lesion over my ribs was bigger and I had to bite down on a washcloth to smother my screams as I cut the scab from my skin. Halfway through, I couldn't take it anymore and leaned over the toilet to vomit. There'd been nothing in my stomach to bring up but bile. If

I'd had my phone nearby, I would've called Astrid to cancel. Every time the scab grew back, I swore I wouldn't cut it off again, but I couldn't help myself. It was like biting my nails. I knew it was gross and that I should stop, but I couldn't.

Astrid and I stood near the wall, apart from the chaos. I looked around for Reba and found her dancing with some people I didn't know. Jarrett and Finn had shown up earlier, but I hadn't seen them in a while.

"So, what made you change your mind about coming?" I didn't think I would've gone to the dance if Astrid hadn't made me. The game had been fun enough—Tripp had sat with me and Reba and the others, though he'd looked uncomfortable the entire time—but the dance wasn't doing it for me.

Astrid rolled her eyes. "There's a concert in Orlando in a couple weeks. Dad said I could go, but only if I went to the dance. So here I am."

"And you dragged me along because . . . ?"

"Because I refuse to suffer alone, obviously."

I snorted. "Wow. Thanks."

"You're welcome."

Reba spotted me and waved from the dance floor.

"Go dance with her."

I laughed and shook my head.

Astrid nodded knowingly. "That's probably for the best."

"What's that supposed to mean?"

"I've seen you dance, Virgil."

I took Astrid's hand. "Come on."

"What're you doing?"

"*We're* dancing."

Astrid tugged her hand back. "Why?"

I looked around at everyone in their suits and dresses dancing like they didn't have a care in the world. I wanted what they had. "Because if people in Merritt are going to laugh at me, I can at least give them something funny to laugh about." This time, I offered my arm to Astrid. She stared at me like I'd lost my mind, but she eventually accepted and let me lead her to the dance floor.

Reba whooped and clapped when we reached her. I wasn't a good dancer, but I threw myself into it. Astrid lasted one song before telling me I looked ridiculous and leaving. I didn't care how I looked. I was having fun. The music drove the monster from my mind for a while; I loosened my tie and let it.

I was sweaty and smiling when Reba pulled me down so she could shout in my ear. "Hey, we're heading to Finn's now. You coming?"

I looked around for Astrid, but she was gone from the spot on the wall where I'd last seen her. She had a car, and I could text her that I'd left.

"Yeah," I said. "Let's go."

* * *

Jarrett drove his truck around the side of Finn's house and parked it by the detached garage. The front yard was a mess of trucks and cars parked haphazardly on the lawn. I could already hear the music blaring from inside the house. Jarrett abandoned us the moment we arrived. Reba stayed behind to check her makeup, and I waited with her.

"I love this song." Reba hadn't stopped dancing since we'd left the gym. It seemed she loved every song she heard.

"Don't know it," I said, mostly to myself. "Deja was the music savant in our group. I just listened to whatever she said was good."

Reba was all smiles in a sparkly sheath dress that looked good on her. She'd flipped down the visor and was touching up her eyeliner. "Deja?"

I nodded. "A friend from back home. She was our DJ. Luca was the gravity well that held our group together."

"What about you?"

"I was . . ." I paused. "I was Luca's boyfriend, I guess."

Reba dug into her purse for lipstick. "Whatever. You had to be more than that."

"Maybe. I don't know. My friends seem to be doing better without me than I am without them."

"You don't know that." Reba finished and swung her legs out of the truck, sliding down from the seat. "Could be they're just putting up a front so you don't feel guilty."

I got out of the truck and shut the door. "Come on. Let's go in."

Finn Duckett's house was a sprawling split-level monstrosity that looked like a drug dealer's villa, except it also had a barn on the edge of the property. To the best of my knowledge, the Ducketts didn't keep any animals. The whole house was ostentatious compared to every other house in Merritt.

"What do Finn's parents do, anyway?" I was standing in the kitchen with Reba and Jarrett. The red cup in my hand was sweating as badly as I was, but I couldn't take off my jacket because I was afraid I'd lose it.

"Finn's mom made a killing in real estate or something," Jarrett said.

Reba tried to cut him off by raising her hand, but she forgot she was holding a drink and ended up sloshing it down her arm. After she grabbed a napkin, she said, "Mr. Duckett's a trust fund kid. Inherited a small fortune."

My head thumped in time to the music, and I tossed back the weak, watery beer. Jarrett handed me another. "If they're rich, why do they live in Merritt?"

Jarrett's brows dipped in the middle. "What's better? Being a little fish in a big city or a shark in a small town?"

It took me a second to work through Jarrett's mixed metaphor. "I guess. But it's Merritt. You really think the trade-off is worth it?"

Jarrett shook his head. More people crowded into the kitchen, but he didn't seem to notice them. "You don't get it yet, do you, Virgil? Being king of the poorest island's better than being a nobody anywhere else. And it ain't even about money."

A girl I remembered from the *Clue* auditions—Cheyenne, I think her name was—slipped her arm around Jarrett's waist and whispered in his ear. His face lit up. "Duty calls."

Hey, wanna see something cool?

Reba and I drifted out of the kitchen and into the sitting room. Deer heads, stuffed and mounted, hung from the walls. Their eyes followed me, the pain of their final breath locked within for eternity. There were people everywhere. Most looked like they went to Merritt High, but a few appeared old enough that it had to have been at least a couple years since they'd graduated.

"Did you really date Finn?" I asked.

Reba laughed so loudly it drew the attention of the others in the room. "Finn can be charming when he wants. Especially when you pry him and Jarrett apart." Reba had changed out of her dress and into a pair of denim shorts with a pink camisole-style top. She still looked stunning. "Truth is, I only went out with Finn because I had a crush on Jarrett."

"Whoa, whoa, wait a second. Back that train up. You what?"

Reba laughed again. "Finn's loud and brash. He's rich. He's on the football team. He's the one with the tricked-out truck his mommy and daddy bought him, and all the fancy toys. But Jarrett's the one in control. He's the leader of the pack."

"He is?" That didn't seem to line up with what I'd seen so far. I hadn't spent *that* much time with Jarrett and Finn, but Finn definitely seemed to have his own ideas for ways to torture me. He was behind postering my locker with monster porn, and I suspected he'd been responsible for doxxing me too.

"Jarrett's mom is the same way. Folks think the Ducketts call the shots because they've got money and they use it to influence the town." Reba shook her head. "But it's the other way around. Mayor Hart pulls all the strings around here."

Merritt politics held zero interest for me, but I nodded along to be polite. "So that's why you wanted to date Jarrett?"

"Well, that and . . ." A wicked smile crept up on her face. "Have you seen him in tight jeans? Damn!"

My phone vibrated, and I fumbled it trying to answer. Luca's face popped up on my screen.

"The boyfriend?" Reba grabbed my phone. "Hi, Virgil's boyfriend!"

I snatched the phone back from her, laughing, and Luca

and I spent a few seconds shouting at each other over the noise before I went outside where it was quieter.

"Are you drunk?" was the first thing he asked.

I chug the beer he gave me to wash away the vinegar taste of him.

"No. That was just Reba. She's cool."

Luca grunted. "Maybe I should call you tomorrow. When you're home and sober." He sounded different. Cold and judgmental. I tried to ignore his tone, to will things to be okay between us.

"No! Talk to me now. I miss you so much."

Pause. "I miss you too, Virgil."

"You can't even believe this place, Luca. At the homecoming parade yesterday, someone threw a park bench through the window of the hair salon, and in the paper this morning the headline read, 'Merritt Residents Overflowing With Homecoming Enthusiasm.' Enthusiasm? It was a riot!"

"Sounds exciting."

"Hardly. I'll take boring with you over exciting in Merritt any day." I raked my hand through my sweat-damp hair. Mosquitoes were already swarming around me, searching for bare skin. "I can't wait to see you at Christmas."

Pause.

Silence.

"I can't come to Merritt for Christmas."

Everyone I love is on the other side of the world.

"Then I'll fly to Seattle," I said. "I'll stay with my mom. Or with Deja. Deja's parents love me."

"Virgil—"

"Don't you want to see me?"

Pause.

Silence.

"I can't do this." Luca's voice sounded muffled, like he was covering the mic with his finger.

Something crashes into me and I hit the moist ground.

"Virgil?" It was Deja.

"Where's Luca? Put Luca back on." I was sweating. No, I was crying.

Deja was talking, and I could hear what she was saying, but my brain kept crashing. I only caught fragments.

". . . really hard . . ."

". . . cares about you, but . . ."

". . . some time . . ."

Words are just words. They don't mean nothing.

"Is Luca breaking up with me?"

Pause.

". . . thinks it's for the best . . ."

I was only messing with you. I ain't no homo.

"Oh."

Silence.

"Virgil?" Jarrett was standing beside me, Finn next to him. I hadn't heard them approach. "You okay?"

Sorry, dude, but I'm with someone.

"No." I collapsed into a white wicker rocking chair. I held my cup to my lips to drink, but it was empty. "I think my boyfriend just broke up with me."

Jarrett's eyes were sympathetic. "Over the phone?"

"Yeah."

Finn poured his drink into my cup. "Forget that prick."

Jarrett's smiling when I catch his eye.

"Wanna talk about it?"

Finn elbowed Jarrett in the side. "This ain't a sleepover."

I drained the cup in two swallows. "I could use another drink."

He tries to hand me a beer, but I wave it off. Grandma will kill me if I come home smelling of alcohol.

Jarrett pursed his lips. "Are you sure?"

"Of course he's sure." Finn held out his hand to help me up. "C'mon. I know exactly what you need."

THIRTY-ONE

I BLINKED.

Blink

Blink

Blink

The world was dark. My eyes felt crusted over and sealed shut with concrete. Something covered my head. Every breath took too much effort. I licked my lips. I tried to lick my lips, but my tongue was sandpaper.

I blinked.

Blink

Blink

Blink

I tried to move my hands but couldn't. They felt bound together behind me. My shoulders burned and sweat coated my body. I shivered. My stomach lurched, and I threw up. The smell of hot cranberries and vodka filled my nose, which made me vomit again. It dribbled out of my mouth and ran down my bare chest.

I blinked.

Blink

Blink

Blink

A tantalizing hint of light danced around my bare feet. Weeds poked up from between my toes. The moon had been full, hadn't it? The moon had been *almost* full. And the sky had been clear. I could see my feet out the bottom of the sack covering my head.

I didn't scream.

"Hello?"

Wanna see something cool?

I squeezed my eyes and tried to remember how I'd gotten here.

The party must've spilled outside. Someone's playing Rihanna. ride ride ride ride.

Not Rihanna. Something else. Something twangy and unapologetically loud. But as loud as it was, I could only hear faint echoes of it carried by the wind through the trees like pollen settling in the fertile ground of my overactive mind.

I wiggled my fingers. They were swollen and numb. My

wrists were bound so tightly that I couldn't reach the knot. I couldn't tell what I was tied to. A tree? A fence post, maybe? It was the only thing holding me up.

I shuddered and breathed in the sour stench of my own vomit. I'd grown accustomed to the smell, but thinking about it for a second triggered my memory of it and I gagged again. There was nothing left in my stomach. A thin ribbon of drool leaked from between my dry lips.

A memory flashed through my mind like lightning, leaving only the afterimage behind.

"You eaten anything today?" Jarrett had asked as he'd handed me another red cup.

Around me, a crowd of people in the kitchen, led by Finn, had chanted, "Drink! Drink! Drink!" and I hadn't wanted to disappoint them.

My ankles weren't bound, but I was scared to move because I feared I'd collapse. I was balanced precariously, my weight divided between my knees and my shoulders. If I fell, I felt like my shoulders would pop out of their joints.

I shook my head, ignoring the dizziness, and tried to throw off the sack. It did me no good.

I don't know where I am. I pull out my phone to call for help, but I don't know who to call. Everyone I love is on the other side of the world.

Except that he didn't love *me* anymore. Luca had broken

up with me and cut the string connecting my heart to my home.

I was crying. No, I was sweating.

I blinked.

Blink

Blink

Blink

"Let me go!" I screamed and thrashed about as hard as I could. Whatever I was tied to shook but didn't give way. My shoulders throbbed and chunks of dried vomit fell out of the sack and onto my chest.

I could feel the mosquitoes feasting on my bare skin. I could see them land on my grotesque, distended belly like it was a distant alien world. I could see them on my chest, clustered around my nipple but avoiding the scabby lesion entirely.

Dude, you don't wanna go wandering out there.

Ain't nothing good in the sprawl at night.

My pocket vibrated. My phone. It had to be my phone. I struggled to reach it, but it was in my front pocket, inches and a million miles away. It might've been my grandparents calling to tell me something happened to my dad at work or my dad wondering where the hell I was. It might've been Deja checking in to make sure I was okay.

I wasn't okay.

Or it might've been Luca calling to say he'd made a mistake. He hadn't meant to break up with me, but the distance had gotten to him, and he'd been having a bad night. He was calling to take it back, to tell me he loved me. But if I didn't answer, he wouldn't know that I loved him too.

"Ha, ha!" I shouted. "Real funny! Let me go!"

Hey, wanna see something cool?

Drink! Drink! Drink!

Don't tell no one about this, all right?

The night symphony paused. Crickets set down their bows; the wind took a breath; the trees stilled their brushes and silenced their leaves.

Blink

Blink

Blink

A howl broke the silence. Rising, rising, cresting the slope, and then sliding down again into the disquiet night.

I don't know where I am. My head feels tight, like the skin around my skull is shrinking. Trees block the sky, and what little light from the moon that does reach the ground is filtered through blankets of Spanish moss draped from the branches.

Ignoring the searing pain in my shoulders, I struggled against the knot binding my wrists. I flung my body around, trying to use my weight to shake loose, but the structure I was tied to held firm.

My heart pounded faster and my breath **soaks my neck, a clawed hand pushes my face deeper into the mud.**

I didn't scream.

My phone vibrated again, but I couldn't reach **it worries me like a dog with a chew toy and then flings me aside.**

I heard it moving in the dark. I heard the sounds of the party as if I were right in the middle of it. Someone was laughing. A girl was saying she was ready to go home. A boy was muttering, "Almost there," over and over. Someone was crying. Their voices grew louder. I heard vomiting, the rumble of an idling engine, the clink of bottles. It was so loud. Much too loud.

And then much too quiet.

Come on. You'll like it.

The wounds on my back and arm itched. The bite on my shoulder ached. The scabs burned like they were acid eating my flesh. Whatever poison the monster had put in me that night in the sprawl called to it now.

Leaves crunched nearby.

I lie on my stomach, my arms askew, and try not to breathe.

I wondered who Luca was going to hook up with now that he was free of me. Probably Jacen Jones. I saw the way Luca had looked at Jacen when he'd passed by in the halls. The way Jacen had looked back. I wondered how long Luca would wait before making a move.

It lowers itself onto my back.

My phone vibrated. I gave up trying to reach it. I gave up trying to escape.

I gave up.

Did you fight back?

"Virgil?"

"Luca?" I didn't remember answering my phone. "Luca, is that you?"

My phone vibrated.

"Virgil? If you can hear me, say something."

A whimper escapes my lips as it rakes its claws across my back.

The symphony resumed.

I clench my eyes shut as tightly as I can and try to pretend I'm sleeping.

The symphony took a breath.

"Virgil?"

I go still and hope it kills me quickly.

Mud squelched nearby.

Everyone I love is on the other side of the world.

The night revealed itself to me. Light invaded the prison of darkness. Reflexively, I flinched.

"Virgil. Thank God I found you."

I blinked.

Blink

Blink

Blink

"Tripp?"

"Come on, Virgil. Let's get you outta here."

THIRTY-TWO

TRIPP DROVE OUT OF MERRITT, AND I DIDN'T ASK WHERE he was taking me. He'd given me a shirt to wear and a pair of flip-flops so small my toes dangled over the edges. The only thing he said to me after we got into his truck was, "Here," when he handed me a bunch of individually wrapped wet napkins that said REAL PIT BBQ on the outside. I used them to clean the puke off my face and chest. I tried wiping the smudges of purple and black from around my wrists, but wet naps don't work so well on bruises.

We pulled into a Waffle House, and Tripp led me inside. I'd caught a glimpse of myself in the mirror, so I knew I looked like I'd been dragged through the swamp facedown, but the waitress who popped by our table didn't seem to notice or care.

Tripp ordered for me. Coffee, water, and a little bit of everything else on the menu because he didn't know what I liked to eat.

"I'm not hungry."

"You gotta get something in you." Tripp sounded like Grandma.

"Luca broke up with me."

Tripp raised his eyebrow. "Your boyfriend from Seattle?"

The word "boyfriend" sounded sharp and harsh inside the Waffle House, with its truck-stop decor, but there were only three other people in the diner and none of them were paying attention to us.

I nodded.

"I'm real sorry, Virgil."

I was only messing with you.

The compassion in Tripp's eyes was too much. He meant to be sympathetic but his pity felt oppressive.

"Restroom." I slipped out of the booth and made my way to the back of the diner. The cramped, claustrophobic restroom smelled like bleach and bacon grease, and the fluorescent lights cast grim shadows on the floor. But it was clean. I ran the water as hot as I could stand it. My arms were dotted with red welts from the mosquitoes, and my eyes were bloodshot.

I scrubbed my hands with soap and water. I washed

my face. I used more soap. I turned the water up hotter. I scrubbed and scalded my hands. I wanted to peel my skin off like a glove.

Under my shirt, the scabby lesion on my torso was as big as an Oreo, the edges were pink and puckered and hot, and more coarse hairs grew from it like clumps of weedy grass. If I'd had my dad's razor, I would've sliced it clean off.

Instead, I scrubbed my hands again and again and again.

Tripp and more food than I could've eaten in a week were waiting for me at the table when I returned. He was quiet until I got settled.

"Are you okay?"

"Do I look okay?" The smell of pancakes and grits and waffles and eggs and sausage and bacon and—I had to fight back the urge to gag.

Tripp shrugged. "You look better now." He glanced at my red, raw hands and my bruised wrists. I dropped them to my lap.

"How'd you find me?"

"Astrid."

I furrowed my brow. "Astrid wasn't at the party." I searched my memories, but they were eggshell fragments strewn across the ground.

At least Tripp had an appetite. He shoveled hash browns into his mouth while he talked. "She said she had a bad feeling about the party, so she was watching pictures from it as they popped up online. She saw some of you and sent them to me."

He looked at me like I was supposed to know what he was talking about. I shook my head.

"You looked pretty drunk. Astrid was fixin' to get you, but I said I'd go since I live closer to Finn's."

I held out my hand. "Let me see the pictures."

Tripp hesitated before he pulled out his phone, tapped the screen a few times, and passed it to me.

Of the hundreds of pictures tagged at the party, only a few had me in them.

There I was with Reba, laughing, drink in one hand.

There I was in the kitchen, standing on a chair next to Finn with my arms raised over my head.

There I was with one arm each slung around Jarrett's and Finn's shoulders, singing, I think.

There I was cuddling an adorable goofy-eyed boxer.

I looked like I was having fun. Some of it even felt vaguely familiar.

Is Luca breaking up with me?

I glanced at Tripp. "These look like normal pictures. What was it that freaked Astrid out so bad she sent you to rescue me?"

Tripp set his fork down. "You don't—"

I kept swiping until I found what I was looking for. There

was no sack on my head yet, so it was easy to tell it was me. My shirt was gone and I was tied to the post of a wood fence in the sprawl. I was alone in the photo, but I couldn't have been alone because someone had to have taken the picture.

I can hear it panting. Feel it moving.

It was tagged MonsterBait.

"Whose account is this?" I didn't give Tripp a chance to answer. I tapped the picture to get to the account profile, but it was a new account with the name A_Holland117. This was the only picture they'd posted. "Who's A. Holland?"

Tripp cleared his throat. "Uh, it's a fake name."

"How do you know?"

"Because . . . uh—"

"Tripp!"

"Alec Holland is the name of one of the incarnations of Swamp Thing. He thinks he's Swamp Thing, anyway. He isn't really, but that ain't important. . . ." Tripp's voice trailed off.

#MonsterBait. It had 237 likes. I couldn't bear to read the comments. "This is why you came to get me?"

Tripp shook his head. "Like I said, Astrid called me, and I was closer and wasn't doing nothing but hanging out with my dad, anyway. I didn't see that picture until I got to Finn's house."

"The sprawl's not safe," I said. "You shouldn't have gone in."

"I wasn't gonna leave you out there."

"Why not? Two hundred and thirty-seven other people did."

Tripp looked up and over my shoulder. I didn't know why until he said, "Heya, Chief Duran."

Merritt chief of police Jodie Duran was wearing running shorts frayed at the edges and a T-shirt with a kitten on the front. Her hair was pulled back in a messy ponytail, and she wasn't wearing so much as a dab of makeup.

"You called the police?!" I scooted toward the edge of the booth. I had to get out of there. The booth, the Waffle House, the whole damn state of Florida.

Duran dropped her hand on my shoulder. "Whoa, there, Virgil. Take a breath. I'm just here to talk."

"I don't want anyone to know what happened!"

Tripp shook his head slowly. "Virgil, they already know."

#MonsterBait

Chief Duran sat down across from me. Tripp moved closer to the window to give her room. We didn't say anything until the waitress came by with coffee for the chief.

"You wanna tell me what happened?" Duran picked at a strip of bacon.

Don't tell no one about this, all right?

"No."

Duran nibbled the bacon and frowned at me. "Will you tell me anyway?"

I didn't want to. I wanted to leave and forget the entire evening, but I suspected the chief wasn't going to give up until I talked. "After the dance, I caught a ride to the party at Finn's house with Jarrett Hart and Reba Daniels."

"How long you been friends with them?"

"Not long."

Tripp cleared his throat. "Finn was the one decorating Virgil's locker with that monster porn." He snapped his fingers. "Oh! And didn't Jarrett admit to putting Kelvin Wright up to scaring you in the Coyote costume the first day of school?"

Duran pursed her lips. "They don't sound real friendly to me."

"They apologized," I mumbled. "They were only messing with me because I was new."

"Uh-huh." Duran tapped the table with her stubby fingers. "So you got to the party. Then what?"

"I had a couple drinks, and then Luca broke up with me—"

"Luca?"

"Virgil's boyfriend from Seattle," Tripp said.

"Ex-boyfriend."

Duran said, "He in town?"

"He's in Seattle. He broke up with me over the phone." I snorted. "He didn't even have the guts to do it himself. He made Deja tell me." I cut off the end of a sausage link and put it in my mouth without thinking. Grease squirted from the meat as I ground it between my teeth. I spit it into my napkin before it turned my stomach inside out.

"I'm real sorry about your boyfriend." Duran had a kind, gentle face that made talking to her easier. "What happened after that?"

I could use another drink.

"I don't . . ."

C'mon. I know exactly what you need.

"It's all kind of . . ."

Drink! Drink! Drink!

Tripp handed his phone to Chief Duran. Her expression betrayed nothing as she flipped through the pictures.

I caught Tripp's eye. "You were right. I shouldn't have gone to the party. Not after last time."

Tripp's chin jutted out. "This ain't your fault, Virgil."

I'm stuck in Merritt, at this party, with the taste of Jarrett Hart still in my mouth.

"Okay."

Duran coughed to get my attention. "You remember anything else?"

I tried, but there was a hole where my memory should've been. When I looked at those pictures, it was like they'd happened to someone else. Not me. "Just waking up tied to the fence."

Blink

Blink

Blink

"I've gotten drunk before, Chief, but I've never blacked out."

I sit down on the couch and it's dark outside. My skin's prickling from the heat and I'm stumbling around. I thought I was sitting.

"It was Jarrett and Finn who tied you up," Tripp said. "It had to be."

I shook my head. "No, they've been decent since—"

"Come on, Virgil. You can't be that gullible."

Chief Duran silenced Tripp with a look. "Buck, why don't you give me and Virgil a minute, okay?"

Tripp looked like he was going to argue. His calm, easy demeanor had been replaced with a rage I'd never seen. There was fire in his eyes, and he was looking for someone to burn. But the moment passed, and he nodded. Duran got up so he could leave.

When Tripp was gone and it was just me and Chief Duran, she folded her hands on the table. "That's a good friend you got there."

"Yeah."

"What do *you* think happened tonight, Virgil?"

Drink! Drink! Drink!

"I don't know."

"Do you think Finn Duckett or Jarrett Hart tied you up in the sprawl?"

Wanna see something cool?

"I don't know."

Duran sighed. "Here's where we're at, then. I could go talk to those boys, but their parents aren't likely to take me questioning them well. Mayor Hart and I don't see eye-to-eye often, and the Ducketts got enough money to make my life miserable."

"Okay."

"I'd also have to call your dad or your grandparents."

"I—"

"And since you can't remember much, unless one of them boys confesses, there ain't a whole lot I can do."

"But—"

"I could drag them down to the station—Lord knows I'd enjoy that—and maybe it'd scare them into leaving you be, but it might wind up causing you a heap more trouble than it's worth."

I understood what Chief Duran was saying, and I definitely didn't want my dad or Grandma and Grandpa involved, but hearing Duran say there wasn't anything she could do made me feel helpless. Tears welled in my eyes. "Someone tied me up out there. Someone left me in the sprawl for that thing to—" I stopped, but it was too late.

"What thing? What was out there, Virgil?"

"Nothing. I was out there."

Duran spread her hands. "I can't help you if you won't talk to me."

"Seems like you can't help me at all."

"If you want me to go after those boys, I will." Duran's sympathetic air nearly set me crying again. "But without evidence, without you being able to identify who tied you up, nothing'll come of it. I won't be able to hold them; I won't be able to charge them."

I didn't scream.

"Anything official I do probably won't help you much, and it'll almost definitely make your life worse. Is that what you want?"

Everyone I love is on the other side of the world.

I didn't see how my life could possibly get much worse.

I can't do this.

But it can always get worse.

"No, ma'am."

Chief Duran paid the bill and led me to the parking lot. She whispered to Tripp and then came around to where I was sitting in the truck. "You still got the card I gave you?"

I nodded.

"Use it, then, all right?"

I nodded again.

"I know this ain't fair, Virgil, and I'm sorry." Duran patted the truck door. "Y'all drive safe now."

Tripp cranked the engine and took off. The world blurred by outside as we drove in silence.

The memories I wanted to recall were lost to me while the ones I wanted to forget stalked me endlessly. "It was out there tonight."

"What was?" Tripp asked.

"The monster."

The smell hits me first. Like a decomposing corpse.

"I heard it in the sprawl."

"Maybe you were just groggy."

Drink! Drink! Drink!

"You said you believed me."

The night symphony pauses. Crickets set down their bows, the wind takes a breath, the trees still their brushes and silence their leaves.

"I do!"

A howl breaks the silence. Rising, rising, cresting the slope, and then sliding down again into the disquiet night.

"The monster was there. Whoever tied me up wasn't playing a prank. They left me out there for it."

#MonsterBait

"I'm sorry I didn't get there sooner." Tripp's voice was tight.

I laughed bitterly. "I felt so helpless. I don't want to feel helpless anymore."

"What do you want to do about it?"

Teeth dig into my shoulder.

"I want to find the monster that attacked me."

It lowers itself onto my back.

"And I want to kill it."

Tripp glanced at me quickly, taking his eyes off the dark, empty road for just a second. "If that's what you want, then that's what we'll do."

I didn't scream.

"That's what I want."

THIRTY-THREE

THEY WERE PREDATORS AND I WAS PREY, AND AT THE EDGES of the cafeteria, buzzards circled waiting for me to die. A howl rose from the north side of the lunch room. Another answered from the west. Laughter spread between them like ripples on a pond.

The harassment had picked up right where it had left off. Phone calls, text messages, notifications of comments across my social media accounts. My phone had been vibrating so much that the battery had finally given up and died.

I would've skipped lunch if that had been an option. I sat alone at my regular table, with the sandwich Grandma had packed spread out before me, and ignored the jeers, taunts, and stares the same way I'd ignored Deja's, Tripp's, and Astrid's phone calls Sunday.

I wore a hoodie despite the heat to cover the bruises around my wrists, and it felt like everyone could see the lesions on my body, glowing through my clothes like brands of shame.

A shadow fell across my lunch, and I glanced up as Reba sat down. She looked hungry.

"Go away."

"Now just wait a second, Virgil—"

"Was it Finn? Was it his idea or was it Jarrett's?" Grandma and Grandpa knew I'd been at the dance and at the party after, so they'd let me off the hook for church Sunday. I was certain they'd heard I was the town laughingstock through the church's gossip network, though, because Grandpa wouldn't look at me and Grandma set me to doing the filthiest chores she could think up when they got home. I'd had a lot of time to think while I was scrubbing toilets and mowing the lawn. It made sense that it was Jarrett or Finn who'd been responsible for binding my wrists and leaving me in the sprawl.

"It wasn't like that."

"Then what was it like, Reba? Was pretending to be my friend so I'd let my guard down and then tying me up and humiliating me always the plan or was it just a spur of the moment decision?"

Reba rubbed her hollowed-out eyes. "You were drunk. I kept telling you to slow down, but you wouldn't listen. You were so cut up about your boyfriend."

"There's a whole chunk of my memory missing. I didn't drink it away."

Reba bit the edge of her thumbnail. "I'm just telling you what I saw. Do you want to hear it or not?"

No, I didn't want to hear what Reba had to say. But I felt like I needed to. I nodded for her to continue.

"We were in the living room and someone asked you about the monster. You lost it, Virgil. You said the monster was real and you were going to prove it."

Drink! Drink! Drink!

"You figured the only way to convince everyone you were telling the truth was to lure the monster out and get it on video."

I stared at Reba, unable to speak. When I found my voice again, I said, "Are you really saying I did this to myself? Is that what you're telling me?"

Tears welled in the corners of Reba's eyes. "I tried talking you out of it, but you wouldn't listen."

"Who did it? Who tied me up? Was it Jarrett? Finn?"

"I don't know. I left before that."

"Who took the picture, Reba?" I held her gaze, certain she knew the answer.

Astrid dropped her bag on the table, breaking the spell. She loomed over Reba with her arms folded across her chest, staring at her from behind a lined, smoky eye. "You've got some nerve."

Reba glanced at Astrid, then me. "I'm telling you the truth, Virgil." She scooted back and scurried away.

When she was gone, Astrid sat down. She skewered me with her disappointment.

"Can we skip the I-told-you-so part of the conversation?"

"No." Astrid glared at me. "Because I told you not to go to the party, and you should've listened."

"Better?"

Astrid frowned and shook her head. "It wasn't nearly as satisfying as I'd hoped it'd be." Her expression softened. "Are you okay? I tried texting you yesterday, but you were clearly avoiding me."

"I was avoiding everyone." I hung my head. "I don't know. I guess I'm okay. Reba said I asked to be tied up in the sprawl. She said I wanted to prove the monster that attacked me was real. But I don't remember."

Someone shouted, "Monster bait!" Laughter filled the cafeteria.

Astrid rested her hand on mine. "Don't listen to them."

I know exactly what you need.

"Why can't I remember?"

My legs feel like jelly. I sit down on the couch and it's dark outside. My skin's prickling from the heat and I'm stumbling around. I thought I was sitting.

Astrid shrugged. "You're a lightweight. It probably didn't

take much to get you blackout drunk. Besides, I heard about Luca. I'm real sorry about that, by the way."

Sunday evening, I'd gone over every picture from the party I could find, but I hardly recognized anything. Astrid and Reba could've been right that I'd had too much to drink, especially because of how upset I'd been about Luca, but I still should've been able to remember *something*.

"We're gonna find out who did this to you," Astrid said. "All right?"

"But Chief Duran says—"

"Duran's decent enough, but that badge of hers is purely decorative. The boys in this town could spray-paint a confession on the water tower and Duran wouldn't do anything about it."

"What if I just want to forget what happened?" I thought about what I'd said to Tripp in his truck Saturday night, and I wasn't sure I had that kind of fight left in me.

Astrid looked around the cafeteria. "Do you think there's a chance they'll let you?"

"No. But maybe I should try anyway."

"It's your choice."

I wrapped up my lunch and pushed it aside. "Why do you care? I mean, I'm sure Uncle Frank told you to watch out for me or whatever, but you don't have to."

Astrid paused as if she'd been prepared to answer questions

but hadn't expected that one. "I guess I just want you to know you're not alone."

"It feels like I am."

"Yeah. It always does."

THIRTY-FOUR

MR. HILLIKER THE DIRECTOR WAS NOT THE SAME PERSON AS Mr. Hilliker the teacher. He stood at the edge of the stage while we sat clustered together in the front two rows of the house seats. "Life as you knew it is over. I don't care about your other extracurricular activities or your families. I don't care about your classes, either, but you *will* keep up with your work so that I don't have to hear from your teachers that you're falling behind."

Hilliker paced along the apron with his hands in his pockets.

"I expect you to be off book by next week. When you are in this auditorium, you will either be rehearsing with me, running your lines, or reading your script. I don't want to see any cell phones out when you're on my time, is that understood?"

Tripp shouted, "Sir, yes, sir!" while the others murmured their agreement.

There were seventeen of us, not including our stage manager, assistant director, and the tech crew, gathered in the theater after school. Mr. Hilliker had split out some of the ensemble roles, and those students would also understudy for the main roles.

"No one pays me to be here," Hilliker continued. "I'm here because I love this place. When I was your age, I didn't have a lot of friends, nor did I have a great home life. What I had was this." He held his arms wide and looked around the theater. "I found a home here; I found friends and a family. And my hope is to provide a safe place for others to find the same. You will not disrespect it or I will kick you out on your ass."

Hilliker held our gazes for a moment and then clapped his hands. "Now, let's get started."

My teeth rattled as Tripp drove down the bumpy dirt road toward his house. He'd invited me over after rehearsal, and it'd seemed a better option than going home, where I'd inevitably turn to my phone to peek at Luca's online life or read what horrible new things had been posted about me. And if I was really unlucky, Grandma would see me sulking and decide I needed something to do.

"Hilliker really takes acting seriously."

Tripp nodded. "He loves the theater more than he loves his wife and kids."

I rolled my eyes, but Tripp was the kind of person who couldn't help laughing at his own jokes. It made it easy to know when he was fooling around, and he looked as serious now as I'd ever seen him.

"So all that stuff about the theater being his home?"

"I heard a little about it," Tripp said. "My dad told me. High school wasn't a good time for Hilly."

It was strange to think of Hilliker as ever being the same age as me. It was weird to think that any of the adults I knew had ever been fifteen. I admit I was curious what Mr. Hilliker had gone through, but I didn't press Tripp for details because it felt disrespectful to go behind Hilliker's back. Truth was, I was pretty sure Hilliker would've been willing to tell me himself if I'd asked.

"How come you drive a stick shift?" I was mildly fascinated watching Tripp wrestle the shifter through the gears.

Tripp shrugged. "It was all I could afford."

"I don't even know how to drive."

"For real?"

"My mom said she was going to teach me when I turned sixteen in December, but I guess she won't be doing that now." I hadn't talked to my mom in a week, but I'd heard my dad fighting with her the other day over something related to the divorce.

"You got a learner's permit, even?"

I shook my head. "It wasn't a priority. I could take a bus or walk wherever I needed to go."

"You must really miss Seattle."

"I . . . **look at the picture of my beautiful boyfriend and perfect best friend, and I envy that they're together and I'm stuck in Merritt, at this party, with the taste of Jarrett Hart still in my mouth.** There's nothing there for me anymore. My mom doesn't want me, and Luca—"

"I shouldn't've brought it up."

"It's all right. It's not like it's ever far from my mind."

Tripp's house sat alone in the middle of an empty swath of land overgrown with grass and weeds. The two-story house looked like it was frozen at the tail end of a long sigh. A few shingles were missing from the roof, the gutters were overflowing with dead leaves and pine needles, the paint was faded in some spots and clean scrubbed away in others, and half of the screens on the windows had tears in them. It was like the before picture on a home renovation show.

Tripp parked the truck and got out. I followed. The front door was unlocked. Inside the house, the air was warm and stale. Newspapers and magazines were stacked neatly against the walls, and there were old radios everywhere.

"Sorry about the mess." Tripp dumped his backpack on the floor and then went around opening windows.

"I think this is the first Florida house I've set foot in that doesn't have air-conditioning."

"We got AC, but . . ." Tripp motioned toward the ceiling where a rectangular piece of cardboard was taped over the vent. "Dad's afraid of being sprayed with chemicals." He glanced at a boom box on the kitchen counter. "Thinks there're messages in the static, too."

The house might've been hot, humid, and full of trash, but it was neat and clean, and I had a feeling Tripp was responsible for keeping it that way. "Is he here?"

"Nah. He's hauling . . ." Tripp scratched his head. "Something. Somewhere."

"He can do that with his condition?"

"Oh yeah. As long as he takes his meds, he's all good. This is just the stuff that bleeds through from time to time."

"My dad dealt with a lot of mentally ill people in Seattle." I felt like I'd made Tripp uncomfortable bringing up his dad, and I started rambling as a result. "There was this guy who spent all day walking up and down the same two-mile stretch of road screaming at the top of his lungs. Dad got called out to help him after he got bumped by a car. Said the guy was incredibly nice. Just that he had a lot to say and wanted to make sure people heard him."

Tripp and I got our *Clue* scripts and sat at a wobbly table in a nook off the kitchen to go over our lines. We hadn't talked about the party since he'd rescued me, but it had been on my mind, and there'd been something I'd been meaning to say. It took me nearly twenty minutes to work up the nerve to say it. "I never got a chance to thank you. For the other night, I mean."

A blush crept into Tripp's cheeks. "You don't have to—"

"I don't know what would've happened if you hadn't come."

It lowers itself onto my back.

"You must think I'm crazy." I winced as soon as the word left my mouth. "I mean . . ."

"I know what you mean."

"You don't have to humor me, though."

Tripp knuckled his cheek, biting the inside. "The messed-up thing about the stuff my dad gets into his head is that he ain't real far off from the truth. He thinks we're being poisoned with chemicals, and we are—pesticides and car exhaust and fumes from factories."

"So you *do* think I made up the monster?"

Tripp pursed his lips and furrowed his brow. "The truth gets a bit twisted in my dad's head sometimes. Maybe it's just a little twisted in yours."

Hot breath soaks my neck, a clawed hand pushes my face

deeper into the mud. Bristly, wiry hair brushes the back of my arms.

"Maybe." I relaxed. "But if you don't believe me, why'd you say you did?"

Tripp dry washed his hands, keeping his eyes on the table. "Truth is, I don't know what attacked you out in the sprawl. You say it was a monster, and maybe it was."

"You said you'd help me find it and put it down."

Tripp looked up and caught my eye. "And I meant it. But I wasn't talking about the monster in the sprawl, I was talking about the monsters that put you there."

Wanna see something cool?

"I should go."

"Chief Duran can't do nothing about those boys, but maybe we can."

"Reba told me I asked to be tied up in the sprawl. She said I was trying to prove I hadn't lied about the monster."

Tripp opened his mouth to argue, but even he'd said Reba was a good person. I hadn't been able to come up with a reason why she would've lied to me, and I doubted Tripp would find one, either. Finally, he said, "That don't mean Finn or Jarrett weren't involved. Maybe one of them put the idea in your head so you'd think it was your doing."

Drink! Drink! Drink!

"Drop it, okay? Please? I only brought it up so I could

thank you. Now I just want to put it behind me."

Tripp's jaw was set and the muscles on the side of his neck were twitching. Then he unclenched, sighed, and nodded once. "But, look, if you change your mind, all you gotta do is ask, and I'll be there."

THIRTY-FIVE

I CARRIED TWO PIECES OF PECAN PIE OUTSIDE TO THE PORCH and sat on the swing beside Dad. I couldn't remember the last time he'd had a day off. When he wasn't working at the firehouse, he was roaming the floors at Target, watching for shoplifters. Dad tried to hide his exhaustion, but it hung off him like Spanish moss.

"How's the musical coming?"

I handed Dad his pie. "Who told you? And it's not a musical. Just a play."

"Your grandma mentioned it."

"I'll bet she did."

Dad took a bite of the sweet, crunchy pie and shut his eyes as he savored it. I'd never met a man who loved pie so much. "Whatever she said to upset you, I'm sure she didn't mean it."

"She said, 'When I was your age, boys didn't participate in theater.' Which, of course she'd say that. She went to an all-girls school."

The lines around Dad's eyes deepened. Weariness drained the color from his cheeks. "I'm trying to get us out of here, Virgil. I really am."

I heard what Dad didn't say. The blame reserved for me. How we might've already been in our own home if I hadn't gotten attacked in the sprawl and wound up in the emergency room. "I just wish they'd leave me alone. There's nothing wrong with theater."

"Your grandparents are from a different time."

"In Shakespeare's day the men played *all* the roles. Does that make Shakespeare a sissy?"

Dad patted my leg. "I know it's tough, kiddo. Just keep your head down and stay out of trouble."

I'd been worried Chief Duran would tell Dad about the party, but nearly a week had passed and she'd kept her word not to. He hadn't heard about it from the Merritt rumor mill or Grandma and Grandpa, either, probably because he was either working or sleeping and didn't have time for anything else. I would've told Dad myself, but he couldn't do anything about what was already done, and there was no use adding to his worries.

"You talked to Mom lately?"

Dad glanced at me with a raised eyebrow. "Are you trying to ruin my pie?"

"She doesn't talk to me either."

"Your mother's concerned about you."

"Silence is a crappy way to show it."

"I've known your mom a long time, so I get how difficult it can be to understand her. She gets caught up in her own world. But she loves you more than anything."

I couldn't tell if Dad was being honest or if he was trying not to be the bitter ex-husband who trashed his kid's mom. "Then why can't I live in Seattle with her?"

Dad flinched, and I might've felt bad except I knew he understood it had nothing to do with him and everything to do with Merritt. "Your mom got an opportunity to do something she's wanted to do for a long time."

"She couldn't have put it off for a couple years?"

"She put it off for fifteen, Virgil."

"Okay, but then why couldn't *we* have stayed in Seattle?" It wasn't the first time I'd asked that question. Dad's answer before had been, "Because I said so." I hadn't expected it to change, but Dad surprised me.

"Because I couldn't bear living in the same city as her."

"You hate her that much?"

"No." Dad's voice was softer. "I don't hate your mother at all."

My phone buzzed. Deja's name and smiling picture popped up on the screen. I stared at it a second before answering. "I don't want to talk to you."

Without needing to be asked, Dad took his plate inside, leaving me alone on the porch.

"Then why'd you answer your phone?" Deja's tone was as cool as mine. "I'm not the one who broke up with you, Virgil."

"No. You did it on Luca's behalf because he was too much a coward to do it himself."

Deja didn't miss a beat. "You're right. He pushed me into that, and I shouldn't have let him. I'm sorry." I heard the unmistakable anger in her voice. She probably wasn't half as sorry as Luca had been after she'd finished with him.

"Okay."

"What's going on with you?" Deja's anger broke like a fever, replaced by concern. "I saw a video of you tied to a fence. Are you okay?"

Laughter, reckless and chaotic, poured from me. "No? I don't know."

"Virgil?"

I told Deja what happened the night of the homecoming dance, and once I began talking, I couldn't stop. "The last thing I remember before being out there is Luca breaking up with me. Luca and the sprawl are forever entwined in my memory now, so when I think of him, I won't think of the first time we kissed or the night he told me he loved me or the way he could make me smile when no one else could. I'll only think of waking up with a sack on my head, tied to a fence, and how terrified I was."

Deja didn't speak for a long time. She didn't tell me she was sorry or try to convince me I should go to the police. She just occupied the silence with me.

When I couldn't take it anymore, I said, "Why'd Luca do it? I don't understand."

"I know."

I could hear the sounds of Seattle behind Deja. The gentle rain, the whirr of a bus passing, the insistent beep of a truck backing up. Those sounds had grated on my nerves once. Now I missed them.

"For the record," Deja said, "I think he made the wrong decision."

"But he doesn't, does he?"

Deja could've given me false hope, told me Luca was being eaten alive by doubt, but that wasn't her style. "No."

My relationship with Luca was over. He didn't love me anymore, and that was the moment it became real. Deja sat on the phone with me while I cried.

"I'm still your friend, Virgil."

"You're *his* friend."

"And yours. Maybe you could come up for Thanksgiving and stay with me."

"Your mom hates Thanksgiving."

"I know."

"She calls it an exploitative holiday for genocidal colonizers."

Deja laughed. "She's not wrong, but I do love pumpkin pie."

The thought of pumpkin pie made me gag.

"Ask your dad. I'll even pay for the plane ticket if you need me to. I got some birthday money—"

"I'll try."

"Don't give me that nonsense." I pictured Deja's stern frown, her one eyebrow raised as she looked down her nose at me. "Do better than try."

I got off the phone a few minutes later. I should've felt better knowing Deja was still my friend, but she was also the last tether connecting me to a world I wasn't part of anymore and that was stretched so thin I feared even it would soon snap.

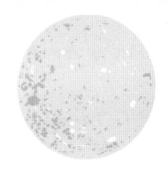

THIRTY-SIX

"WANNA SEE SOMETHING COOL?" JARRETT UNBUTTONS
*his shirt, sliding it off and letting it fall to the muddy ground.
He unbuttons his shorts and drops them around his ankles. He
unbuttons his skin and slips out of it too.*

"Sorry, dude, but I'm with someone."

"It's cool."

"Not for me."

*Jarrett crosses the distance between us faster than my brain can
process. He slides one fingernail down the front of my T-shirt, slicing
through the cotton, turning my favorite shirt into a rag. He digs the
end of his nail into the scabby lesion on my chest. It's a zipper. Jarrett
unzips my skin to my navel and then steps back and laughs.*

*"Don't tell no one about this, all right? I was only messing
with you."*

"Whatever you say."

"I ain't no monster."

Jarrett's knees pop as the joints reverse, bending backward now. He falls to the ground and cries. A hand bursts from his chest, and Luca claws his way free. He's covered in blood and thick gobbets of rotting meat. His face is red, his eyes are red, his smile is white.

"Luca?"

"Just came to take what's mine."

A whimper escapes my lips as he rakes his claws across my back. As he punches through my spine and tears out my heart. I think I'll die from the pain, but I don't. I'll live with the hurt forever.

I finish unzipping my skin and leave it behind.

"What am I supposed to do now?"

"You're a monster, baby," Luca says. "Be a monster."

I shut the door to the carport quietly behind me. My bed-sheets were balled up under my arm, and I only breathed when I was sure I'd made it through the house unnoticed.

"What're you doing, Virgil?"

I yelped and turned around to find Grandma standing at the washing machine.

Grandma was in her housecoat with her hair in rollers. "Are those your sheets? I do sheets on Sunday."

"I know."

"Today's Friday."

"I know that too." Which meant there must've been a good reason I was sneaking around the house trying to wash them. But of course Grandma couldn't be asleep like a normal person. It was barely dawn, so she'd probably been awake for hours planning how she was going to ruin my weekend, the month, and the rest of my life. "I needed to wash them and I didn't want to bother you with it."

Grandma held out her hands. "Well, I'm doing a load, so let me have them."

"I can take care of it." I hugged the sheets to my chest.

Irritation flashed across Grandma's face. "I don't have time for your foolishness this morning, Virgil."

"I said I can do it myself."

Grandma rolled her eyes. "I raised two boys. Whatever you've done to your sheets, I promise I've seen it before."

"It's—"

Dad popped his head out the door. "Mom, have you—" He stopped when he saw me. "Virgil? What're you doing up?"

"Oh my God. Does nobody in this house ever sleep?"

"He's soiled his sheets," Grandma said, "and he's too embarrassed to let me wash them."

"I didn't soil my sheets!"

"This might be something else." Dad frowned in Grandma's

direction. "Something only a father would understand."

"Please, Tommy. Who do you think washed yours and Frankie's socks when—"

"It's mud!" I shook my sheets out to reveal the brown streaks staining the cotton. "There's mud on my sheets. I woke up with mud on my sheets and I have no clue how it got there." I threw the sheets on the ground. "You want to wash them so bad? Go for it." I turned and stormed inside, shoving past Dad on my way in.

I knew I'd crossed the line yelling at Grandma, but I wasn't going to sit around and wait to get scolded. I grabbed clean clothes, locked myself in the bathroom, and turned on the shower.

The scab over my ribs was still getting bigger. The one on my thigh was the size of a slug. A new one had appeared on the underside of my right bicep, thick hairs sprouting around the border. Every time I cut off a scab, it grew back. I should have left the scabs alone or told Dad so he could take me to the doctor, but I couldn't. I kept cutting them off and they kept returning. That pain was one of the few things I could count on.

Jarrett unzips my skin to my navel and then steps back and laughs.

I was sick. There was something wrong with me. Dr. Nalick had been wrong. The monster had infected me with a disease that was changing me. I wasn't sure into what, but

I was scared it was only a matter of time before I woke up in bloody sheets instead of muddy ones. It felt inevitable.

Taking a shower hadn't helped me avoid the consequences of my outburst. Breakfast was waiting for me at the kitchen table. So were Dad and Grandpa.

"Sit," Grandpa said.

I obeyed without hesitation.

Grandpa folded his hands on the table. "The first thing you're going to do after you've finished eating is apologize to your grandmother."

The plate was swimming with maggots. "I'm not hungry."

"You're going to eat."

I looked to Dad for help, but he was sitting with his chin against his chest like he was fifteen again. "Dad?"

"I'm going to make an appointment with a therapist for you, Virgil."

Grandpa sighed. "The boy doesn't need a therapist. He needs the business end of a belt."

Dad caught Grandpa's eye. "I don't beat my child."

"Leave the melodrama for your son, Thomas. We spanked you and Frank, and it's a good thing we did."

"How do you figure that, Dad? I'm a forty-year-old man with a failed marriage living at home again, and Frank's an alcoholic. What good did whipping us with your belt accomplish?"

"I have to get to school."

Both men turned to me as one and barked, "Sit!"

I remained seated.

Dad set aside his argument with Grandpa and gave me his full attention. He raked his hand through what was left of his hair. "You *will* apologize to your grandma, and then you and I will discuss the rest of your punishment this weekend."

"Will that be before or after the chores I'll already be assigned as penance for being attacked?"

Grandpa looked at Dad as if to say, *See?*

Through clenched teeth, Dad said, "Go to school. Now."

I didn't wait for him to tell me twice. I grabbed my backpack and took off. Grandma was on the porch swing reading a book. She didn't look up.

"I'm sorry, Grandma."

Nothing.

"I shouldn't have yelled at you."

"No. You most certainly should not have."

"I didn't . . ."

Grandma looked at me over the top of her book. "You didn't what, Virgil?"

I didn't want you to see the mud. I didn't want you to know that I'm scared because I don't know how it got there. I didn't want you to look at me the way you're looking at me now. I didn't want you to look at me with the same disbelief as the night you picked me up from the emergency room. "I didn't want to cause any problems."

"And how did that work out for you?"

"About as well as everything else since I moved to this crappy town."

Grandma slipped a bookmark between the pages of her book and set it in her lap. "My daddy used to say that if it smells like manure everywhere you go, check the soles of your own boots."

I furrowed my brow. "Okay?"

"Have you ever considered that Merritt isn't the problem, Virgil?"

"Well, no—"

Grandma picked up her book. "Maybe you should."

THIRTY-SEVEN

"WHAT THE HELL IS THAT? YOU GOT AIDS OR SOMETHING?"

I was trying to get out of my shirt as quickly as I could so that I could change into my gym clothes, but the words hit me and I got tangled in the sleeves, making me more vulnerable. I finally managed to yank my shirt over my head. Grady was standing a couple lockers down, staring at the scab over my ribs.

I shrugged. "Can't have AIDS if you've never had sex."

Grady's eyes narrowed and looked at me like I'd asked him to solve a trigonometric equation. After a moment he shook off his confusion and shouted, "Dude, I think Knox's got AIDS. *And* he's a virgin!" The steam that hung in the air carried Grady's voice to the other side of the locker room, eliciting laughter. Great. I'd given them more ammunition they could use to mock and harass me. Not that they needed it.

I tugged on my shirt, changed into my shorts and sneakers, and walked as quickly as my dignity would allow to the PE field.

Of course, everyone was looking at me and whispering. Under normal circumstances, I would've been swearing along with the others at Coach Munford's announcement that we were going to be running laps most of the period, but I was grateful I didn't have to deal with the forced social interaction imposed by team sports.

When it came to running, I fell pretty squarely in the middle of the pack. I let my mind drift while my legs kept pace. Of course, it drifted right back to the fight I'd had with Dad and my grandparents that morning. Then back to waking up in muddy sheets. No matter how hard I strained to reach into my memory, I couldn't recall how I'd gotten so filthy, and that terrified me.

What had I been doing outside in the middle of the night? Where had I gone? What had I done? My body felt like a chrysalis, and I didn't know what was going to emerge when I completed my transformation.

"What the hell's Grady going on about? How'd you get AIDS if you're a virgin?" Jarrett must have fallen back from his position at the front of the pack so he could talk to me. That or he'd lapped me from behind.

"I don't have AIDS. And Grady's a dick for saying that.

First of all, HIV is totally treatable these days. Second—"

"Don't shoot the messenger." Jarrett glanced at me. "You look like you're itching to shoot someone, though."

"Gee, I wonder why."

Carrying on a conversation while jogging was difficult for me, but Jarrett hardly seemed winded. "Reba said she told you I had nothing to do with dumping you in the sprawl. Finn didn't either."

Drink! Drink! Drink!

"Right. I tied myself to the fence and somehow managed to take a picture from five feet away with my hands bound behind my back."

Jarrett didn't respond. He didn't run away, either.

"What happened that night? I remember Luca breaking up with me. You and Finn were there." I shook my head. "The rest is a blank until I woke up in the sprawl again."

"It was a party. You had a couple drinks; we all hung out and had a good time."

"Reba said I asked to be strung up."

Jarrett looked over to catch my eye. "I wasn't around for none of that."

Come on. You'll like it.

"You were with someone?"

Jarrett nodded. "Can't say who, though, so don't ask."

"Convenient."

"Right." Jarrett bit back a laugh. "Except no one gives a shit who *you're* hooking up with."

"You think people care that you're gay?"

"I already told you I ain't a homo."

"Bi? Pan? Curious?"

Jarrett didn't say a word. I heard his answer loud and clear, though.

"I hate this town," I said.

"Most folks around here wouldn't care," Jarrett said. "Only *my* folks."

"Sorry," I muttered. Growing up in Seattle, it'd been easy to forget there were still parts of the country and the wider world where being queer could get you killed.

Don't tell no one about this, all right?

We jogged in silence for a couple minutes before I worked up the nerve to say, "If you were hooking up with someone at the party, how do you know it wasn't Finn who tied me up in the sprawl?"

Again, Jarrett didn't answer.

"Oh."

"Finn really ain't gay, though." Jarrett kept his voice low. "So don't say a word unless you're looking to die."

"I won't."

Jarrett's expression said he wasn't joking, and I believed him. "Me and Finn have been friends since kindergarten. He's the only other one who knows about me." Jarrett shrugged. "Sometimes he gets drunk and we fool around. It don't mean nothing to him."

It was unlikely that the two people I had the most reason to suspect of leaving me in the sprawl were each other's alibis. But if Jarrett and Finn had been the ones who'd tied me up, I had a feeling Finn, at least, would've devised a story that didn't involve him fooling around with Jarrett. I was sure there were any number of girls at Merritt High who would've enjoyed being his alibi.

Hey, wanna see something cool?

Jarrett brushed my arm with the back of his fist to get my attention. "I'm real sorry for what went down, though. If I'd been around, I wouldn't've let it happen."

Why did he have to sound so sincere? The cynical part of me examined every word he'd said, looking for cracks in his story, but I found none. When Jarrett said he wasn't involved, when he said he was sorry, I believed him.

"I just wish I knew what happened. Maybe Reba's right and I asked to be tied up in the sprawl, but I don't know."

Jarrett didn't say anything else while we were running. At the end of class, I showered fast—sticking close to the corners and shadows and avoiding the curious eyes of people looking for the lesions Grady had sworn he'd seen—and then changed back into my regular clothes. When I fished my phone out of my locker, there was a message from Jarrett with a video attached.

Hope this helps.

I played the video.

The music was loud, and a hundred voices were competing to be heard. Whoever was recording the video wandered through the house. They stopped in the living room where people were sitting on the couch and on the coffee table—anywhere there was room.

"Bullshit!" a voice shouted.

There I was, leaning against the wall near the doorway to the dining room. Reba was standing nearby, shaking her head. I still had my shirt on. I was holding a red cup.

". . . and I'll prove it! There's a monster out there!"

I couldn't see who I was arguing with or hear what they said.

"I'll be the bait." I slurred my words as I spoke. "I'll go out there right now and wait for that monster. Then you'll see."

Reba grabbed me and shoved me into the other room. That's where the video ended.

Blink

Blink

Blink

#MonsterBait

THIRTY-EIGHT

AFTER CHURCH ON SUNDAY, DAD TOOK ME TO TASTY CONES.
I avoided looking at the spot in the parking lot where I'd collapsed. One of the Hunt children, Nine of Eleven maybe, shrieks
in terror. Every conversation in the parking lot skids to a halt as the
child's sound splits the night, doing the one thing I've been unable
to do. Mrs. Hunt drops her uneaten cone. Pastor Wallace shouts,
"What in the Yankee Doodle?!" Coach Munford says, "That ain't
blood is it?" while Missy Pierce slaps his arm and says, "Call the
police, stupid!"

We took our ice cream cones and walked back toward
Main Street. Dad picked a park bench, seemingly at random,
to sit at. The toe of my sole remaining sneaker catches in a pothole,
and I stumble forward, shredding my palms and knees on the asphalt.
My jeans, which hang around my hips with little more than prayer,

are already ruined. I crawl until I reach a bench I can lean on to help me stand.

Strawberry ice cream dribbled down the sides of Dad's hand as he idly licked it. He seemed as disinterested in his cone as I was in mine. "I need you to be straight with me, Virgil. What's going on with you?"

It had been a couple days since my meltdown, and I'd been hoping we had all agreed to pretend it hadn't happened. Grandpa was back to ignoring me and Grandma had resumed talking to me, if only to tell me what chores needed doing.

"Nothing's going on. Everything's fantastic." I licked the chocolate blob perched atop the cone, trying to stay ahead of it melting, but my throat closed up as soon as the thick, sugary stuff touched my tongue.

Dad frowned. "I talked to your teachers. Only Mr. Hilliker had anything good to say about you. The others said you sleep during class, rarely turn in homework, and don't participate. If it weren't for your test scores, you'd be failing most of your classes."

"But I'm not failing."

"That's not the point."

"Then what is?" I wasn't trying to be a smartass, but I definitely came across as one.

"You're not a C student, Virgil. You got so upset when Mrs. Jahari gave you a B in eighth-grade math that you didn't shut up about it for a month. You used to care about your grades."

I shrugged.

"Then there's your sleepwalking—"

"How is that my fault?"

"And you're still sleeping in your closet."

My ice cream was melting over my hands, and I gave up trying to stop it. "So what if I am?"

Dad eyed me, lingering on my midsection. "What about your weight? Do you think I haven't noticed how thin you've gotten?"

I resisted the urge to cradle my belly and push in the bulging fat. "You were skinnier than me when you were my age. I've seen the pictures."

Dad finally gave up on his cone and threw it away. He tried to clean his fingers with a napkin, but it was a lost cause. "Tell me what's wrong, Virgil. This isn't you."

I don't know what's happening to me.

And I'm terrified. "I'm fine."

"You're not fine."

"How would you know? You're always working. You're barely a part-time dad."

A couple folks were walking their dogs in the park behind us, lingering nearby, pretending not to listen. By dinnertime, the whole town would know what Dad and I had talked about.

"That's not fair." Dad couldn't hide the hurt in his eyes.

"Weren't you the one who said life isn't fair? Or was that Grandpa?"

Dad sucked in a breath and held it, staring me down, probably hoping I'd blink or start sobbing so we could have a touching father-son moment. I did neither. "I'd make you quit the school play, but since acting's the one class you're doing well in, I don't want to mess that up."

I didn't tell him it was an extracurricular activity and therefore not tied to my grade. "Isn't having to live in Merritt punishment enough?"

Dad ignored me. "You're going to come home right after rehearsal every day. Your grandmother's agreed to help you with your homework despite how you've been treating her."

"That's not going to work with my schedule—"

Dad smacked the ice cream cone out of my hand and sent it flying onto the sidewalk where it splattered in front of Mr. Griffin's shih tzu, who made a valiant attempt to lick it up before Mr. Griffin yanked the leash and pulled his dog away.

"Do I look like I'm joking, Virgil? You *will* do as you're told. There will be no more parties, no more football games, no more friends. From now on, you'll go to school, go to rehearsals, and then come home. Period."

"This isn't my home."

Dad shook his head. "Neither's Seattle. Not anymore. It's past time you accepted that."

THIRTY-NINE

MR. HILLIKER PACED BACK AND FORTH ALONG THE FRONT of the stage, knuckling his spine. "You're not supposed to be funny, Virgil."

I'd been in the middle of a scene with most of the rest of the cast when Mr. Hilliker had stopped us. "But I thought this was a comedy."

"It is, but *Wadsworth* doesn't know that. Part of the comedy comes from playing it seriously." He looked at the rest of the cast in turn. "That goes for all of you, *Tripp*."

Tripp pointed at himself. "Why're you calling me out?"

Mr. Hilliker didn't bother answering. Nor did he need to. Tripp was genius when it came to the physical comedy, but he still hadn't nailed the voice of his character, and each attempt was more outlandish than the last.

"From the top of the scene, please."

The theater was the one place in Merritt where I felt normal. Mr. Hilliker was strict, but I felt like I was becoming a better actor because of him. It made it that much easier for me to pretend everything was okay.

Everything was not okay.

True to his word, Dad had locked down my life. When I wasn't at school, I was at home doing homework or chores. I also had my first therapy appointment, but it hadn't gone so well. Pastor Wallace was Merritt's only licensed therapist, and while he'd been nice enough, I was pretty confident Jesus wasn't the answer to my problems. Dad said he'd try to find a therapist outside of Merritt.

Tripp elbowed me in the side when Mr. Hilliker let us go for the day. "What's *he* doing here?"

I didn't know what Tripp was talking about at first, but I followed his sight line to the back of the house where Jarrett was sitting with his feet up. He looked like he was sleeping.

"Don't know and don't care." I gathered my belongings from where I'd dumped them by the front row.

"You wanna come hang out at my house? I've been doing some reading about cryptids, and—"

"I told you I'm grounded."

"For how long?"

I spread my hands. "Forever?"

Tripp hung his head. "Oh."

"Sorry."

No matter what happened, Tripp bounced back quickly. He never seemed to stay angry or depressed for long. "It's cool. I could try to get Hilly to give us a pass for lunch tomorrow. I'll tell him we're running lines or something. Or maybe I could drop by your house."

"Maybe. I'll have to ask."

Mr. Hilliker called Tripp over, so I headed outside. I tried to avoid looking at Jarrett, but his head popped up as I neared, and he stood and fell in beside me.

"Can we talk?"

Since Jarrett had shown me the clip where I'd volunteered to prove there was a monster in the sprawl, I hadn't exactly been avoiding him, but I hadn't welcomed seeing him either.

"My grandma should be here soon." I kept walking until I reached the roundabout where Grandma normally picked me up.

"It'll only take a few minutes, but not here." Jarrett usually projected an aura of ease, but right then he seemed anxious enough to climb out of his skin.

Come on. You'll like it.

"Whatever you have to say, just say it."

Jarrett shoved his hands in his pockets and agitated like a washing machine, looking everywhere but at me. "It's just, ever since you showed up in Merritt, I've had this feeling like we're the same—"

No matter what I say, Jarrett hears the answer he wants to hear.

"God, Jarrett, Luca *just* broke up with me, like, two weeks ago."

Drink! Drink! Drink!

"Besides, I'm not into you that way." My shoulders fell. "I don't think I'll ever feel that way about anyone again."

"That's not . . ." Jarrett shook his head.

A car horn that sounded like a goose being murdered cut Jarrett off before he could elaborate. Grandma had pulled up in a busted white VW Jetta instead of her Cadillac. I left Jarrett standing on the sidewalk and trotted toward Grandma.

"New car?" I slung my backpack onto the floor and climbed into the passenger seat.

"Your grandfather rescued it from a dealer for three hundred dollars."

"Smells like he overpaid."

Grandma cracked a smile. The first I'd seen in days. "I told him the same thing." The car had a manual transmission, and Grandma eased through the gears like she'd been born with a shifter in her hand. "Are you and the Hart boy friends?"

I honestly don't know. "Not really."

"Good."

"You don't like him?"

"I don't care for the family."

"Why not?" I was sure Grandma had a reason; I just wasn't sure it was a good one. She wasn't exactly known for being open-minded.

"Garrett Hart was trouble when he was Jarrett's age. You'd do well to steer clear of them."

I couldn't help laughing. "Wait, so Jarrett's dad's name is Garrett?"

"They're not a particularly creative family." Instead of driving home, Grandma drove past the house to an old field, where she parked the car and shut off the engine.

"Did you bring me out here to murder me, Grandma? I know I've been a pain in the ass, but—"

Grandma leveled a frown at me. "Language, please."

"Sorry."

She unbuckled her seat belt and reached for the door. "Switch places with me."

I had a ton of questions, but I did as I was told.

"You've never driven before, have you?" Grandma asked when we'd both gotten settled.

It felt strange to be sitting behind the wheel. "No, ma'am."

"Well, I think it's time you learned. With your father

working all the time, your grandfather and I can't be running you around everywhere."

I chuckled. "Not like there are too many places I can go, seeing as I'm grounded for the rest of my life."

"You deserve your punishment, Virgil. However, once your grades are where they ought to be and you've proven that you can be respectful and responsible . . . Well, I think this will be a suitable starter car for you."

The floors, which had no mats, were scuffed and worn, the dashboard was cracked, the radio was missing completely, the fabric seats were torn, and the headliner was drooping. It wasn't much of a car, and I wasn't sure how it was actually running, but that made me love it even more. "You're giving me this?"

Grandma looked at me like I should've known better. "You're going to earn it by continuing to do chores, by watching your mouth, and by doing whatever your grandfather and I ask of you."

"I can deal with that."

"You'll also need to learn to operate this vehicle well enough to convince me that you are a safe and courteous driver, and it will need some work before it's roadworthy."

My sixteenth birthday was less than two months away, but I hadn't given much thought to getting my driver's license. I hadn't needed one in Seattle. But Merritt was home now whether I liked it or not.

"I don't know anything about fixing cars."

"Luckily, your grandfather does." Grandma smiled. "I will teach you how to drive, and he will help you fix this unfortunate mess."

Accepting the car felt like admitting I'd been wrong, and while I felt bad about some of the things I'd said, I'd meant others. "Why are you doing this?"

Grandma didn't answer immediately. She ran her hand along the dash as if she could read the memories left behind by the car's previous owners. A delicate smile touched her wrinkled lips. "My memory isn't what it used to be, Virgil, but I *do* recall what it's like to be young sometimes, and I know it is not always easy."

Everyone I love is on the other side of the world.

"Oh."

"I know it seems difficult to believe now, but you *will* get through this. You will find your way, and you will grow into the man I know is inside you." She patted the gearshift. "Now, listen closely. Your left foot rests on the clutch and your right foot handles the gas pedal and the brakes."

I did my best to pay attention, but I couldn't stop thinking about what she'd said and wondering if it was a man inside of me or a monster.

FORTY

THERE WAS SOMETHING CATHARTIC ABOUT WATCHING the Coyotes blunder their way up and down the field while Astrid provided snarky commentary that earned her scowls from everyone within earshot. It was also nice *not* to be the person everyone was staring at or talking about for once.

Despite Dad's decree that I not be allowed to go anywhere other than school, Grandma had said I could go with Astrid to the game. Dad was at work and, "What he doesn't know won't hurt him," Grandma had said. "Just this once."

I suspected Astrid's sudden enthusiasm for high school football had less to do with the game and more to do with springing me from my self-imposed prison of despair. I wouldn't have been surprised to learn Uncle Frank had bribed Astrid to spend time with me, though I had no idea how they'd managed to convince Grandma and Grandpa to set me loose for the evening.

"I can't believe Grandma's teaching you to drive." Sitting beside me on the bleachers, Astrid looked more out of place than I did. She'd dyed her hair bright lime green and painted her nails to match. Grandpa's reaction when he'd seen her was to ask where she'd hidden her pot of gold.

"She didn't give me much choice. I'm still not sure if it's a reward or part of my punishment."

Astrid laughed. "Is it awful?"

"Surprisingly, no." Driving lessons after rehearsals over the last week had grown into something I looked forward to. "Grandma's an okay teacher. She knows what she's talking about, and she's patient."

"'Patient' isn't a word I associate with Grandma."

"I'm as shocked as you are."

Astrid flared her nostrils. "Do you think they'll give me a car if I yell at them?"

I snorted and laughed. "Did you see the piece of crap I'll be driving? It's like a quarter step up from a riding lawn mower."

I was having fun. For a brief moment in time I had forgotten about Luca, forgotten about the 347 notifications on my phone alerting me to comments people had left for or about me, forgotten about the sprawl, forgotten about the lesions expanding across different regions of my body, forgotten that I called Merritt home now. I forgot and began to enjoy myself. Then Jarrett and Reba climbed the steps and made their way to some empty seats nearby. Jarrett caught my eye and smiled.

Come on. You'll like it.

I looked at my shoes.

"You okay, Virgil? Should we leave?"

I glanced up through my lashes. Jarrett wasn't looking at me anymore, but Reba was. She waved before settling into her seat.

"I'm okay."

I wasn't okay. I didn't know how I felt seeing Jarrett and Reba, especially after Jarrett had sent me the video proving I'd practically begged to be tied up in the sprawl. I'd shown the video to Tripp but he'd insisted someone could've put the idea in my head—and he made no secret of who he thought that had been. The video evidence didn't change that I'd been to two parties at Finn's house and had wound up in the sprawl both times.

Teeth dig into my shoulder.

Astrid didn't speak for a while. We watched the game, neither of us really interested. During a time-out, she turned to me. "I was talking to Katie Lynn Farmer. She said she's heard things about Finn."

Don't tell no one about this, all right?

I frowned. "Whatever you heard, it's none of our business."

Astrid's eyebrows dipped to form a V. "Sure . . . uh, but Katie Lynn said she's heard whispers that girls who get cozy with Finn at his parties often wake up the next day unable to remember much." She paused and fixed me with a pointed stare. "What'd you think I was gonna say?"

I ain't no homo.

"Nothing."

"If you know something else, Virgil—"

I wasn't trying to protect Jarrett or Finn so much as trying to avoid being the person who outed them. "You know how much drinking goes on at those parties. Half the people there probably don't remember much the next day, and the ones who remember probably wish they could forget."

I chug the beer he gave me to wash away the vinegar taste of him.

"What if those girls weren't just drunk? What if Finn put something else in their drinks?" Astrid spoke in her regular voice as if she didn't care that everyone could hear her.

I don't know where I am.

"I have to pee." I stood and shoved my way to the end of the row, knocking into people and causing a ruckus. I muttered apologies until I was free, and then I ran, trying to catch my breath. I rounded the corner near the concession stand and stumbled into a man's back.

"Don't touch me!" The man whirled around. He was tall with willowy limbs, a round stomach, and a bowed back.

"I didn't—"

"Who are you?" Salt-and-pepper stubble covered his cheeks, and there was a familiar quality to his eyes.

"Dad, calm down!" Tripp barreled toward us, and the resemblance came into focus. He reached where we were standing and threw himself between me and his father. "It's all right, Dad. Virgil's a friend."

Mr. Swafford eyed me suspiciously. "You sure?"

"I wasn't looking where I was going. I bumped into him."

"It's fine." Tripp kept hold of his dad's arm. "Dad's having a rough day."

Mr. Swafford huffed. "You don't gotta talk about me like I'm not here."

"Sorry, sir," I said.

"I'm gonna go find seats." Mr. Swafford pulled away from Tripp and ambled toward the bleachers.

Tripp let out a long, exhausted sigh. "He only got back from a run this morning. I told him he should stay home and sleep, but he loves the games."

"It's cool."

"I would've asked you to come with us, but I thought you were grounded."

Guilt tackled me from all sides. "I should've called you—"

Tripp waved me off. "Don't worry about it."

"The game was Astrid's idea, and Grandma was feeling generous. Truthfully, I think she's running out of chores."

"She could send you to my house." Tripp's easy grin slid into place.

"Don't give her any ideas."

Tripp glanced after his dad. "Anyway, I should get going. See you Monday."

Tripp took off, and I hung out for a few more minutes before returning to Astrid. She spent the rest of the game on her phone, and I spent it trying to ignore Jarrett and Reba. Thankfully, they paid as little attention to me as I did to them. The game ended without the Coyotes putting a single point on the board.

On the way home, Astrid turned down the music and said, "I thought you wanted to figure out what happened to you."

I tried to turn the music up again, but Astrid slapped my hand away. "What? I just want to forget it happened, okay?"

Astrid's knuckles turned white as she gripped the steering wheel. "You think if you starve yourself, it won't happen again because what kind of monster wants to attack someone who's just skin and bones? You think, eventually, the nightmares will go away and you'll be able to sleep in your own bed without keeping the lights on. You think, you *hope*, that one day you won't flinch when someone touches you."

"Astrid, I—"

"Try hiding all you want, Virgil, but that monster's never gonna stop stalking you until you turn around and face it."

I knew what Astrid was trying to say, what she was trying to do, but she didn't understand, and I wasn't sure how to make her. "What if *I'm* the monster, Astrid?"

You're a monster, baby. Be a monster.

"You're not a monster."

"But how do you know?"

"Because, Virgil, monsters don't ask themselves if they're monsters."

I wanted to believe Astrid.

But I didn't.

FORTY-ONE

ROUGH HANDS SHOOK ME AWAKE, AND I LEAPT LIKE A CAT and tried to fling myself backward. I slammed my head against the underside of the shelf in the closet and kicked the louver door off the hinge before smacking into the wall.

"What the hell is wrong with you, Virgil?!" Dad stood in the middle of my room holding his hands up where I could see them.

"I . . ." My head hurt, and I was confused.

Dad looked at me like I was a violent stranger. After a moment he shook his head. "Get showered and dressed. We're leaving in twenty minutes."

"Where're we going?"

"Shopping. You're going to the Halloween Jamboree with Astrid tonight, and you need a costume."

I did as I was told, but I complained the entire time.

"But *why* do I have to go to the Halloween Jamboree?" According to Tripp and Astrid, the jamboree turned the entire park in front of Main Street into a carnival. Tripp had been giddy as he'd explained it. Astrid had been far less enthusiastic. "And how did Uncle Frank convince Astrid to go? I was under the impression she'd rather eat broken glass."

Dad and I were in Target, standing in the costume aisle. It'd been picked over so thoroughly that my choices were pretty grim.

"Because it's time we become part of this community." Dad held up a sad mummy mask and then returned it to its hook. "I think part of your problem is that neither of us has committed to living here, and we're going to change that tonight."

Right. Because the real issue wasn't that I'd been attacked by a monster and then spent the next couple months being constantly harassed about it or that I'd left behind my friends and lost my boyfriend. It was that I hadn't spent enough time dressed in a costume letting the entire town judge me while I stuffed my face with candy apples.

A thought occurred to me. "Wait. You're going, too?"

Dad nodded. He'd picked up a generic zombie makeup kit and was reading the back. "I've got friends of my own."

"Like who?"

"Like none of your business."

A familiar voice barged into the conversation. "Don't let your daddy fool you, Virgil." Jodie Duran clapped Dad on the back. "I'm the only friend he's got around here."

Dad's face lit up and he threw his arms around her. "Jo-Jo!"

Jo-Jo? I mouthed.

Duran punched Dad in the shoulder. "I will shoot you in the foot if you call me that again."

Dad rolled his eyes. "You're off duty."

"That does not mean I'm unarmed."

The pair of them were talking and laughing and swapping jokes. I couldn't remember the last time I'd seen my dad smile so much. I'd assumed he was as miserable living in Merritt as me, but maybe he was only miserable *because* of me.

"Hey, Virgil." Duran cuffed my shoulder. "What's the good word?"

I forced a smile and held up a tube of silver makeup. "Just getting a costume for the jamboree."

Duran's eyebrows rose. "You're going?"

"Halloween's my favorite holiday."

Dad slung his arm around my shoulders. "We used to have a costume contest at the station back in Seattle. Virgil and I won every year."

"Remember when I was seven and we did the chest-bursting alien costume?"

"You were the cutest larval xenomorph in the city." Dad beamed.

Chief Duran shook her head.

Someone in a red shirt caught Dad's attention. He said he'd be right back and ran off.

Duran motioned at the makeup I was holding. "Robot?"

"Not quite. I'm still putting the idea together. I haven't got a lot of options, seeing as we waited until the last minute."

"I hear Harper's giving you driving lessons."

It was weird hearing Grandma's actual name, and it took my brain a second to make the connection. "Yeah."

"Before he retired, Chief Coleman used to call her the Daredevil of Merritt because of the way she tore around the back roads like speed limits didn't apply to her."

"Seriously?"

Duran smiled. "It was a game between those two. He never could catch her, though."

The idea of my grandma speeding around town and being chased by the sheriff was ludicrous, and yet I believed it.

"How're you doing with everything else?"

I shrugged. "I'm learning more than I ever wanted to know about fixing cars with my grandfather. It's not as boring as I thought it would be."

Duran lowered her voice. "That's good, but I meant about the other thing."

Something crashes into me and I hit the moist ground.

"Oh."

Duran held up her hands. "Don't worry. I haven't told your daddy what happened, but I'd be surprised if he hasn't seen the video floating around."

Which one? "Thanks for not telling him." I didn't think there was much chance of Dad not finding out about the second party eventually, either, but I hoped he remained ignorant. I didn't want to give him another reason to be disappointed in me.

Chief Duran frowned out one side of her mouth, and her thick eyebrows dipped. "Are you sure you're all right? If you need to talk—"

"I'm okay. I'm fine."

Dad returned, stumbling into the awkward silence that had risen between me and Duran, but he was oblivious to it. "Sorry about that. Just trying to switch my days off."

Chief Duran nodded at Dad and said, "I should get going, but I'll see you tonight, Tommy."

"Six?"

"Sounds good." Duran turned to me. "And remember what I said, Virgil. My door's always open." She ambled away.

Dad watched her go, a strange, dreamy expression on his

face. Then he looked at me. "What'd Jo-Jo mean about her door being open? You're not in trouble, are you?"

"It's nothing. She was just being friendly." I handed him the silver makeup to put in the basket. "Come on, I need to find a bodysuit."

FORTY-TWO

THE HALLOWEEN JAMBOREE WAS THE KIND OF GATHERING I would've sworn only happened in poorly written TV shows about small towns. Main Street and the park had been transformed with bales of hay and Styrofoam gravestones and carved pumpkins ranging from an incredibly detailed Merritt Coyote to one that looked like it'd been attacked with an ice pick and a claw hammer. Little booths with games and concessions ringed the park, and harried parents herded sugar-high ghosts and ghouls and fairies and superheroes from one end of the jamboree to the other.

"We don't have to do this. We can bail, and no one will miss us." Astrid was wearing her usual costume, which most people in Merritt already thought was spooky, but with the addition of a pair of cat ears and a fake nose piercing. Actually, the nose ring was real, but she'd convinced Uncle Frank and Aunt Kelly it was part of her costume to give them time to adjust to seeing her wear it.

"Where else are we going to go?"

"Anywhere?"

I ignored Astrid and grabbed my costume out of the back of Astrid's car. I slipped the straps over my shoulders and adjusted it. "How do I look?"

Astrid stood back, eyed me up and down, and shrugged. "Like a weirdo."

"I'm a UFO."

"Yeah, I get it. And it looks good. I'm just not sure why you put so much effort into it."

I touched the silver foam torus that encircled my torso. "It wasn't *that* much work." It had only required Styrofoam, silver paint, tinfoil, and the bodysuit I'd finally found. I'd even borrowed silver nail polish from Astrid to do my nails, which had earned me a frown from Grandpa.

Astrid wrinkled her nose. "Oh, God. You actually like Halloween, don't you?"

"I have no idea what you're talking about."

"You're one of those people who decorates his yard and goes to school in a costume even when no one else does."

I tried to cross my arms over my chest, but my spaceship got in the way. "I never had a yard."

"But if you'd had one—"

"Fine! I would've decorated it. I would've been the kind of person who made his neighbors hate October because I would've turned my yard into a horror show. Are you happy? You've outed me. I like Halloween."

Astrid mimed gagging. "I'm going to need a candy apple before I vomit." She took off, leaving me to struggle through the crowd after her.

Despite the looks folks kept throwing my way, the atmosphere of the Halloween Jamboree was festive, and I found myself having fun. A group of eighth graders performed an impromptu rendition of Michael Jackson's "Thriller" that they'd clearly spent a great deal of time rehearsing, the costume contest was surprisingly competitive—my favorite was a mother-daughter duo who'd dressed as Morticia and Wednesday Addams—and even though the games were rigged, I couldn't stop trying to toss a ring around a bottle so I could win a cheap plastic coyote head. Every business, it seemed, had set up a booth in the park. Dr. Kaluuya, dressed as Dracula, was handing out fake fangs and toothbrushes, and Birdie's Bridal was offering everyone the chance to have their portrait taken as a corpse bride. Even Merritt Baptist Church had a booth, and it was easily the scariest. Pastor Wallace, set up right across from the haunted bounce house, was sermonizing about the dangers of drinking, masturbation, premarital sex, gender nonconformity, and the homosexual lifestyle. Astrid gave him the finger each time we passed.

It was a good thing Astrid and I hadn't left early, because we definitely would've been missed. We ran into the grandparents, and I rode the Ferris wheel with Grandma. I found Dad in his Where's Waldo? costume hanging out with Chief Duran, who was dressed like an ear of corn. Everyone in Merritt was at the jamboree.

"Damn!" Tripp was standing a couple feet away holding up his phone. "Every time I try to snap a picture of you, it comes out fuzzy."

"Ha. Ha."

Astrid gave him a flat stare. "What're you supposed to be?"

Tripp held out his arms. "Y'all really don't see it?"

"I see you dressed in a filthy suit." He was wearing a tan suit that was a little short in the arms and legs and had leaves stuck to it. There was also what looked like a flyer wrapped around his thigh. His hair, which was usually kind of a mess, was swept back like he'd been standing in a wind tunnel.

Tripp snapped his fingers. "Forgot one thing!" He reached around back and pulled out a microphone.

I shook my head. "Still don't get it."

"Weather reporter during a hurricane!"

"Eh. Needs work."

"We can't all be UFOs."

"I hate Halloween," Astrid mumbled. "I'm gonna go scare some kids. Find me when you're ready to leave."

Tripp watched Astrid walk away, and his expression reminded me of Dad at Target watching Chief Duran. "Has she got any friends other than you?"

"She says she does, but I honestly don't know."

Tripp dragged me to get a hot dog even though I wasn't hungry, and we sat off to the side to watch people. I'd only taken a small bite of my dog by the time Tripp finished his. He wiped ketchup off his chin with his napkin. "Hey, so I've been doing some reading about what might've attacked you in the sprawl, and I had a few ideas you might find interesting."

"I thought we went over this."

"No, I know. It's just I keep thinking what if there *is* something out there? Something no one's ever seen? Or something everyone knows is haunting the sprawl but no one talks about? I read accounts of people seeing things you wouldn't believe."

I silently counted to five before responding. "I know you mean well, Tripp. You're the only person who isn't family who's stuck by me since I got here."

Tripp bumped my knee with his. "That's 'cause we're friends, right?"

"Yeah. It's just, I don't know what happened to me in the

sprawl. I don't know what attacked me. The only thing I do know is that I want to forget it happened, and I want everyone else to forget about it too. Okay?"

"Of course. Whatever you want."

"Thank you."

Tripp clapped me on the back. "You had your fortune read by Abigail Rucker yet?"

"Of course there's a fortune-teller in Merritt. Why wouldn't there be?"

Tripp dragged me toward the center of the park. "She's not really a fortune-teller, but she sure thinks she is. Takes the whole thing as serious as Pastor Wallace takes saving your soul from the sin of solo sex." He cackled at his own joke, and I couldn't help smiling.

"What is that guy's problem, anyway?"

"Major mommy issues. There are some stories—"

"Oh look, here we are." The fortune-telling booth was a little larger than the others, with a curtain of burgundy silk hung across the entryway. I was grateful the line to get in was short because, even though I'd asked, I didn't actually want to hear about Pastor Wallace's messed-up childhood.

I had to take off my spaceship to fit inside the tent, and I left it leaned against the side of the booth. I felt exposed wearing only the bodysuit, but it wasn't the most revealing costume I'd seen that night.

"Buckley Swafford," the fortune-teller said in a drowsy voice as we entered. A sign behind her declared her to be Madame Rucker. "And you must be the young Knox boy I've heard so much about."

"Do people in this town really have nothing better to do than talk about me?"

"Not from them." Madame Rucker turned her eyes heavenward. "From *them*."

"I'm out of here."

Tripp grabbed my arm to prevent me from leaving, and we approached Madame Rucker's red-velvet-cloaked table. The entire setup looked like one of Mr. Hilliker's productions. There were tea candles, tarot cards, and even a crystal ball. And Madame Rucker was dressed in a gauzy gown that was as tacky as it was cheap.

Tripp sat on the stool in front of Madame Rucker. She took his hand and stared at his palm. Then she had him draw three cards from her tarot deck. Deja had tried her hand at reading tarot in seventh grade. She was the kind of person who became obsessively focused on one thing for a while and then got bored and moved on. Before tarot it had been watercolor painting. After that, she'd learned to juggle.

Madame Rucker turned the first card over. "Ah. The Empress, for your past. A powerful woman who's had an enormous influence on you." She turned the middle card over. "The Page of Cups represents your present. Someone has come into your life who has surprised you. Someone sensitive, maybe with their head in the clouds."

"I'm standing right here," I muttered, which made Tripp snort.

Madame Rucker glared at me before turning over the final card. "The Hanged Man reversed represents your future." She narrowed her eyes, taking in the three cards. "You've been stuck for quite some time, and moving forward will require you to sacrifice something dear to you, but you're unwilling." She looked him in the eye. "You have to let go or you'll never move forward."

Tripp sat at the table for a second before standing. Madame Rucker's reading had sounded like vague nonsense to me, but Tripp looked a little shaken as he stood.

Madame Rucker motioned for me to take a seat.

"You know? I think I'm good."

Tripp nudged me toward the stool. "Come on, Virgil. You gotta do it."

Madame Rucker wore a smug grin. "Scared of what *your* future holds?"

Annoyed, but figuring the fastest way out was through, I sat down, shuffled the cards, let Madame Rucker scan my palm, and then chose three cards from the deck.

Madame Rucker turned over the first card. "The Three

of Cups. You were happy where you were before. You had a circle of friends you trusted."

"Everyone knows I hate it here."

The second card was the Two of Pentacles. "Very interesting. You're trapped between two worlds. Trying to balance too much, and failing at both. You have to decide which to stay in and which to leave behind."

"I'm so glad I didn't pay for this."

Madame Rucker turned over the final card, and her eyes widened dramatically. "The Tower reversed."

"Yeah? And?"

"There's change coming." Madame Rucker's voice quavered. "You're changing, and it's going to be painful. But you'll have to tear down the old before you can become something new."

He unbuttons his skin and slips out of it too.

"What the hell does that mean?" I stood to leave, but Madame Rucker grabbed my wrist.

"You're going to change, Virgil Knox; you haven't got a choice. But what you become will depend on you."

I yanked my hand away and left. When I got outside into the muggy air, I leaned forward with my hands on my knees and tried to breathe.

You're a monster, baby. Be a monster.

Tripp followed me out. "You okay, Virgil?"

"I'm fine. That was stupid. Let's just go." I went around the side of the booth to get my UFO costume, but it was gone. "Great. Of course someone took it."

"Took what?"

I looked around and almost immediately spotted my costume hanging from the tallest branches of an oak tree. I pointed it out for Tripp. "I hate this town."

"Don't stress. I can get it."

I didn't scream.

"Forget it. Just, whatever, I'm going home. I shouldn't have come." I took off walking toward Grandma and Grandpa's house.

Tripp jogged after me. "Don't go, Virgil." I didn't answer him. "At least let me give you a ride."

While I knew accepting a ride from Tripp meant having to listen to him talk, it was better than walking home in the dark in a shiny silver bodysuit. I nodded and changed course toward the field where everyone had parked.

As we cleared the crowds, Astrid appeared from the shadows. "Hey, where're you boys sneaking off to?"

"We're not sneaking—"

"Don't care," she said. "Just take me with you."

"Fine by me," Tripp said.

"Whatever. Let's just go."

FORTY-THREE

FROM THE TOP OF THE WATER TOWER, I COULD SEE THE lights from the Halloween Jamboree. The sprawl was out there, too, cloaked in shadow. I could feel its tendrils reaching out, whispering to the darkness within me.

Wanna see something cool?

"You know what the really messed-up thing is?" Astrid had been ranting about how much she hated Merritt and everyone in it, including our family, for the last ten minutes.

"I'm sure you're going to tell us," I mumbled. I sat as near to the edge as I dared, but I kept my legs pulled in. I wasn't afraid of heights, but I didn't enjoy them either.

"I actually want to be a vet like Grandpa."

"Really?" I asked.

Astrid nodded. "I used to hang out at Grandpa's office

after school. I loved watching him work, and sometimes he even let me help. I saw him save a dog that'd tangled with a fox, and I knew right then that I wanted to be a veterinarian."

"What's that like? Knowing what you wanna do with your life, I mean." Tripp sat with his legs dangling over the side, swinging them back and forth.

"It's inconvenient."

"How come?" Tripp asked.

Astrid blew out a noisy sigh. "Because everyone thinks I'm planning to go vet school and then come back to Merritt to set up shop like Grandpa did. You know he never sold his old offices? He's been letting them sit vacant, saving them for me, and he thinks I don't know about it."

I'd only lived in Merritt a couple months, and I already couldn't wait to get out. The idea of growing up in Merritt and living in Merritt and dying in Merritt gave me vertigo.

"I can't even get good drugs here," Astrid added.

Tripp snorted. "I got mushrooms in my freezer back home if you want some."

"For real?"

"Uh, yeah?" Tripp shrugged. "I sell them sometimes. They're supposed to be good for depression."

Astrid cackled. "Right, because I'm sure that's what most of your buyers are using them for."

I ignored Astrid and looked around her to Tripp. "Do they actually work?"

"Don't know. Never tried them."

Astrid's laughter faded. "Wait, seriously? You've never been tempted? I'd do anything to get a break from Merritt for a while. Even eat a couple of mushrooms that you dug out of a pile of cow manure."

"Of course I'm curious," Tripp said. "But I read psychedelics can trigger certain mental illnesses in folks who're predisposed to them, and that ain't a chance I'm willing to take."

I wanted to tell Tripp he was going to be okay, but I couldn't know that for sure. Tripp deserved better than empty platitudes or false hope.

Astrid bowed her head. "I'm worried about turning into my dad, too." She lifted her eyes to look at me and Tripp in turn. "If you ever see me drinking, you better punch me. Hit me so hard you break my jaw. Anything to keep me from becoming him."

Uncle Frank's alcoholism was the worst-kept secret in our family. He wasn't a mean drunk or a blackout drunk. He was a gregarious, friendly drunk. But every time Uncle Frank cracked open another beer, everyone around him cringed.

"Except there ain't nothing *my* dad can do. He can't swear off booze and go to meetings. He does everything he's supposed to and it still ain't enough. Half of Merritt treats him like a leper and the other half like a charity case."

I nudged Tripp with my knee and tried to catch his eye. "We don't have to talk about it."

"Yeah," Astrid said. "I didn't mean to bring it up."

Tripp waved us off. "The worst part is how folks watch me like I'm a bomb fixing to blow any minute."

"You're not a bomb," I said.

"I might be." Tripp leaned his head against the railing. "I'm near the age it started for my dad, and if I'm like him, there ain't a damn thing I can do to stop what's coming."

What was I supposed to say to that? Mr. Swafford's mental illness wasn't his fault—it didn't make him a bad person—but I wouldn't have wished it on anyone. Developing schizophrenia like his dad would complicate Tripp's life in ways that were difficult to predict. It wasn't fair.

"What about you?" Astrid nudged me. "Who are *you* afraid of becoming?"

Tripp was watching me, waiting for an answer. He'd been dying to ask me why I'd gotten so upset at Madame Rucker's, but he'd kept his questions to himself. "We won't say nothing. Water Tower Rules are in effect."

Astrid said, "What rules?"

"Water Tower Rules," Tripp repeated. "I just made them up."

I was hoping Astrid and Tripp would argue until they forgot about me, but I wasn't that lucky. After clarifying the rules of the water tower, they returned their attention to me.

"I don't know—"

Astrid huffed. "That's not fair. We bared our souls to you."

Tripp rested his hand on her arm. "Give him a second."

I licked my lips. "Ever since I was attacked in the sprawl, I feel like there's less and less of me. My mom doesn't want me, Luca doesn't love me, most of the town thinks I'm delusional and a liar. I wake up every day to messages and comments from people telling me to go back to the sprawl and let the monster finish me off, and there are mornings when that doesn't sound like a terrible idea."

#MonsterBait

"I'm not afraid of *who* I might turn into. I'm terrified of *what* I *am* becoming."

Tripp dropped Astrid off at the jamboree where she'd left her car and then drove me back to my grandparents' house. He pulled into the driveway, but I didn't get out.

"What's up, Virgil?"

We weren't on top of the water tower anymore, and I felt bad dragging our conversation down to earth with us, but I couldn't shake the questions rattling around my brain. "What will you do if it turns out you *are* like your dad?"

Tripp scrubbed his hand through his hair. "I don't know."

"But there's got to be a solution, right? It's not fair that you might become something you've got no say in."

"It ain't like that. My dad didn't become something else. He's still my dad."

I traced the scab on my torso through the bodysuit. It burned and itched.

Jarrett unzips my skin to my navel and then steps back and laughs.

"But aren't you afraid of what the disease will do to you?"

"Sure, but I'd still be me." Tripp cocked his head to the side. "You got something on your mind?"

You're a monster, baby. Be a monster.

"Is this about what Rucker said to you?" Tripp asked. "Because you know she's full of shit, right? Last year, she told Edna Echols she was gonna come into a bunch of money, and three months later Edna lost everything because she'd invested in some shady Ponzi scheme."

I could feel something moving inside me. Feel it scrabbling at the back of my ribs, struggling to escape. "She said I'm going to change. That I haven't got a choice."

"I also heard her say what you change into is your decision."

"What if it's not?"

I waited for Tripp to reassure me, to tell me that we always had a choice. To tell me that life was never so cruel as to force us to become something we didn't want to become without giving us a way out. But I should've known better.

"I don't know, Virgil. I suppose you'll have to do the same as the rest of us and make the best of what you get."

FORTY-FOUR

I STOOD AND WATCHED HELPLESSLY AS THE TOOLBOX FELL and spilled Grandpa's wrenches and screwdrivers across the driveway. My brain didn't register what was happening quickly enough for me to stop them.

Grandpa slid out from underneath the Jetta and wiped his face with a cloth. He was wearing a mechanic's coveralls over his khaki pants and button-down shirt. "What the devil has gotten into you today, Virgil?"

I scrambled to collect the tools—many of which I'd learned the uses of since I'd started helping Grandpa fix the Jetta. "Sorry. I didn't sleep well last night."

"I know. I heard you stomping around at dawn."

"You did?" I froze.

"After I came home from Vietnam, I got insomnia from

time to time. Taking a walk's not a bad way to beat it." Grandpa fixed me with an iron stare. "Just be a little quieter if you don't mind."

"Yes, sir."

It'd been over two weeks since Halloween, and while the lesions hadn't grown worse, my dreams had. Grandpa hadn't heard me going for a walk to help me sleep; he'd heard me returning from the sprawl. I'd woken up in the swamp with leaves in my hair, mud under my fingernails, and no idea how I'd gotten there.

"I'm proud of you, Virgil."

I finished sorting the tools—Grandpa was particular about how and where they were stored. "You are? I mean, I feel like I'm more of a hindrance than a help out here."

Grandpa smiled. "You'd never make it as a professional mechanic, but you're hardly the disaster your father was."

"Thanks?"

"You're trying, though, and that's what counts. However, that's not what I meant."

"Sorry, Grandpa, but I'm lost."

"Not as lost as you think you are." Grandpa drank from one of the tumblers of lemonade Grandma had brought us earlier. Grandpa hadn't aged like a flower, withering over time, he'd aged like a whiskey, distilling with the years into an even more potent version of himself. "I'm proud of how you handled that mess that happened to you in the sprawl."

It was the first time Grandpa had mentioned it since the night it happened.

"You do realize I'm still sleeping in the closet, right?"

"I knew men who came home from the war and let the trauma consume them." Grandpa never talked about his experiences in the military. But he might've been the one person who understood the fear festering inside me. I could tell him about the nightmares and the scabs and how I was afraid of what I was becoming, and he would understand it in a way no one else could.

"How'd *you* get past it?"

Grandpa's eyes were distant for a moment, like he'd left his body and traveled elsewhere. Maybe he had. Maybe he'd traveled back in time. "I took everything that happened to me, and I put it in a box. I shut the lid, locked it, and stuffed it into the darkest corner of my soul, never to be opened again."

That wasn't the answer I was expecting, but I probably should have. "Wait, so you're saying you just pretended what happened to you in Vietnam never happened?"

Grandpa nodded. "I know your father wants to send you to therapy and let you talk about your feelings, but talking about feelings never did anyone a lick of good. You just take that pain, you put it away, and you fill the space where it was with better memories."

Hot breath soaks my neck, a clawed hand pushes my face deeper into the mud.

Grandpa didn't want to talk about what had happened to him. He didn't want to hear what had happened to me. He wanted me to keep quiet and put it behind me.

"You're a Knox man, Virgil. I'm glad to see you've started acting like one."

It lowers itself onto my back.

Grandpa set his lemonade on the bench and held out his hand. "Now, pass me that socket wrench so we can finish up."

"Yes, sir."

FORTY-FIVE

MR. HILLIKER WAS LOSING IT. WE WERE LESS THAN A MONTH from opening night, and rehearsals had been running longer into the evenings. Mr. Hilliker began nitpicking every perceived mistake, and his patience with us had an exceptionally short fuse.

"I don't care if Austin missed his line," Hilliker was saying. "You have to improvise. The show doesn't stop because someone missed a line *they should've known by now*!"

Tripp elbowed me in the side and whispered, "Don't worry. This is just how he gets."

Mr. Hilliker heard Tripp and rounded on him. "And you. Don't think I don't see you trying to make the others laugh. This isn't the Buck Swafford Comedy Hour. Say your lines, hit your marks, and leave the jokes at home."

Tripp's smile vanished. "Yes, sir."

Hilliker went on like that for another ten minutes, pointing out every mistake we'd ever made since the dawn of time. Nothing was good enough. Katie Lynn was saying her lines too quickly; Georgia was mumbling hers. Brian's blocking was off; Alex's was too robotic. The only person he hadn't corrected that night was me, which made me nervous.

Hilliker heaved a long sigh and waved his hand through the air. "We're done here. Let's get it right tomorrow, people."

I turned to leave the stage, but Mr. Hilliker asked me to stick around. I told Tripp to let Grandma know I'd be out in a minute. When the others had scattered, I went to the edge of the stage and sat, waiting for Hilliker to lay into me the way he had the others. I figured whatever he had to say was so awful that he didn't want to embarrass me.

"How you holding up, Virgil?"

It wasn't the question itself that made me suspicious, it was the way he'd asked it. He sounded sincere, but I sensed he had an ulterior motive.

"All right, I guess."

Mr. Hilliker stroked his beard. I'd noticed he did that whenever he was unsure of what to say. "I know this has been a rough couple months for you—"

"Yeah. But I'm fine."

"Are you?"

Mr. Hilliker possessed a kind of gravity that drew words from me, and despite Grandpa telling me to shove my feelings in a box, I couldn't help but let them out. "I mean, no one's taped monster porn to my locker since homecoming, but that doesn't mean I don't hear them talking about me. And I think that's the worst part. They're all talking *about* me—calling me a liar, saying I made the whole thing up, saying I went to the sprawl and let something attack me for the attention—but not one of them has bothered to talk *to* me. They say I'm the liar, but they're the ones making up stories about what happened that night. They don't care about the truth."

Mr. Hilliker spoke softly. "For what it's worth, I don't think you made it up."

I searched Hilliker's face for the lie—he was an acting teacher, so surely he was skilled at pretending—but his sympathy seemed genuine.

"Have you talked to anyone about what happened to you?" Hilliker asked.

"I talked to Tripp, a little. And Astrid, too."

"Quite a talented actress, your cousin."

"She is?"

Hilliker nodded. "I had her for drama in ninth grade. Never could get her to try out for a show, though. I keep hoping she'll audition, but alas . . ." He coughed. "But I meant, have you talked to a professional?"

"Oh. Yeah, my dad's looking for a doctor. He hasn't found one yet."

Mr. Hilliker finger combed his beard again. "It's just that I see you holding back—"

"That's the character, though. Wadsworth is reserved. He's keeping secrets."

"To a degree." Hilliker paced a tight circle in front of me. "But *you're* still holding back. There's something in you, a well of emotion, that you're not allowing yourself to tap into."

A whimper escapes my lips as it rakes its claws across my back.

"I'll try harder."

"It's not about knowing your blocking and your lines. You've got that."

"Then what is it?"

Mr. Hilliker stopped and stood in front of me with his hands on his hips. As we'd gotten closer to December, he'd started to look more like Santa Claus, which made it difficult to take him seriously. "Being an actor isn't about faking emotion, Virgil. It's about communing with it. It's about becoming friends with the darkest parts of yourself and tapping into those raw feelings."

"And?"

"And I'm not sure you're able to do that in your current condition."

"Sir?"

"Curtain's up in less than a month," Hilliker said. "It's not a lot of time, but maybe it would be best if we let Nash take over your role."

Nash Galloway was my understudy. A ninth grader who couldn't act his way out of a clear plastic bag. "Are you cutting me?"

Instead of answering my question, Hilliker said, "Do you know why I cast you?"

"Because I nailed the audition?"

Hilliker chuckled. "I've been teaching drama for twenty years. The theater department barely has the funding to keep the lights on in here, and *Dracula's* a cheap play to license, so I've watched more Renfields than you can imagine." He paused. "You've never been through a hurricane, have you?"

I shook my head.

"Right before the storm hits, after folks have boarded up their homes and made their preparations, there's this space when everything is calm but you can feel the chaos about to be unleashed. That quiet chaos is what you gave me. It's a rare gift you have, but I haven't seen so much as a hint of it since that audition."

I feel its poison in my blood.

"So you're cutting me because I'm not good enough, but you're replacing me with Nash? He's the worst actor here!"

"I'm trying to coax the best performance I can from each of you, but I'm worried about pushing you too hard, Virgil. To do your best, you need to be in touch with your emotions, and I don't think you're ready for that."

Grandpa wanted me to put my feelings in a box and hide them away. Hilliker demanded I expose them onstage for the entire town to see. I was scared of what would happen if I did either, but I'd do anything to stay in the show.

"Please don't cut me. This is the only good thing in my life right now. I hate it in Merritt, but I can't go home. I've lost my boyfriend and my friends. Without this show, I won't have anything to look forward to." I hadn't meant to cry, but tears ran down my cheeks and fell from my chin.

"Damn it." Hilliker's resolve crumbled fast and hard. "Look, get into therapy, okay?"

My nose was running, and all I had to wipe it with was the back of my sleeve. "I had a session with Pastor Wallace, but—"

"That man's not qualified to counsel you on what to have for supper." Hilliker tapped his lips. "I might know someone. He's not taking new patients, but he owes me a favor. I'll talk to him and then call your dad, if that's okay."

I wasn't sure if I could speak without crying again, so I nodded instead.

"Good."

When I felt a bit more composed, I said, "So you're not going to cut me?"

Mr. Hilliker sighed. "No. You're a damn good Wadsworth."

"Thank you."

"But you could be an exceptional one."

"I want to be."

"Then I'm going to have to push you, Virgil, and I need to know you can handle it."

You're a monster, baby. Be a monster.

"I can."

Mr. Hilliker pursed his lips and eyed me warily. "I suppose we'll see."

FORTY-SIX

GRANDPA AND I WERE AT THE AUTO-PARTS STORE ORDERING a door handle for the Jetta to replace the one that refused to open when it was hot out, which was practically every day. I'd spent the morning helping Grandma relocate her gardenia bushes from the side of the house to the front yard, and Grandpa hadn't given me a chance to shower or change before dragging me to the shop with him. My jean shorts were filthy, my T-shirt was holey, and I definitely stank. Grandpa didn't notice because twenty years of smoking had killed his sense of smell.

While Grandpa was chatting with Adeline, the woman who owned the shop, I hung out with Ratchet, Adeline's golden retriever. Getting up was tough for the old dog, so I knelt on the floor to give him some love.

The bell dinged when the front door opened, and I hoped that meant a customer who'd interrupt Grandpa and Adeline so I could go home. I was exhausted, and I still had to work on my lines. I'd barely escaped Mr. Hilliker cutting me, and I wasn't going to give him any reason to reconsider.

"Hey, Virgil. **Wanna see something cool?**"

Jarrett reached over my shoulder and scratched Ratchet behind the ears. Jarrett didn't stink. He smelled like sandalwood and pepper.

I ducked around and out of the way, rising to my feet to face Jarrett. He was wearing a sleeveless shirt, a pair of blue board shorts, flip-flops, and aviator sunglasses slightly too large for his face. "What do you want?"

Jarrett flipped the sunglasses to the top of his head. "Reba says hey."

"She knows where to find me."

"She thinks you're mad at her."

"I'm not."

Jarrett raised an eyebrow. "Are you pissed at me? I tried telling folks to leave you alone about the monster stuff, but gossip's got a mind of its own and—"

"I'm not mad at you, either. I'm trying to put that stuff behind me."

Ratchet struggled to stand, and nudged my hand with his wet nose. Apparently he'd decided it wasn't right that two people were standing within optimal petting distance but weren't petting him. I idly scratched his head.

Jarrett pursed his lips, eyeing me and tapping his fingers against his thigh. "Hey, so I'm taking my boat out to Lake Barton. Wanna come?"

"No, I—"

Grandpa butted in. "Jarrett Hart. Good to see you, son."

"And you, Mr. Knox. How's your shoulder?"

Grandpa rubbed his right shoulder. "Better. Mostly." He glanced at me. "Sometimes Jarrett tags along when his father and I play golf."

"Oh," I said.

"How's your mother?"

Jarrett flashed a smile. "Already working on her reelection campaign."

"Hardest working woman in Merritt, that mother of yours." Thankfully, Grandpa didn't seem interested in loitering. "Are you ready, Virgil?"

"Yeah, I—"

"Actually, I invited Virgil to come out on the boat with me. Maybe do a little fishing." Jarrett looked me up and down. "Smells like he could use a bath, too."

That earned him a laugh from Grandpa. No one, it seemed, was immune to Jarrett's charm.

"It's okay," I said. "I'm sure Grandma has chores for me to do at the house."

Grandpa clapped my back. "No, you should go. You've earned a break."

It looms over me, framed by the night and the stars and moss-choked oak trees.

"But I'm grounded. Dad said—"

"Your father's at work until tomorrow. I'm giving you permission now." It didn't feel like Grandpa was allowing me to go so much as forcing me.

Jarrett took advantage of my hesitation and slung his arm around my shoulder. "Come on, I just have to grab a part for the trailer and then some ice at Tracee's, and we can go."

"I assume you won't be drinking, Mr. Hart," Grandpa said as Jarrett dragged me away.

"Not for another five years, sir."

Jarrett cracked open a beer and took two gulps before letting out a satisfied sigh and wiping his mouth with the back of his hand. "This is what life's all about, Virgil."

Lake Barton wasn't large as lakes went, but it was the biggest body of water near Merritt, and we weren't the only folks taking advantage of the warm, sunny Saturday afternoon.

"Where are the others?" I sat on a bench at the back of the boat with my legs spread out in front of me. Despite my misgivings, I was enjoying the afternoon. It reminded me of the first days of spring in Seattle when we'd emerge from the dark after the long winter, sun starved and weary, to bask in the promise of brighter days to come.

Jarrett shrugged. "Reba's working, Finn pissed off his dad and got himself grounded, and I can't handle hanging out with Chuck on my own. Finn likes him, but I think he's a dick."

"Guess it's lucky you ran into me, then."

"You got that right." **I thought you said you weren't into it.**

I tilted my face toward the sky and shut my eyes, but I could feel Jarrett watching me. I could sense him staring. I didn't want to give in, so I ignored him for as long as I could before I opened my eyes again. "Problem?"

"How do you do it?"

"Do what?"

Without his friends around, without the rest of Merritt watching him, Jarrett was different. He was still self-assured, still laid-back, like there was nothing in the world that could touch him, but a layer of polish was gone, and I could see the scuff marks.

"Deal with folks talking about you? I mean, I heard a joke about you last week that involved you working in a zoo so you could be closer to the animals, if you know what I mean."

I knew what he meant.

"Don't it piss you off? I seen the shit they post about you online—"

"You've written some of it."

Jarrett caught my eye. "Finn. Not me. I never posted nothing."

"You and Finn are practically the same person."

"Nah." Jarrett shook his head. "Finn's got his own ideas about how things in Merritt work. He thinks he can do anything he wants. Sometimes I don't know if he sees the rest of us as real people, right? Like the whole of Merritt's a toy his mommy and daddy bought for him to play with."

His lips hit the side of my nose, his chin grazes my cheek, and his hands are everywhere.

"But you're different?" I asked.

"Yeah."

"Except you paid a kid to dress up in the Coyote costume to scare me on the first day of school."

Jarrett hung his head. His hair fell over his eyes. "I only did it because, well, folks expect things of me, you know? Finn and those boys were egging me on, and if I'd said no they would've done it anyway and—"

"And they would've made fun of you for refusing," I finished.

"Yeah." A film of shame clung to that one word. "I ain't like you. I can't shrug off things the way you can."

I snorted. "I didn't shrug anything off. It's just that I don't have the room in my head to worry about every rumor being spread about me because there's a monster taking up the space. I never left the sprawl, Jarrett, and that monster's still on my back, breathing in my ear."

"It can't hurt you."

"It already did! It's inside me! I feel it!" My hands trembled and my knees shook. I hugged them to my chest.

Jarrett watched me, sucking his lower lip. After a few seconds he stood, stripped off his shirt, and dove over the side of the boat. His head broke the surface a moment later. "Come on, Virgil."

"I'm fine here."

Jarrett held his hands up. "I won't try nothing. I told you I'm not into you like that."

Don't tell no one about this, all right?

"I'm not wearing swim trunks, and there's nothing worse than soggy denim."

I expected Jarrett to keep pressing the issue, but he shrugged and dove under the water. He swam like he was part fish.

"What's the temperature like?" I leaned over the side and skimmed the water with my fingers.

"Warm as a bath." Jarrett ducked under, popped back up, and spit a stream of water at me. "Come on. Wash some of that dirt off."

I let out a harried sigh. "Fine." I kicked off my jean shorts, but left my shirt on.

"Nice boxers."

They were covered in pumpkins. Dad had gotten them from work on sale after Halloween. I flipped off Jarrett and dove in. When I hit the water of Lake Barton, I felt clean in a way no scalding hot shower had been able to make me feel. I let the water wrap around me, I let it into my mouth, I let it pour down my throat. I let it fill me and wash the dirt and poison away. I knew the feeling wouldn't last, so I enjoyed it while I could.

"I'm probably gonna wind up mayor, like my mom," Jarrett was saying. We were floating on our backs in the water, and I'd asked him what he planned to do after high school. I liked listening to Jarrett talk. Not so much the words, but the lazy, easy way he made them sound.

"Is that what you want, though?"

"I dunno. Does anyone our age ever get to do what we want?"

"Sometimes."

Jarrett sounded skeptical. "Not me. It's probably better my folks got my future planned out, anyway. If they gave me that kind of rope, I'd probably get tangled in it, trip, and fall flat on my ass."

"From where I'm sitting, you seem like you've got everything figured out."

Jarrett chuckled.

"I'm serious."

"I know. That's why I laughed." Jarrett was quiet a moment. "You gonna be a firefighter, like your dad?"

"Probably not."

"What're you gonna do then? Run off to Hollywood and become a movie star?"

I laughed so hard I got water in my mouth. "I'm not a good actor. It's just something fun to do. I get to be someone else when I'm onstage. I don't have to be me anymore."

I didn't expect Jarrett to understand since he seemed to love being himself, so I was surprised when he said, "Sounds nice."

My skin was starting to feel tight. I hadn't put on sunscreen, and I didn't want my arms and legs to burn. I climbed out of the water and sat under the shade of the canopy on the boat. Jarrett followed a minute later. He tossed me a towel. His skin was already deeply tanned, so he sat in the sun to let it dry him off.

I hung the coarse towel around my shoulders. Jarrett was eyeing me again.

"What?"

"You can take off your shirt. I don't care if you got scars. I already seen them, anyway."

It worries me like a dog with a chew toy and then flings me aside.

I pulled the towel tightly around me.

"You gotta let it go, Virgil."

"Let it go." I sneered. "Right, like it's that easy. What do you even know about it?"

Jarrett stood and turned his back toward me. He raised the right leg of his shorts up as high as it would go. His skin underneath was pale white, but that wasn't what made my breath catch in my throat. Four jagged lines scored the underside of his thigh, from the outside up almost to his buttocks.

"I was twelve when it happened." He let his shorts fall and sat back down.

I didn't scream.

"You knew I was telling the truth this whole time? You let Finn bully me, you let this entire town think I was a liar, you let me think I needed to prove to everyone I wasn't delusional by letting them hang me up as bait."

"I told you I wasn't around when that happened. I would've stopped you."

"But you knew?!" I couldn't decide whether I wanted to pick Jarrett's brain—force him to tell me everything he could remember about his own attack—or punch him in the face until he begged me to stop. "How could you let them harass me when you knew I was telling the truth?"

Jarrett sighed. "Because they weren't serious. They were only joking."

"It wasn't funny!" I shouted. "I sleep in my closet every night because I'm terrified the monster's going to find me!"

"It won't."

"How do you know?" My voice carried across the water. "How are you okay with what happened to you?"

Deep grooves were etched across Jarrett's forehead. "Because it ain't a big deal. It's just something that happened. You ain't the first person to get attacked out there. The rest of us just don't feel like we gotta run around talking about it all the damn time."

"Why the hell not?!"

"Because we just don't. And neither should you." There was a finality to his voice that made me forget what I was going to say.

I didn't understand how Jarrett could pretend that nothing had happened. How he could treat being attacked like some rite of passage that, having survived, I should immediately forget.

The smell hits me first. Like a decomposing corpse.

I couldn't forget. How could he?

I wanted to ask. I wanted to demand he tell me how he made it through the day without reliving the horror and fear.

I lie on my stomach, my arms askew, and try not to breathe.

But I didn't.

"I saw the scab on your leg." Jarrett's voice pulled me from the murky depths to the surface. "When you jumped in the water."

My boxers barely covered the lesion. The cuff must've ridden up when I raised my arms to dive into the water earlier.

"You got any others?"

Jarrett didn't want to talk about the attack, and I didn't want to talk about the scabby lesions. But one of us had to concede, and it was always going to be me.

I pulled off my wet shirt, turned to the side, and raised my arm to show him the one on my ribs. "This is the one Grady saw in the locker room. There's another on my back." I touched the soft, pink flesh on my chest. "I cut this scab off this morning."

Jarrett's face paled. "You cut it off?"

"Yeah."

"Why the hell would you do something like that?"

I didn't know how to answer anymore. "Because I keep hoping one time I'll cut it off and it won't grow back, and that's how I'll know I'm finally safe."

Jarrett peered closely at the pale pinkish wound. "How bad did it hurt?"

"Pretty bad."

Jarrett bobbed his head. He unstrapped his watch and tossed it on the bench. He turned his arm over to show me a lesion similar to mine.

He plants his hand on the door and leans against it with all of his weight. He's got a scab the size of a quarter on the underside of his wrist.

"What am I turning into?" If Jarrett had been attacked when he was twelve, then he'd had four years to figure it out. Surely, he had the answers.

Jarrett narrowed his eyes. "You ain't turning into nothing."

"But the monster did something to me, right? It poisoned me. I've been having these nightmares and sometimes I wake up in the sprawl covered in filth and mud."

You're a monster, baby. Be a monster.

"What the hell attacked me in the sprawl?"

Jarrett licked his lips. I was sure he was going to give me the answers I'd been searching for since I'd woken up in the hospital. But he either didn't have them or wasn't willing to share. "When you're ready to know, you'll know." He leaned forward and patted my knee. "C'mon. We should be getting home."

No matter how I glared at him as we drove the boat back to the ramp and loaded it on the trailer, Jarrett didn't say another word until we reached my house, and then all he said was, "See ya around, Virgil."

FORTY-SEVEN

LUCA CALLED WHILE I WAS DOING HOMEWORK WITH Grandma. I never would've expected her to be such a good tutor, but my grades were improving and I was pretty sure I'd be ready to pass my driver's test by my birthday. Whether or not Grandpa and I would be finished repairing the Jetta was another story.

"Are you planning on answering that?" Grandma eyed my phone.

I was working on quadratic equations, which were my least favorite equations. I glanced at the screen, saw Luca's name, and shook my head. "We're busy."

"That's the fourth time he's called."

"He can call four hundred more. I don't care."

Grandma was reading a mystery novel while I worked,

pausing when I had a question. She dog-eared the page and set the book down. "It's okay to be angry at him for hurting you."

"I know."

"It's okay to forgive him, too."

Grandma was the last person with whom I expected to wind up discussing my failed relationship, but there we were. "What if I don't want to forgive him?"

"That's your choice, Virgil, but you're going to live a long time. You'll be lonely if you reach your end years with an abundance of enemies and no friends."

My phone buzzed again. Grandma picked up her book and retreated to the other room.

I answered the phone. "Hey, Luca."

"Oh," he said, like he was surprised to hear my voice. "What's up, Virgil?"

"I don't know. You called me."

Luca spoke fast like he was overstimulated or strung out on caffeine. "Right. I did do that." He paused. "How have you been? Merritt still the worst?"

"Yes."

Drink! Drink! Drink!

"Everyone here misses you so much. Especially Kris. She said the vibe in the theater isn't the same without your energy."

I laughed in spite of myself. "Of course she did." I resisted enjoying the conversation. I resisted Luca's charm. "I'm playing Wadsworth in *Clue*."

"How's that going?"

"Honestly? It's kind of a mess, but also fun. I think being in that play's the only thing I enjoy about Merritt. Well, that and my grandma's driving lessons."

Luca laughed. "*You're* learning to drive?"

"I am. And I'm not terrible at it either."

"Yes, you are, dear!" Grandma shouted from the other room.

I took the phone outside to the carport and sat on the back of the Jetta despite the mosquitoes that immediately dive-bombed my exposed skin. "What's this about, Luca?"

I'm stuck in Merritt, at this party, with the taste of Jarrett Hart still in my mouth.

"First off," Luca said, "I need to apologize."

"Okay."

"I shouldn't have made Deja break up with you for me. That was a dick move."

Everyone I love is on the other side of the world.

"You deserved to hear it from me." Luca's voice caught in his throat. "I just thought it would be better for both of us. We can't be what the other needs with so much distance between us. But I love you, and that will never ever change. I hope you know that."

Something crashes into me and I hit the moist ground. My phone slips out of my hand and spins off into the dark.

"Did you call to break up with me again? Once wasn't enough? You needed to break my heart a second time? Do you know what I went through that night?"

"Virgil, I'm sorry. This wasn't how I meant for this to go, but I wanted you to hear it from me and not from Deja or see it online—"

"See what?"

"I'm going out with Avi Warner and—"

Teeth dig into my shoulder.

"I still want to be your friend and—"

It lowers itself onto my back.

"When you come home, we can all hang out and—"

A whimper escapes my lips.

"Say something, Virgil. Please?"

I go still and hope it kills me quickly.

"Don't call me again, Luca." I hung up the phone and blocked his number.

I didn't scream.

FORTY-EIGHT

DR. APELGREN WAS AN ANCIENT MAN WITH A MUSTACHE that curled up at the ends, a conspicuous toupee, and an office in a strip mall sandwiched between a dog groomer and an iPhone repair shop. But he'd come highly recommended from Mr. Hilliker, so Dad had set up the appointment, and Grandma had driven me there.

I settled onto a lumpy couch and crossed my arms. "What should I talk about?"

"What would you like to talk about?"

I eyed the therapist suspiciously. "Are you going to do that thing where you answer every question I ask with another question? Because I really hate that."

Dr. Apelgren smiled. His teeth were brown from coffee or smoking. I couldn't tell which. "Is this your first time in therapy, Virgil?"

"Kind of." I didn't consider my session with Pastor Wallace worth mentioning.

"I thought so. Why don't you tell me why you're here?"

My parents are divorcing, my boyfriend broke up with me twice, I was attacked by a monster, I blacked out at a party and woke up tied to a fence—though I also may have asked for it to be done—and I hate Merritt and want to go home to Seattle, except I don't because everyone I love is not *on the other side of the world.*

"My drama teacher thinks I've got emotional problems and might cut me from the play if I don't talk to you."

Dr. Apelgren's face lit up. "Ah, Jim Hilliker. Good man."

"Yeah. He's the one who gave me your name." I wasn't sure what to say. I wasn't going to spill my feelings to the first old dude who asked, no matter how fancy his mustache.

"I spoke to your father yesterday."

"You did?"

Dr. Apelgren nodded. "We had a nice chat on the telephone. I require it of the parents of my adolescent patients."

"Did you talk to my mom?"

"Would you like me to?"

"She hasn't got time for me, so I doubt she'll make time for you."

Dr. Apelgren shifted in his seat. The only real emotion he'd shown was the smile when I mentioned Mr. Hilliker.

"Thomas says you're sleeping in the closet and that you're sleepwalking and having nightmares. Would you like to discuss that?"

"Did he tell you I was attacked by a monster?"

"He mentioned you were attacked, but I believe he said the attacker was a bear or an alligator."

A laugh bubbled up and escaped, bitter and sharp.

"It wasn't an alligator or a bear?"

"Sure."

Dr. Apelgren paused before answering. "Adapting to change can be challenging. Human beings are quite resilient, but too much change can overwhelm us. There's no shame in needing help."

I didn't know what I was supposed to get out of this. I wanted Dad to stop worrying about me and I wanted Mr. Hilliker to believe I was capable of performing, but I didn't know how talking to Dr. Apelgren would achieve either goal.

"It's okay, Virgil. This is only our first session. We're just getting to know each other. Change doesn't happen in a day."

Change. The word stuck in my head, bouncing around like a fragment of a song I couldn't escape. "Is it possible to choose what we become or are we bound to turn into whatever's inside us, no matter what?"

Dr. Apelgren's thick, wiry eyebrows rose slightly. "What are you afraid of turning into?"

"I don't know."

Dr. Apelgren tapped his fingers on his knee. "I reject the belief that some people are born bad. I think we each have within us the capacity for good *and* for evil. Does that answer your question?"

No. "Yeah."

"Excellent!" Dr. Apelgren clasped his hands together and smiled. "Why don't we schedule your next appointment, and we can talk more about this then?"

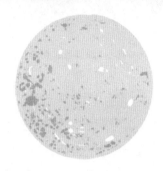

FORTY-NINE

"DRINK! DRINK! DRINK!"

Finn Duckett binds my hands to the fence post. His hair hangs in his eyes, dripping sweat. His grin is manic; his eyes are red.

Jarrett watches from the shadows.

"Is that tight enough?" I ask. "Don't want me to accidentally escape, do you?"

"Don't worry," Jarrett says. "You can't escape." He leaps from the dark and sinks his teeth into Finn's neck. Finn doesn't fight. His eyes roll back and he moans.

ride ride ride ride ride.

"Don't tell no one about this, all right?" Finn murmurs. "I ain't no homo."

Jarrett's skin splits open. He cracks like an egg, and coils of wet, slithering worms fall out, undulating on the dead leaves *and dirt. The shell that was Jarrett crumbles to dust. The worms crawl into Finn—through his ears, up his nose, into his mouth. They fill him as he writhes, and then he bursts open, spraying blood and gore across the swamp. Bits of Finn splatter my face and chest.*

The wind whispers, "You're a monster, baby. Be a monster."

Life wasn't terrible. After my last conversation with Luca, I finally changed my phone number, which put a stop to the random calls and harassing messages. I also deactivated my social media accounts. People still talked about me, but their whispers had become little more than senseless white noise.

I spent the rest of the weekend thinking about Jarrett's revelation that he'd been attacked by a monster when he was twelve and wondering what he knew that he wasn't telling me. I was also curious why he'd decided to tell me. Did it make us friends? Did I want to be his friend? I had never wound up in the sprawl tied to a fence while hanging around with Tripp.

And speaking of Tripp, I'd been working up the nerve to talk to him and Astrid about Jarrett's attack, but I kept putting it off because it wasn't my secret. I could swear Astrid and Tripp to secrecy, but I couldn't guarantee they'd abide by that promise if they felt they had a good reason to break it. Still, I needed to talk to someone, and they were the only people I trusted.

Tuesday morning I'd decided to finally tell them. I'd texted Astrid and Tripp and told them to make sure they came to lunch. After showering and changing from PE, I was heading toward the cafeteria when Jarrett and Finn fell in on either side of me.

Jarrett draped his arm around my shoulders. "C'mon, Virgil, we're eating out today."

I tried to steer them in the direction of the cafeteria, but they were both bigger than me. "We can't skip. Not today."

Finn scoffed. "Told you he wouldn't go."

"Of course he will."

I tried to duck under Jarrett's arm. "No, I won't."

Jarrett stopped and locked eyes with me. "Aren't we friends?"

Words are just words. They don't mean nothing.

"Well, yeah, but—"

"Then, as a friend, I'm asking you to go."

Behind me, Finn was whispering, "We're getting ribs," over and over in a singsong pattern.

Jarrett playfully punched my shoulder. "It'll be fun."

No matter what I say, Jarrett hears the answer he wants to hear.

I sighed. "Okay, but we have to be back for sixth period."

Jarrett cheered. Finn shouted, "We're getting ribs!"

Twenty minutes later we were sitting in the back of Jarrett's truck and I was watching Finn and Jarrett gnaw on barbecue ribs. The sound of their chomping and the juice dribbling down their chins made me nauseated.

"Hurry up and eat." Finn motioned at the Styrofoam container in front of me with a chewed-on bone.

It was the smell that really got to me. **Sweet in a way that fools my brain for a fraction of a second before I realize it's rotting flesh.**

"I'm good." I tried to eat some of the coleslaw that had come with the meal, but even that turned my stomach.

"Hey, so what's the deal with you and that crazy freak you hang out with? You got a hard-on for him or something?"

Jarrett smacked Finn's arm. "Dude."

"What?"

"Tripp's my friend," I said.

Finn was glaring at Jarrett even as he spoke to me. "He's still probably gonna wind up crazy like his crazy dad."

"His dad has schizophrenia, and there's nothing wrong with him *or* Tripp." I was doing my best to keep my anger in check.

"If you say so." Finn shrugged. "I get why you'd hang out with that cousin of yours. She's creepy hot."

My lip curled. "Ew?"

"But I can't see no reason to spend time with Tripp unless you're trying to bang him. Or trying to get him to bang you. How's that work, anyway? You negotiate that first or what?"

Jarrett tossed a bone down and wiped his mouth with a napkin. "Christ, Finn. What's gotten into you?"

"Me? What's gotten into *you*? I'm just trying to keep our good friend Virgil here from sticking his dick in crazy."

"Shut the hell up, Finn." Jarrett's voice was so low I almost didn't hear him.

Finn rolled his eyes and picked up another rib. Jarrett snatched it out of his hand and threw it across the parking lot.

"What the hell'd you do that for?"

Jarrett motioned after it with his chin. "Be a good dog and fetch it."

I had no idea what was happening, and I wished I could disappear.

"I told you to watch what you say."

Finn radiated rage. "So, what? You bring the fag along and now I can't talk the way I want? Choke on a dick, Hart."

"Get out."

"It's fine," I said.

Finn squared his shoulders, ignoring me. "Or what?"

Jarrett inhaled deeply and exhaled slowly. "You know exactly what."

I lie on my stomach, my arms askew, and try not to breathe.

Finn sat still, every muscle tense. Jarrett remained loose and relaxed.

Finn blinked. Cussing under his breath, he grabbed his drink and stood. He kicked my lunch out of the truck before hopping over the side. "How am I supposed to get back to school?"

Jarrett shrugged. "Start walking, I suppose."

After that, there didn't seem to be much use hanging around, so we tossed our trash and drove back to school.

"Sorry about Finn."

I felt awkward about the entire situation and didn't know what to say. "You didn't have to do that. I wasn't that upset." I forced a laugh. "Go along to get along, right?"

Jarrett bobbed his head. "Sometimes. Other times you gotta stand up to folks or they won't respect you. That's doubly true of Finn."

"Oh."

"But don't worry. I'll make sure nothing happens to you. You're one of us now."

"Okay."

We pulled into the school parking lot and Jarrett killed

the engine. He turned in the seat and stopped me from getting out. "Hey, you ever find out who recorded that video of you being tied up in the sprawl?"

Drink! Drink! Drink!

"No, why?"

Jarrett let me go. "No reason."

FIFTY

MY FAMILY HADN'T CELEBRATED THANKSGIVING MUCH in Seattle. We'd had a dinner—sometimes Granny would come into town to stay with us—but we hadn't bought into the whole celebration because of its history of colonialism and genocide. Folks in Merritt didn't see it quite the same way. History teachers at school were still using textbooks that framed settlers as benign and generous people who'd tamed the wild lands of America and brought knowledge, Jesus, and beads to the Tribal nations. They even talked about Christopher Columbus like he was a hero. Arguing about it nearly earned me a detention, so I kept my mouth shut after that and tried to get through the school day without drawing attention to myself.

The only place I was happy to be seen was onstage. Mr.

Hilliker seemed pleased with my performance since our talk, and he hadn't suggested replacing me again.

"All right," Hilliker said during our last rehearsal before the holiday break. "While I want you to enjoy your Thanksgiving, I also want you to be thinking about the show. We'll have two more rehearsals before dress rehearsals, and then that's it, kids. Opening night."

We'd grown tight as a group, staying late to run lines and help the art department paint flats. We'd scurried around the catwalks to help the tech team set the lights. Over the past few weeks we'd started to feel like real actors. I didn't know if I'd remain friends with anyone in the cast other than Tripp after the show ended, but until closing night, these people were my best friends in the world.

"I'm proud of the work you've put in," Hilliker went on. "I'm probably going to shout a lot during dress rehearsals as I slowly lose my mind and the rest of my hair, so I want to tell you now how proud I am of each and every one of you. You're the best group of thespians I've had the pleasure of directing."

Tripp nudged me. "I bet he says that to all the thespians."

I shushed him, not wanting to ruin this moment for Mr. Hilliker. Maybe he did say it to every cast of every show, but I had a feeling he was always sincere.

When Mr. Hilliker finally let us go, I gathered my things and followed Tripp to his truck. Grandma was too busy preparing for Thanksgiving to pick me up, so I'd asked Tripp for a ride home. On the way, I apologized for standing him and Astrid up for lunch and told him where I'd been, what had happened, and about Jarrett's revelation that he'd been attacked by a monster, too. I left out what Finn had called Tripp and his dad because I was sure he'd heard it before and didn't need to hear it again. It hadn't taken us long to get home and we sat outside on the porch steps while I finished.

"You sure been spending a lot of time with Jarrett Hart."

I spread my hands. "Everything I just told you, and that's all you've got to say?"

Hardly anything seemed to surprise Tripp or throw him off. His expression remained placid. "Just 'cause Jarrett says he got attacked by a monster don't make you the same. You and him are nothing alike. That's if he's even telling the truth."

"I saw the scars. Besides, why would he lie?"

"No idea, but I told you we used to be friends, so I know a little something about him." Tripp leaned back, resting on his elbows. "Nothing ever stuck to him. Didn't matter if he got caught with his hand in the cookie jar, he never got in trouble for it. I guess, all I'm saying is it can't hurt to be skeptical where he's concerned."

Grandma stuck her head out the door. "Virgil, it's getting near suppertime."

"Hi, Mrs. Knox." Tripp turned around and waved.

"Good evening, Buckley. You're welcome to join us. Catfish, fried okra, and black-eyed peas."

Tripp cringed at the sound of his name but perked up at the mention of food. "Are you sure it's okay?"

"I wouldn't have asked otherwise." Grandma smiled, and I was happy to see her warming up to Tripp. "Y'all finish up out here and then come on in and set the table."

When the door closed behind Grandma, I turned back to Tripp. "I get what you're saying about Jarrett, I really do—"

"But?"

"He understands what I went through."

"Even though he won't talk about it with you or tell folks it happened so that they'd know you were telling the truth?" Tripp shrugged. "If you say that helps, then I'm happy for you, but you got people who believed you from the start, and maybe we don't know exactly what you went through in the sprawl, but we're here for you anyway."

Maybe Tripp was right. It's not as if Jarrett had told me anything new. I still didn't know what had attacked me or what was happening to me with the lesions. Tripp had no reason to believe me, but he had, and he'd stood with me while Jarrett had known I was telling the truth and had let everyone believe I was lying.

"Thanks, Tripp." I stood and offered him a hand. "Come on. Grandma will get cranky if she has to ask us a second time to come inside."

FIFTY-ONE

THANKSGIVING DINNER WAS AT UNCLE FRANK'S HOUSE, AND it was a disaster from the moment we showed up with food that no one had asked for.

"I told you Kelly was cooking." Uncle Frank scowled at Grandma.

I stood in the doorway holding a warm casserole dish full of stuffing balanced in one hand and a bag with pies in the other. Dad was lucky he'd had to work. People were always setting fire to their houses and yards on Thanksgiving while trying to deep-fry turkeys.

Grandma wore her best smile. "And bless her heart for going through all that trouble on our account, but it doesn't hurt to have a backup plan."

"A backup in case of what, Mom?"

Grandma shoved a dish of butternut squash at him. "Are you going to let us in or do you intend to make us wait outside all afternoon?"

Uncle Frank's ears turned red. "You always do this, Mom. She's going to think you don't trust her."

"Watch your tone, son," Grandpa said.

"This is hot. And heavy?" I refused to stand in the doorway while Grandma and Uncle Frank started World War III, so I ducked into the living room and dropped my dishes off at the long folding table that had been set up. It was supposed to rain, so our plan to eat outside had been foiled.

Aunt Kelly was in the kitchen, and she took the news Grandma had brought a backup dinner with far more grace than Uncle Frank had. All she said was, "That just means more leftovers for everyone."

Uncle Frank cracked open a beer.

I wanted to find Astrid, but she was hiding in her room. RJ, Ciara, and Jimmy dragged me into a game of *Mario Party* before I could find her. I finally managed to sneak away after getting my ass handed to me twice. Those kids were ruthless.

"Hey? It's Virgil." I knocked on Astrid's bedroom door. "You in there?"

"Come in." I could practically hear her rolling her eyes.

Astrid was sprawled across her bed reading. Her room

looked like a thrift store had thrown up on her floor. I didn't understand how she could live surrounded by so much chaos.

"What're you reading?"

"A book." Astrid sighed, slipped a bookmark between the pages, and turned her attention to me. "Has the fighting started yet?"

I pulled the desk chair out and sat, propping my feet on the corner of the bed. "Grandma brought over almost an entire emergency dinner, and Uncle Frank kinda lost it, but your mom's taking everything in stride."

"You can thank her lord and personal savior, Xanax, for that."

"Maybe Uncle Frank should've taken a couple."

Astrid's smile vanished in an instant. "Don't even joke about that. The booze is bad enough."

I felt chastised and didn't know what to say next.

Astrid shifted on the bed, pulling her legs up. "Tripp told me you ditched us at lunch to hang out with Jarrett and Finn."

Grateful for the change of subject, I said, "I didn't so much ditch you as I was coerced into skipping."

"Sure you were."

"Seriously!" I doubted Tripp had told Astrid much more than where I'd been, and I wasn't in the mood to drag that mess back into the open right then. I could tell her everything that had happened with Jarrett another time. "So you and Tripp are talking?"

"Yeah. And?"

"Nothing." A smirk crept up on my lips. "Do you talk a lot when I'm not around?"

It took a second, but Astrid got what I was not-so-subtly hinting and gave me the finger. "Tripp's my friend, dickhead."

"He could be more."

"He *could* be, but if he were, if I wanted that from him, it wouldn't be any of your business."

I held up my hands in surrender. "Sorry. It's just that you'd be so cute together."

"If you love him so much, why don't you date him?"

I looked away, fidgeted with my thumbs. "Tripp's cute—"

"He's like a puppy whose paws are too big for his body and can't figure out how to walk and talk at the same time."

"But, he's totally into you—"

"He is not!" Astrid said.

"Besides, the idea of another person touching me makes me want to crawl out of my skin. When someone gets too close to me, when they bump me in the hallway or when someone pats my arm or touches me in any way, it's all I can do to not scream until my lungs burst. But I don't scream. I never scream."

The admission lay like a corpse on the bed between me

and Astrid, both of us looking at it, unsure what to do.

In a quiet voice, Astrid said, "Sometimes, you can scream night and day and folks still won't hear you. Especially in Merritt."

"How would you know?"

"There're a lot of different ways to scream, Virgil."

I looked closely at Astrid, at her green hair, her pierced nose, her clothes. Had she been screaming this whole time and I hadn't noticed? "Astrid, did something happen—"

"We're not talking about me."

"But—"

Astrid arched her eyebrow. When I didn't argue with her, she relaxed. "Look, if you ever need to let out what's inside you, I've got plenty of hair dye."

"Thanks, but I'm not sure letting what's inside me out is safe for anyone."

A hand clamped over my mouth. I tried to open my eyes, but there was cloth wrapped around my head.

"Don't make a sound," a voice whispered.

Hot breath soaks my neck.

I went limp. I clamped my eyes shut.

My body left the floor. I floated through the house and out the door, making no sound as I traveled.

Voices hissed.

"He was *in* the closet. That's a joke begging to be told."

Blink

Blink

Blink

"What the hell'd you hit me for?"

I'm crying. No, I'm sweating.

My body touched the ground again.

"Try not to move around."

The world shook and vibrated. I was in the back of a truck. We were moving. I wasn't bound, I could've removed the blindfold, but I left it in place. The air was warm against my bare skin.

His tongue slips into my mouth, and then he backs away, laughing.

Without my phone, I was helpless. Useless.

It lowers itself onto my back.

The truck stopped. We hadn't been driving long. Hands grabbed me under my arms and lifted me out. Leaves crunched under my feet. My toes dug into dirt. I recognized the smell.

Ain't nothing good in the sprawl at night.

"Come on. Almost there," a voice said. Louder. No longer afraid of noise.

I stumbled as we walked. **Mud squishes under my shoes.** I knew exactly where I was.

We stopped. My blindfold was yanked away.

Blink

Blink

Blink

Jarrett stood to my right, illuminated from behind by the truck's headlights, his languid grin made sinister by shadows.

Finn stood to the left. He wore a sleeveless shirt and denim shorts with a half-empty pint bottle of Jack tucked into his pocket.

Neither was looking at me. I followed their gazes to a tree where Worm was tied up, gagged, his chin against his chest, his sweat-soaked hair hanging forward. Chuck stood beside him, grinning like a hunter showing off his prize kill.

"Surprise," Jarrett said.

Chuck lurched forward. "What the hell took you guys so long?"

Finn sneered. "Scared of the dark, Chucky?"

They fought. Their words were mosquitoes buzzing.

"What the fuck?!" My voice echoed through the night, silencing the boys.

Finn approached and slung his arm around me—I didn't scream—he reeked of whiskey and sweat. My skin crawled. "I know I gave you a heap of shit since you been here." He motioned at Worm with his chin. "This here's my apology."

"Dylan's the one who was recording you that night," Jarrett said.

Worm's name was Dylan. I'd forgotten. Knowing made it worse.

Finn crossed to the tree, grabbed Dylan by the hair, and yanked back his head. He pulled the gag down. "Tell him what you did, Worm."

Dylan's eyes were wild and frightened.

Finn smacked him across the face. "Go on and tell him."

"I only did what I was told!" Dylan's voice cracked.

Finn replaced the gag. He took a swig from his bottle.

Chuck pulled a fat Sharpie from his pocket and uncapped it.

Jarrett leaned closer to me. "Finn asked around and found out Dylan put the idea of proving there was a monster in your head. He tied you up and took the pictures and video. He made you think it was your idea."

Drink! Drink! Drink!

"I don't remember."

"You just heard it from Dylan's own mouth." Jarrett shrugged. "Anyway, Finn wanted you to know he was sorry."

"By kidnapping and torturing a kid?"

Finn's menacing laugh drew my attention away from Jarrett. Chuck stepped back so I could see that he'd written EAT ME across Dylan's bare chest. Finn got out his phone.

He and Chuck took selfies with Dylan in the background.

Jarrett shouted, "Don't forget to tag it!"

#MonsterBait

"Now you really are one of us." Jarrett was grinning again.

Finn poured some whiskey onto the gag in Dylan's mouth and laughed. "Come on, let's get outta here."

Dylan's head popped up. He squirmed and screamed.

"We can't leave him," I said.

"It's what he deserves!" Finn shouted, stumbling toward the truck.

"Monster *bait*!" Chuck cackled.

I dropped my voice so only Jarret could hear. "You know what could happen if we leave him."

"Don't worry. I'll come back after I drop y'all off."

"No." I didn't scream. I went to the tree to untie Dylan. I didn't care that he'd tied me up or taken the pictures. No one deserved to be left alone in the sprawl.

Jarrett stood back and watched.

Without the ropes holding him up, Dylan's legs gave way. I pulled his arm around my shoulders and helped him to the truck.

Finn looked disappointed when he saw me with Dylan. "What the hell, Knox? He woulda been fine."

Chuck leaned across to Finn and said something too low for me to hear. They cracked up laughing.

Jarrett tried to get Dylan's other arm, but the kid jerked away and almost sent us tumbling to the ground. Jarrett held up his hands and got in the truck.

When we were moving, Dylan pulled the gag from his mouth. He was saying something, but the wind drowned him out.

"What?"

Dylan's eyes flicked up to catch mine. "I'm sorry." That's all he said, over and over. As soon as we pulled in front of his house, he leapt from the truck and dashed inside.

I slid open the back window and stuck my head in. "You guys shouldn't have done that."

Finn tossed back the rest of the Jack. "You're welcome."

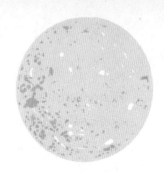

FIFTY-TWO

NEARLY EVERYONE IN MERRITT ATTENDED CHURCH. IT WAS expected, and folks talked unkindly about anyone who didn't make an appearance. The pageantry of Sunday mornings had less to do with celebrating the Lord than with being seen and gossiping about the neighbors. Religion had never played a major part in my life. I didn't not believe in the possibility that something greater than myself existed, but I didn't spend much time thinking about it either. That Sunday morning I spent most of service thinking about the sprawl. Every time I closed my eyes, I saw Dylan tied to the tree, blubbering and shaking. I'd been part of that. Finn and Jarrett and Chuck had made me complicit. Yet, in a twisted way, kidnapping Dylan had been Finn's attempt to make amends for the hell he'd caused me. Knowing Dylan had probably been the person who'd taken the original #MonsterBait photos hadn't made me feel any better about what Jarrett, Finn, and Chuck had done.

From where I was sitting with Grandma and Grandpa, I could only see the backs of Jarrett's and Finn's heads, and I hadn't been able to find Dylan at all, which didn't surprise me. Tripp was there with his dad. Uncle Frank, Aunt Kelly, Astrid, and the kids had shown up late and were seated at the rear of the church. I wasn't sure if I was going to tell Astrid and Tripp about Dylan. Dylan's #MonsterBait picture was probably all over social media, but no one knew I'd been involved. I hadn't been in on the plan, and I'd prevented the boys from leaving Dylan alone in the sprawl. I'd saved him from my fate. I wasn't guilty of anything, so there was no need to confess. Right?

When service ended, we filtered outside. Grandma went off in search of new gossip and Grandpa left to find his friends. I stood alone under the shade of an old oak tree, grateful for the quiet. It didn't last.

"Heya, Virgil." Reba sauntered toward me and leaned against the tree. She wore a pretty yellow sundress and had on a pair of dark glasses, even though the sky was overcast. The summer heat had finally broken and ushered in a taste of fall.

"Reba."

"How you been? Feels like I haven't seen you in forever."

I shrugged. "*Clue*'s opening next week, so most of my time's been eaten up by rehearsals."

"I already bought my tickets."

"You might be the only one."

"Oh, I don't know. I doubt you'll draw the same crowd as the Coyotes, but there still isn't much to do in Merritt. A lot of folks will show up in the hopes of seeing someone fall off the stage."

I snorted.

Reba motioned to where Grandma was talking to Pastor Wallace. "Old Wallace looks like he's ready to eat his tongue. What's your granny saying to him?"

She hadn't been thrilled by his sermon demonizing gay marriage, but I wasn't sure if that's why she'd sought him out. Either way, I cleared my throat and affected a warbling falsetto. "Well, bless your heart, Pastor Wallace, I didn't realize you were such an expert on the homosexual lifestyle. Tell me, where did you acquire your experience?"

Reba dropped her voice an octave to play along. "Well, uh, I spent a summer in San Francisco spreading God's word to as many men as I could find. They were very receptive to my teachings."

"I'll bet they were." I couldn't keep from laughing, and Reba lost it too. Grandma threw a glare in our direction, so I pulled Reba toward a retention pond on the side of the church. A group of ducks waddled toward us, interested until they realized we had no food for them.

Reba stopped and turned toward me. "About what happened at the party—"

"I put that behind me." At least I was trying to.

"I'm sorry I didn't stop it. I should've taken you home."

"You didn't do anything wrong." I'd thought I was mad at Reba, but nothing that had happened at Finn's house had been her fault. She hadn't poured the drinks in me, and she hadn't tied me to the fence.

"I didn't do anything right, either." Reba cast her gaze down. "Did you ever learn who was responsible for leaving you out there?"

I nodded.

"Was it Jarrett or Finn?"

"Neither."

Reba's eyebrows rose. "You sure about that?"

"Pretty sure." I couldn't remember what had happened that night, but, even so, my brain was already compositing Dylan's face into the hazy memories. There he was with the rope. There he was holding the phone. "Jarrett and Finn helped me find the person responsible."

#MonsterBait

Reba took off her sunglasses and caught my eye. "Do you trust them?"

"No, but the person who did it told me himself." I shrugged. "Besides, Finn and Jarrett weren't around when I was being tied up."

I ain't no homo.

Reba slipped her sunglasses back on. "Did I ever tell you why I broke up with Finn?"

"I think you mentioned whiskey dick once."

"That was a joke."

"Oh."

Reba resumed walking around the lake, so I followed. "I only went out with Finn for a few months, but it didn't take long before I started hearing stories of girls at his parties getting blackout drunk even though they swore they didn't have more than a couple beers."

Drink! Drink! Drink!

"Mostly they were younger girls, ninth and tenth graders, so I assumed they couldn't hold their liquor. But there was a girl, Skylar Montrose. She didn't drink, I knew she didn't, but there she was, at one of Finn's parties looking like she'd spent the entire night doing keg stands.

"She passed out on one of the couches upstairs, and boys took *pictures* of her." I didn't need the look Reba had given me to understand what kind of pictures she meant.

"I don't know how much further it would've gone if I hadn't found her and taken her home."

"That's why you broke up with Finn?"

Reba shook her head. "He convinced me he didn't have anything to do with it. I told you Finn can be charming when he sets his mind to it." She clenched her fists. "The next party he threw, I blacked out. I woke up the morning after in Finn's bed feeling like I'd been hit by a school bus."

Hey, wanna see something cool?

"Did he . . . ?" I couldn't bring myself to say the words.

"No. Finn said he found me stumbling around outside and that if he hadn't taken care of me, something awful could've happened." Reba shivered. "It was a threat. Finn wanted me to know he could do anything to me anytime, and I was helpless."

"Damn, Reba—"

"I broke up with him a couple weeks after."

"But you're still friends with him?" I was trying to process what Reba had told me. "You go to the parties and hang out with him and Jarrett even though you think Finn's drugging people?"

"Being one of the boys is the best way to keep an eye on them. I see a girl at Finn's house who looks a little too drunk, and I make sure she gets home safe."

Drink! Drink! Drink!

There was so much to unpack. I believed Reba, obviously, and I believed Finn was capable of everything Reba had said.

More than capable—willing and eager. My respect for Reba went up a hundredfold for having the courage to spend time with the person who'd drugged her so she could attempt to prevent it happening to other girls.

"Do you understand why I'm telling you this, Virgil?"

My wide-eyed, confused stare must've given away that I didn't.

"The way you were acting that night at Finn's house reminded me of Skylar."

C'mon. I know exactly what you need.

"Are you saying you think Finn drugged me?"

Reba spread her hands. "Obviously, I can't be sure, but I thought you should know before you get too cozy with those boys."

I caught sight of Grandma waving me down. I wanted to continue talking to Reba, but Grandma wouldn't tolerate being kept waiting. "I have to go."

"Sure," Reba said. "If I don't see you before the play, break a leg, all right?"

"Thanks, Reba."

FIFTY-THREE

OUR FIRST DRESS REHEARSAL WASN'T A CATASTROPHE.
Despite the sounds of hammering from backstage, we ran through the entire play without stopping. I flubbed a couple lines, Tripp came out in the wrong costume once, and there were a few other minor mistakes, but we worked through them and the show went on.

In the dressing room afterward, Tripp popped up behind me. He was practically vibrating. "We did it!"

"Mostly." I tried to sound serious, but I couldn't suppress the euphoric high I was riding.

"Sure, I came out in the cop's costume when I was supposed to be dressed as the maid, but no one noticed but Hilly."

"That's because he was the only person in the audience."

"Don't get hung up on details, Virgil."

I snickered, which turned into a laugh that Tripp joined. It wasn't even that funny, but we were cracking up so hard a couple of the other boys threw us sidelong glances and shook their heads before dashing out the door.

When Tripp had regained his composure, he said, "Hey, what happened at church Sunday? I heard from Ashlynn that your grandma murdered Pastor Wallace on the church steps? I always leave before the good stuff happens."

Grandma had refused to tell me what she'd said to Pastor Wallace, but according to whom you heard the story from, Grandma had either castigated the pastor until he cried or threatened his life under the eye of God and the whole congregation. "You know my grandma. Actually, though, something did happen."

It had been tough in the moment to process what Reba had told me, but I'd had plenty of time at home and I still wasn't sure what to make of it. If anyone could help me sort it out, Tripp could. I told him everything Reba had said.

Tripp had finished cleaning his makeup off and was changing into his regular clothes. "I remember Skylar and the pictures."

"You weren't . . . You didn't—"

"Hell no." Tripp threw me a look that said I should've known better than to ask. "You know, she ended up moving?"

Considering what I'd been through, I believed it. "Do you think it's true? About Finn drugging people?"

"Don't know, but it sure sounds like something he'd do."

I sat on the counter. "Do you think Finn might have drugged *me*?"

Drink! Drink! Drink!

Tripp looked up from lacing his sneakers. "Why? You got nice legs, but you ain't really Finn's type."

Don't tell no one about this, all right?

"Maybe he did it to mess with me."

"And the second time?"

I opened my mouth to reply, before fully considering Tripp's question, but stopped when it hit me. "Wait, what?"

Tripp shrugged. "The first party you went to, maybe he put something in your drink to mess with you. But why would he have done it the second time? Weren't you supposed to be friends?"

I'd only been thinking about the second party. **#MonsterBait** I hadn't even considered that I might've been drugged at the first party.

I don't know where I am.

Maybe I drank too much at the party after the homecoming dance, maybe so much that I blacked out, but I'd hardly drunk at all on the night I was attacked.

It lowers itself onto my back.

Which would mean that Finn was responsible for me being in the sprawl that night. He was responsible for what happened to me.

"Virgil?" Tripp touched my arm, and I started and bumped into the mirror behind me. He held his hands where I could see them. "You're all right, Virgil."

"What if he did drug me?" I spoke the words, not so much for Tripp as for myself.

Tripp cleared his throat to get my attention. "Maybe you should tell the chief."

"I've got no proof." A thought occurred to me. "I could get proof. Finn probably keeps whatever he's using in his room. If I could get in there—"

"Don't. Please?"

"But—"

Tripp's expression veered toward pity. "Look, after what you been through, I get that you wanna do something. You wanted to hunt down the thing that attacked you and then you wanted to find out who strung you up in the sprawl. Now you wanna go hunting around Finn's house."

I threw up my hands. "You were willing to help me before. Why won't you help me now?"

"I never said I wouldn't help. I just think maybe this is bigger than you and me. Tell Chief Duran. Let her handle it."

"What if she won't?"

Tripp looked around the dressing room. "We gotta focus on the show, so how about we'll talk to Duran and give her a chance to do the right thing. If she won't, when the show's done, you and me'll go play detective. Okay?"

I wanted to go after Finn right then, but Tripp was right. I couldn't get sidetracked and let the cast down. Besides, Chief Duran might surprise me if I let her. "Okay. We'll wait."

Tripp and I finished cleaning up and headed out. Mr. Hilliker stopped me at the exit.

"You did a good job tonight, Mr. Knox." Some of Hilliker's anxiousness seemed to have burned off. I wouldn't have called him calm, but he was certainly less manic.

"Thanks. I'm still a little shaky near the end."

"You've got this. You're performing on a level way above the others, though I'll kick your ass if you tell anyone I said so."

"Really?"

Hilliker glanced at his foot. "Do you doubt me?"

"Not that. About the acting?"

"You're good, Virgil. Really good. Keep at it and who knows how far you could go."

It was the first time I'd ever felt like I had a talent. That maybe there was something I was meant to do with my life. I didn't know if acting was that thing, but I liked knowing it could be. "Thanks, Mr. Hilliker."

"Compliments are free, son."

"Not for that. For giving me somewhere I feel safe."

It was difficult to see behind the beard, but I was pretty sure he was grinning.

FIFTY-FOUR

I DRESSED OUT FOR GYM AS QUICKLY AS POSSIBLE. EVEN though no one was paying attention to me, I could feel them looking at the scabs on my chest and leg. I could feel them wondering what was wrong with me.

I'd called Chief Duran like I'd promised Tripp. She hadn't sounded surprised to hear from me. After I told her my story, she'd asked a couple questions and then told me to stay away from those boys and that she'd handle it. I didn't know what that meant, but it was the day before opening night, and I had to put everything that wasn't the show out of my mind.

When I reached the field, Coach announced we were playing flag football. He paired us off into teams and flipped a coin to see who controlled the ball first. I was almost as bad at flag football as I was at soccer. I couldn't pass to save my life, and I could barely catch, either. My only benefit to the team was that I could run, but no one expected Zach Willis, our team's quarterback, to hand the ball off to me. Which was why I was so shocked when he proposed doing exactly that.

"You want to do what?" I said in the huddle when he explained the play.

The other boys snickered.

Zach was the human equivalent of mayonnaise on white bread, so it wasn't in his nature to make jokes, especially about football. "All you gotta do when I toss you the ball is run straight down the field. And don't get turned around and run the wrong way, either."

He broke the huddle before I could persuade him this was a terrible idea. The boys on the other team looked bigger than usual. They were growling and grunting like a bunch of feral hogs. Maybe I could drop the ball when Zach tossed it to me. Fumble it and let the other team grab it. Doing so would've surprised no one.

Jarrett snapped the ball to Zach and set the play into motion. To me, it looked like the boys were scrambling every which way without a plan. I couldn't keep track of who was where or what was going on. Everything was so loud.

"Virgil!"

I turned toward the voice calling my name, and Zach pressed the ball into my hands and shoved me toward the end zone. The moment I held the ball, the other players blurred and a path emerged. I saw where I needed to go.

So I ran.

I was going to do this. I was going to score. No one could touch me.

My legs feel like jelly.

The path narrowed, but I could still make it. I didn't see Luke Ashford coming at me from the left. **He crashes into me and I hit the moist ground.**

"Sorry, Coach." Luke brushed the grass off his hands. "Got a little carried away."

Coach chuckled.

I limped to my feet.

Zach called the huddle. Same play.

Snap.

I ran.

This time it was Drew Feeney who tackled me, crashing into me from behind. **I lie on my stomach, my arms askew, and try not to breathe.**

Coach chuckled.

Same play.

Snap.

Run.

Alex Boyce **pushes my face deeper into the mud.**

Zach tossed me the ball. I refused to take it. He picked

it up and shoved it into my hands and propelled me toward the end zone.

I didn't scream.

I ran.

Luke, his face a determined mask, barreled toward me.

It lowers itself onto my back.

I go still and hope it kills me quickly.

Coach Munford blew the whistle and sent us to the locker rooms to shower and change. I limped back, my skinned knees bleeding, my body battered and bruised. None of the boys said a word to me as they jogged past. They'd spent the last forty minutes taking their aggression out on me, but now I didn't exist.

When Jarrett passed, I grabbed his arm. "What the hell was that about?"

Jarrett jerked away. "You should try out for the team next year. You'd make a hell of a tackling dummy." He took off, leaving me to hobble to the locker room alone.

FIFTY-FIVE

ON MY WAY TO THE CAFETERIA, I SPOTTED DYLAN. I CALLED to him, but he ignored me, forcing me to hold my ribs, grit my teeth, and chase after him. "Hey! Wait up!"

Dylan turned so quickly that I skittered back and hit a bank of lockers. "Leave me alone!"

I held up my hands. "I didn't have anything to do with what happened in the sprawl. I didn't tell them to do that to you."

"You think I care about that?" A cut ran across Dylan's bottom lip. Freckles dotted his cheeks. He looked so much younger than I remembered. "You got no idea what I went through. Always doing every damn thing they said. 'Worm, clean my boxers. Worm, run and set up them bottles. Worm, fetch that girl's number.' I did *everything* they asked. And I did it for nothing."

Stragglers heading to class or lunch paused to watch, but Dylan's glare sent them on their way again.

"You can get through this. Changing my number helped—"

Dylan's brow knit together. "I don't care about being called some names. All I wanted was to play varsity. Think that's gonna happen now?"

"You're upset about football?"

"Obviously."

It was difficult to drum up much sympathy for Dylan not making the varsity team, but I tried. "Well, look, I'm sorry for what they did. I didn't know they were going to do it, and if you need help or someone to talk to—"

"You really don't understand nothing, do you?" Dylan sneered. "Just leave me alone."

Dylan stalked off. That hadn't gone the way I'd expected. I couldn't blame Dylan for not wanting my help. I'd barely been capable of helping myself. At least Dylan wouldn't have to worry about monster porn showing up on his locker unless Finn coerced another JV player with graphic design skills into being his thrall.

Astrid and Tripp were already at our table when I arrived in the cafeteria. Their conversation cut off, replaced by a guilty silence.

"What?"

"We weren't talking about you," Tripp said.

Astrid threw him a dirty look. "Really?"

I winced as I collapsed into my seat.

"What's that about?" Astrid asked.

"Football game got a little rough during PE today." I dug the banana out of my lunch because it was the only thing I thought I could stomach.

"We played flag football when I was in Munford's class." Tripp had a slice of pizza, fries, and a chocolate chip cookie spread in front of him.

"We were supposed to, but some of the boys didn't get the message." I told them what'd happened. How Zach kept forcing me to take the ball, and how every play wound up with me getting my face shoved in the dirt.

I glanced toward Jarrett and Finn's table, but it was empty.

"Why would they do that?" Astrid looked ready to skin someone alive. "Is this some dumb testosterone thing?"

I looked to Tripp for a clue, but he shrugged with his hands. I was about to respond with a glib comment when I spotted Reba walking toward us. She sat down beside me.

"Hey, Reba," Tripp said. He was smiling. Astrid was not.

"Hey, y'all."

Astrid leveled an unfriendly stare at Reba. "What do you want?"

Reba ignored her and looked at me. "You okay, Virgil? I heard you had some trouble during PE."

I grimaced thinking about it. "No permanent damage. I think."

"We were trying to work out why the boys went after him," Tripp said.

"Not that anyone's needed a reason before," Astrid added.

Reba drummed her fingers on the table. "You know anything about Chief Duran questioning Finn this morning?"

Tripp caught my eye. I hadn't told him yet that I'd called Duran.

Reba must've seen the look that passed between us because she shook her head. "What the hell were you hoping to accomplish?"

Astrid looked back and forth between me and Reba. "What did I miss?"

"I had to do something, Reba."

"Shit, Virgil." Reba leaned her head back and sighed. "You've got no idea the hornet's nest you've kicked over."

"Is someone going to tell me what y'all are talking about?" Astrid asked.

I held Reba's gaze for a moment longer before turning my attention to Astrid. "Reba told me she thinks Finn's been slipping roofies in girls' drinks at his parties. It might also explain why I can't remember how I wound up in the sprawl the night I was attacked. I told Chief Duran—"

Reba cut me off. "And she showed up at the Ducketts' house at six o'clock this morning to question Finn. Do you wanna know how that turned out?"

"She arrested him and we won't have to worry about him no more?" Tripp's attempt at humor fell flat.

"Hardly," Reba said. "The Ducketts have already called for

the chief's removal. If she's still got a job this time next week, it'll be a miracle."

I should've known better. Not only had telling Chief Duran accomplished nothing to stop Finn, but Duran was in danger of losing her job.

"You did the right thing," Tripp said, as if he were reading my mind.

Astrid smacked Tripp's arm. "You knew about this?"

"So what happened today in PE was payback?" I looked to Reba for the answer.

"More like a message." Reba glanced around and then stood. "I should go. Be careful, Virgil."

"Great." I buried my face in my hands. "I really screwed this up."

"Maybe, but if any of them come near you again, I will end them in the most painful ways I can imagine." Astrid's voice cut through my misery, and I almost smiled.

"She's scary, Virgil, but she's right. We got your back."

When I took my hands away, Astrid and Tripp both looked determined in their own way to stand by me. Maybe telling Duran about Finn potentially drugging people at his parties hadn't resulted in the outcome I'd hoped for, but I didn't regret doing it. And knowing Astrid and Tripp were there for me made me feel like I could survive whatever was to come.

"Thank you. Both of you." I motioned at Tripp's cookie. "You gonna eat that?"

FIFTY-SIX

IT WAS A RARE NIGHT THAT DAD WAS HOME FOR SUPPER.
With Thanksgiving past and the holidays truly upon us, he'd
been working even more at Target and picking up extra shifts
at the firehouse, too. Dad was exhausted—he didn't even try
to pretend he wasn't—but he said the overtime pay made up
for it.

"Think you'll be ready for your driving test in a couple
weeks?" Dad wore a hopeful smile and seemed more relaxed
than he had in days. It probably helped that my sessions with
Dr. Apelgren were going well and I hadn't gone for a night-
time stroll since Jarrett and Finn had kidnapped me.

"I don't know. I've got the basics down, but driving on
the highway makes me nervous."

Grandma smiled. "Oh, I think you'll be just fine."

"Cars running well, too," Grandpa said. "The boy's got a knack for cars you and Frankie never had."

Dad chuckled. "That talent must've skipped a generation."

"Did your father ever tell you about the time he put motor oil in his gas tank?"

"Do we have to tell this story, Dad?"

Grandpa went on, unconcerned. "He thought he could make his gas last longer."

"Jeez, Dad. You didn't?"

"I was seventeen!"

My phone buzzed. I pulled it out without thinking, which earned me a sharp look from Grandma. I held it up. "It's Mom."

Dad nodded. "Go on, then."

I heard Grandma and Dad arguing about whether I should be excused from the table to take a call from Mom, but I ignored them and went outside to the porch. Mom called so rarely that I wasn't willing to take the chance she'd still be able to talk after I finished dinner.

"Hey, Mom."

"Virgil! How are you?" She sounded like she'd been drinking. Her voice was slightly louder than normal, her words a bit more exaggerated.

"I'm okay. *Clue* opens tomorrow night, so I'm anxious about that."

"I love that movie. Who're you playing? No, wait. Let me guess. Colonel Mustard?"

"Wadsworth. I'm the lead, remember? I told you this already."

"Right. That's right. You did. You know, I just adore Tim Curry. Do you remember when we used to watch *The Rocky Horror Picture Show* and sing the songs together? You had such a beautiful voice."

"I still do."

Mom made a noncommittal grunt.

"Cool, so did you have a reason for calling me other than to tell me you think puberty destroyed my singing voice?"

"Don't be melodramatic, Virgil. And I did, actually."

I was starting to wish Dad had taken Grandma's side and made me wait to answer the phone. "Well? Are you finally buying me the pony I've always wanted?"

"I'm flying you home for Christmas."

Everyone I love is on the other side of the world.

I heard the words, but they didn't quite register. "What?"

"I've already bought your ticket. You'll have to miss a day of school, but teachers never assign important work before winter break, anyway."

"How long?"

Mom was quiet a moment. "Well, I was going to talk to you about that when you were here, but how would you feel about coming home permanently?"

All I'd wanted since the day Dad and I had arrived in

Merritt was to go back to Seattle. But there was nothing for me there anymore. Besides, I had friends in Merritt now. People who'd been there for me when I'd needed them. People who had my back.

"Virgil?"

"I don't know, Mom."

"I thought you hated Merritt."

"I do."

It lowers itself onto my back.

Mom's voice became a blur of nonsensical words. She was offering me the one thing I thought I'd wanted. Escape. I touched the scab over my ribs through my shirt. In returning to Seattle, I might escape the monster that had attacked me in the sprawl all those weeks ago and had been hounding me since. Or I might simply carry it with me to a new city where it would continue to terrorize me.

"I thought you'd be happy," Mom was saying. "You don't know what I gave up to do this for you, Virgil."

"Can we talk about it later? We were right in the middle of supper."

Mom's enthusiasm chilled. "Fine. I'll speak to your father, too. But you *are* coming home."

I wasn't sure how we'd gone from discussing whether I wanted to move back to Seattle to me no longer having a choice. "Sure, Mom. Love you. Bye." I hung up without waiting for a reply.

Dad looked up when I padded into the kitchen and sat down. "What'd your mother want?"

She wants me to move back to Seattle. She wants me to leave Merritt and live with her again. Return to the school where I'd be forced to see my ex-boyfriend and his new boyfriend. She wants me to abandon you and Grandma and Grandpa and Astrid and Tripp. She wants me to leave everyone I love on the other side of the world. "Nothing."

FIFTY-SEVEN

I SAT IN THE STAGE LEFT DRESSING ROOM TRYING TO APPLY eyeliner without stabbing myself. It wasn't going well, and I was still holding it together better than most. Jesse was convinced he'd forgotten his lines, Mackenzie couldn't find her shoes, and Tripp was going around giving people impromptu pep talks that made them cry.

"And if you miss a line," he told Alisha Spinnaker, "keep going. No one'll notice."

"Why not?" Her lower lip trembled.

"I just mean they won't be paying attention to you, so you don't gotta worry."

Alisha ran out of the room.

"Damn. Did it again."

I glanced at Tripp in the mirror. "Stop trying to make people feel better, and finish putting on your makeup."

We were less than twenty minutes until showtime. Mr. Hilliker was somewhere going over stage directions with Miley Hennessy, our stage manager. He'd already sweated through one shirt and jacket. Thankfully, he'd brought spares.

Tripp pulled a stool to the counter next to mine. I wasn't worried about him getting ready on time. In addition to his role as the maid, he had a couple of scenes where he had to change quickly so he could play someone's dead body. Tripp could switch costumes faster than anyone in the cast. "You're a long way from the kid who didn't know where to sit in Mr. Hilliker's class."

I thought back to the first day. It had only been a few months, but it felt like a lifetime ago. "You bet him I'd be the first to sit down, didn't you?"

"Hilly likes to see who the boldest students in his class are gonna be."

"How'd you know I'd be the first to sit?"

Tripp wore a sober expression. "Anyone with the nerve to show up after what you went through had to be brave."

"I was annoyed, not courageous."

"Don't matter what you call it if it gets you where you need to go."

I'd gotten lucky finding a friend like Tripp. I could've

wandered through the semester alone, but I'd found someone willing to get a little lost with me. I didn't know what would happen going forward. It seemed obvious Finn knew I'd gone to Chief Duran about him, and I had a feeling he was going to take it personally. I didn't know if my mom would really make me return to Seattle or if she'd change her mind. I had no idea if the monster inside me was going to tear free or if I could continue fighting it. Everything was awful, but with a friend like Tripp, it also wasn't so bad.

"Thanks."

"Don't mention it." Tripp clapped my back and stood. "Also, if you think you might need to puke, do it *before* the show. The folks in the front row'll thank you."

FIFTY-EIGHT

I DIDN'T NEED TO THROW UP. IT HELPED THAT MY FIRST scene was with Tripp. He was onstage when the curtain rose, preparing the house. He'd wanted to wear a traditional French maid's costume, but Mr. Hilliker had convinced him he simply didn't have the bosom to pull it off. Instead, he wore a slim black suit, and was primly polishing a glass while a TV droned in the background.

I stood in the wings waiting for my cue.

One moment I was Virgil Knox, a timid, confused nearly sixteen-year-old high school student, the next I was Wadsworth, a proper butler with mysterious intentions who was quite possibly not who he appeared to be. From the moment I opened my mouth, the world outside the stage ceased to exist. I forgot my bruised ribs and skinned knees, the scabs on my body, my mom telling me she wanted me to come home, the monster I was becoming, the boyfriend who'd broken up with me. Everything disappeared.

During the dinner scene, when I finally exited the stage for the first time, Mr. Hilliker was waiting. He clapped me on the back, grinning. "You're doing well, Mr. Knox."

"Who is Mr. Knox?" I asked. "Is he another guest?"

Mr. Hilliker chuckled. "Keep it up."

And I did. We all did. The entire cast tore through the show like the words had been burned into our bones. There were no flubbed lines, no missed cues. During dinner, Cook dropped a glass she hadn't meant to drop, but everyone played it off like it was intentional, and the show went on.

I felt more alive than I had since moving to Merritt. Nothing compared to the exhilaration of performing, of playing off the other actors, our energy feeding one another, driving one another to be better than we thought possible. We were phenomenal. It was a special kind of magic we cast that night.

As the show neared its end, I felt invincible. I locked the cop in the library, returned to the group, and then waited for my next scene after the cop and the maid were murdered.

Holding a small flashlight, I stood in the center of the stage and lit my face. The telephone ringing in the background was the only sound. I looked for the light panel so that I could turn on the rest of the lights.

A howl rose from the back of the audience. I froze.

A few titters sounded out beyond the darkness.

I shook my head. It was nothing.

Another howl, closer.

This wasn't part of the show, but no one in the audience knew it.

The night symphony pauses. Crickets set down their bows, the wind takes a breath, the trees still their brushes and silence their leaves.

A hulking form with long, muscled arms and powerful legs detached from the shadows and leapt onto the stage, barreling straight toward me.

Something crashes into me and I hit the moist ground.

I scrambled backward until I struck the wall.

It looms over me, framed by the night and the stars and moss-choked oak trees.

The flat behind me fell, causing a chain reaction that took out the bookshelf, which toppled into the table. Like dominoes, the entire set tumbled down.

Teeth dig into my shoulder. It worries me like a dog with a chew toy and then flings me aside.

It bared its teeth. Its lips pulled back in a twisted imitation of a smile.

The monster tilted back its head and **a howl breaks the silence. Rising, rising, cresting the slope, and then sliding down again into the disquiet night.**

It leaned closer.

Hot breath soaks my neck, a clawed hand pushes my face deeper into the mud.

I didn't scream.

Bristly, wiry hair brushes the back of my arms.

I didn't scream.

My shoulder burns where its teeth penetrated me, and I feel its poison in my blood.

Mr. Hilliker and Tripp ran onto the stage from the wings.

It lowers itself onto my back.

The monster turned and fled, leaping off the stage and sprinting into the audience. I huddled with my knees pulled to my chest, shaking.

Blink

Blink

Blink

"Lower the godforsaken curtain!" Hilliker yelled.

Tripp knelt in front of me. "Virgil? Virgil, are you hurt?" He snapped his fingers in front of my face.

I didn't scream.

I cried.

FIFTY-NINE

I SAT ON THE EDGE OF THE STAGE AND HUGGED MY KNEES to my chest, unable to look anyone in the eye. No one had blamed me for ruining opening night, but they hadn't needed to.

"So you got no idea who might've been in that costume?" Chief Duran had been in the audience and had asked me to stick around and answer some questions. Grandma and Grandpa, who'd come to see the show with Astrid, Uncle Frank, and Aunt Kelly, stood off to the side.

"It wasn't a costume." My voice was little more than a whisper.

Duran cocked her head. "Say that again?"

Tripp barged into the conversation. "It was obviously Finn! Maybe Jarrett, too! You know as well as I do those assholes did this!"

Mr. Hilliker rested his hand on Tripp's shoulder. "Watch your language, Mr. Swafford."

"Why on earth would Finn Duckett or Jarrett Hart be involved?" Grandma asked.

I didn't answer Grandma's question. I didn't need to. Chief Duran knew the answer. This had been another message. Retribution for ratting out Finn. He was never going to leave me alone.

"You should have Nash take my place for the rest of the show's run," I mumbled.

Mr. Hilliker stroked his beard. "If that's what you want, son, but I don't think that's the answer."

Grandpa was frowning. "We don't give up, young man."

Mr. Hilliker kept talking. "We'll post ushers at the doors and search bags to make sure nothing like this happens again."

I clench my eyes shut as tightly as I can and try to pretend I'm sleeping.

Everyone was talking at and around me. Telling me what to do and how to feel. It didn't matter if Hilliker kept it from happening again. The damage had been done. Just like my memories of Luca were entangled with the monster in the sprawl, so now was the stage. I'd never be able to go out there again without hearing the monster's howl and feeling its claws rake across my back. Finn Duckett had taken from me the last place I truly felt safe, and I'd never get it back.

"I'd like to go home."

Chief Duran glanced at my grandparents and nodded. Grandma sighed and Grandpa jingled the keys in his palm. Mr. Hilliker said, "That's right. Go on home and get some rest. We'll talk about this more tomorrow."

"I mean Seattle. I'm going home to Seattle." I slid off the stage and exited the theater.

SIXTY

GRANDMA KNOCKED ON MY BEDROOM DOOR. AGAIN. "YOU can't waste all day in bed, Virgil."

Joke's on you. I'm in the closet.

"Come on out and get some breakfast and then we'll go driving."

I curled deeper into my nest of blankets. Every time I shut my eyes, I saw the monster. The one that leapt onto the stage superimposed over the image of the one that attacked me in the sprawl. They were the same. I'd only been able to sleep when I finally passed out, and even then my dreams were filled with the monster. Sometimes the monster attacked me; sometimes I was the monster.

I'd heard Dad come home early that morning, but he'd only stayed long enough to shower and change for a shift at

Target. I wasn't sure if Grandma or Grandpa had told him what had happened during the performance the night before.

Everyone thought it had been a person wearing a monster costume—the theater had been dark, so I understood how they could make the mistake—but it hadn't been. It had been *the* monster. It was real. Right there in front of me. Jarrett had tried to warn me. **There are monsters in Merritt, but they don't live in the sprawl.** I should've listened.

Someone knocked on my door, but the sound was too timid to be Grandma. "Hey, Virgil, it's Tripp. I'm coming in, so I hope you don't sleep naked."

The bedroom door creaked.

"Virgil?"

As much as I didn't want to see anyone, I doubted I could convince Tripp to leave me alone. I wouldn't have been surprised to learn Grandma had invited him over to lure me out of my room.

"In the closet."

Light spilled into my sanctuary. Tripp stood over me. "There's a joke somewhere in here."

"You're looking at it."

"Kind of sad for a joke."

I looked up. "What do you want, Tripp?"

Tripp was wearing a pair of board shorts and a tank top like he'd been on his way to the lake and had decided to stop off and try to cheer me up first. He sat down cross-legged outside the closet.

"Came to check on you. Astrid was gonna come, but I thought you might not appreciate being yelled at until you stopped moping."

"I'm not moping."

Tripp shrugged. I knew he was there to convince me not to drop out of *Clue*—we had a performance that night, a Sunday matinee, and then another run the following weekend—but I wasn't going to change my mind. The show would have to go on without me.

"You really moving back to Seattle?"

I answered with a grunt.

"When'd that happen?"

"Thursday. My mom called and told me she'd worked it out."

"And you honestly wanna go back? To the boyfriend that bailed on you and the friends who forgot you existed? I mean, don't get me wrong, you do what you gotta do, but it just seems like there ain't much left in Seattle worth returning to."

"Nothing in Seattle ever attacked me."

"Fair enough."

Tripp still hadn't brought up the show, and I kept hoping he'd leave. Instead, he sat with his fingers laced together, twiddling his thumbs. A minute or two passed, though it felt like an hour. "I ever tell you why my mom ain't around?"

"No, but it sounds like you're about to."

Tripp threw me a sharp warning glare that maybe joking about him while he was discussing his mom wasn't the smartest idea. "My mom never did like Merritt. Grew up here, but hated it all the same. Couldn't wait to leave. Then she met my dad and got pregnant with me.

"They got married 'cause that's what you do when you live in Merritt and you're pregnant and your family don't believe in having babies out of wedlock. My mom figured she'd grow into being a mother, but she never did take to it."

Tripp looked up and caught my eye. "This was all in a letter she left me. I ain't pretending I know what was going on in her head."

I didn't know what to say, so I said nothing.

"One day, while Dad was working, she decided she couldn't stick around no more. Packed a bag, wrote a letter, dropped me off at my dad's folks' house, and left. Never heard from her again. Since my grandparents died, it's just been me and Dad."

"I'm sorry, Tripp."

Tripp shrugged. "Don't be. I don't blame my mom. I'm not mad at her. Everyone deserves to be happy, and she couldn't be happy here."

"I know the feeling."

"Do you? Because I might be mistaken, but you looked pretty damn happy when we were up on that stage."

It looms over me, framed by the night and the stars and moss-choked oak trees.

"I was, but . . ." My voice cracked. "The monster did something to me in the sprawl. If I stay, I'll turn into a monster, too."

You're a monster, baby. Be a monster.

"Nah. You couldn't be a monster if you tried."

"You don't know me."

"I feel like I kinda do, but let's say you're right." Tripp crossed his arms over his chest. "You think running away's gonna keep you from turning into a monster?"

"I—"

"If the monster's inside you, won't it just tag along wherever you go?"

Tripp had voiced my own fears, but there had to be a way to ensure I left the monster in Merritt. When I moved back to Seattle, I wanted to be able to forget Merritt and everything in it.

"I'll figure it out," I said.

"I'm sure you will." Tripp paused, watching me. "There's nothing I can say to make you change your mind about quitting the play, is there?"

I shook my head.

"We both know it was Finn Duckett who ruined the show last night, though, right?"

I nodded.

Tripp let out a long, frustrated sigh. "Look, if you wanna let Finn and Jarrett and all the boys in Merritt like 'em keep you from doing something you love, I can't stop you. If you wanna let them run you out of town, I can't make you stay. But it seems like a real shame to let them win."

"Let them win?" I laughed wildly. "How the hell am I even supposed to play when the game is rigged?"

"Shoot, Virgil, the game's *always* rigged. But you keep playing anyway, otherwise you're just wasting everyone's time." Tripp patted my leg and stood. "Hope to see you at the show tonight."

SIXTY-ONE

OF COURSE FINN WAS THROWING A PARTY. HE'D RUINED THE
one thing I actually enjoyed about Merritt, and he needed
to celebrate. Reba sent me a message about it, but didn't say
why. Maybe she was asking for help. Maybe she thought I
could find proof of Finn's crimes that Chief Duran could use
to arrest him and keep her job. Regardless of Reba's reason,
I admired her. She had every cause to hate Finn and Jarrett,
but she kept putting on a smile and going to the parties so she
could try to keep other girls safe.

Hey, wanna see something cool?

I had no intention of going. Even if I captured video of
Finn dropping pills into someone's drink, I doubted Chief
Duran or Mayor Hart or anyone in Merritt could do any-
thing, because it wasn't only Finn. It was the entire culture

of silence in the town. It was the way Jarrett knew I'd been telling the truth about being attacked but had kept quiet. It was the way the veneer of respectability was more important to folks than people's actual safety. It was the way everyone in town was comfortable turning away so that they didn't have to see the rot eating away at Merritt's roots. Going to Finn's party, bringing him down, would change nothing and would probably only lead to more humiliation for me.

Words are just words. They don't mean nothing.

Not everyone stood by and watched, though. Reba was trying. Tripp had gone out of his way to support me. Chief Duran must've known what would happen if she questioned Finn, and she'd gone ahead with it anyway. Even Astrid fought Merritt's complacency in her own weird fashion. Doing nothing, if there was even a slim chance of changing things, would make me as complicit as the rest of them. But hadn't I endured enough?

Around suppertime, I started to get hungry. I hadn't eaten all day, and I'd only left my room to use the bathroom. I was surprised to find Grandma and Grandpa sitting with Dad at the kitchen table.

Dad looked up when I entered. "Good. I was just coming to get you." He looked exhausted. A layer of stubble made his cheeks appear sunken in, and his eyes were painted with the bruises of lost sleep.

"What for?" I looked around the kitchen. It was early, but Grandma usually had dinner started by now.

"If we hurry, I can get you to the theater in time for the show."

I folded my arms over my chest. "I'm not going."

"Don't let some clown in a costume make you act like a fool," Grandpa said. "In my day—"

"I don't care what they did in the Middle Ages, Grandpa." Anger was a whisper in my chest. A quiet growl.

"Watch your tone, Virgil." Grandma stared down her nose at me.

Dad cut through the noise. "You *are* going to the show. I can't force you to perform, but at the very least you owe it to the cast to support them from the audience."

"I don't owe anyone a damn thing." My voice rose. "Grandpa tells me to pretend what I'm feeling doesn't exist, like that ever helps anything. Grandma punishes me with never-ending chores when I'm the one who got hurt. And you just disappear."

"I've been working—"

My pain grew louder. "I needed you, Dad! I needed someone to tell me it wasn't my fault! That it was okay to hurt! That it was okay to be afraid! But you weren't here! You left me with them!" I pointed at Grandma and Grandpa. "And all they want is to sweep it under the rug because we can't have folks in Merritt talking about us, can we?"

I saw tears in Grandma's eyes. Pain etched across Dad's face. Even Grandpa had gone pale.

"You can't hide from what happened to you," Dad said.

"Of course I can't! Because the monster didn't stay in the sprawl. It lives in here." I poked my sternum. "And in here." I pointed to my head. "I'm the monster now! I'm the thing people should be afraid of! And it didn't have to be this way. All you had to do was listen! All you had to do was pretend to care!"

My voice filled the kitchen. It shook the walls and rattled the windows. I was an earthquake. A tornado descended from the sky with no objective but to destroy.

I waited for an apology. For one of them to admit they were sorry and tell me they wished they'd listened to me in the emergency room. But shame had rendered them mute. Or maybe it was fear. Of me. Of what I was and what I was becoming.

I stormed out of the house. I didn't know where I was going, but I needed to leave. The bicycle had a flat tire, but the Jetta was sitting in the driveway and Grandma usually left the keys in the ignition. So what if I didn't have my license?

ride, ride, ride, ride.

I got in the car, cranked the engine, and fled as fast as the Jetta would take me.

SIXTY-TWO

I SNUCK INTO THE THEATER AFTER THE SHOW HAD STARTED and sat in the back row. I was surprised by how many seats were filled. Most folks probably hoped for an opportunity to witness another disaster. Unfortunately for them, the only disaster on stage was Nash Galloway. Not that I could blame him. The kid had never expected he'd have to play the lead, and I think the only reason Mr. Hilliker chose him as my understudy was because we wore the same size suit.

Tripp was the star that night, but the other cast members each had an opportunity to shine. The hours and weeks of hard work had paid off. The show was hilarious, sometimes unintentionally so, and the audience seemed to genuinely enjoy themselves. I was ashamed that I was allowing fear to prevent me from being onstage that night. But, like my memories of

Luca, the theater was tainted for me now. My mind would forever draw a straight line from the stage to the sprawl.

I hated them for that. I hated Finn and Jarrett and everyone in Merritt who had laughed at my pain, who had called me a liar or told me I'd deserved what I'd gotten. I hated myself for the small part of me that believed them.

Near the end of the show, I crept out quietly to avoid being seen. I wasn't sure where to go, but I couldn't return home to face whatever wrath awaited me. Not yet.

"I knew you'd show up." Astrid was leaning against the railing by the stairs leading down from the theater doors. She'd dyed her hair neon orange, and was wearing all black.

"What're you doing here?"

"Came to see how you are. Your dad called my dad. He's worried about you." Astrid shoved her hands in her pockets. "Did you really steal a car?"

I rolled my eyes. "They bought the car for me, so it's not actually stealing, is it?"

"You don't have a license."

I ignored her and walked toward the parking lot. Astrid jogged to catch up.

"What's going on with you, Virgil? Why aren't you in there?"

I stopped by the Jetta. "You know why. And don't tell me I'll get over it with time. That's bullshit, and you know it."

Astrid pursed her lips. "Yeah, you're right. It's bullshit. What are you gonna do about it? Run home to Seattle? Spend the rest of your life sleeping in your closet?"

"Maybe."

"Well, that's——" Astrid stopped, took a breath, and said, "Fine. Look, you deal with your trauma however you need to. I'll support you no matter what."

"I don't need support. I need . . ." I stalled out, unsure what to say.

"What, Virgil?"

I shook my head. "Finn's having a party tonight, and I think I might go."

"Why the hell would you do that?"

"To confront Finn, maybe? Or talk to Jarrett. He knows something about what's happening to me."

Astrid breathed in, flaring her nostrils. "All right." She went around to the other side of the car.

"What're you doing?"

She looked at me like I'd asked why the sun rose in the morning and set in the evening. "Do I think going to Finn's party is a terrible, *terrible* idea? Yes. But I did just say I'd support you no matter what." She motioned at the door. "You gonna let me in?"

I unlocked the doors. When Astrid was buckled in beside me, I glanced at her. "Thanks."

"No one should have to face their monsters alone, Virgil."

"What if I'm the monster?"

Astrid shook her head. "You're not, but if you were, I'd still go with you."

SIXTY-THREE

THE CROWD GATHERED AT FINN DUCKETT'S HOUSE SATURDAY
night was barely half as large as it had been the night of the
homecoming dance, and I still felt boxed in, pressed on all
sides with no way to escape. But because there were fewer
people, I stood out more as I entered through the front door.
I could hear them thinking:

What's he doing here?

#MonsterBait!

Drink! Drink! Drink!

Astrid slipped her arm through mine and led me deeper
into the house. Those people didn't matter. What they
thought didn't matter. Every single one of them felt as alone
and scared as I did. They talked about me because so long
as they did, they could be assured no one was talking about

them. In high school, the best defense was a good offense.

Bass-heavy rap shakes the furniture, and the white boys in the living room shout along with the words—all the words—without the slightest hint of self-awareness.

I spotted Reba in the kitchen and asked Astrid to find Jarrett or Finn or anyone who knew where they were.

"Don't drink anything you unless you open it yourself," she said. "Actually, maybe you shouldn't drink anything at all."

"I won't."

We split up. Reba saw me and peeled away from the group she was talking to. Her hair was big and bouncy, and she looked relaxed in jean shorts and a sleeveless top. "You came."

The scabby lesions itched. I fought to not scratch them. "I want this to be over."

Reba's eyes softened. "You might be asking for too much."

She was probably right. The best-case scenario was that I found what Finn had drugged me with, turned it over to Chief Duran, and she was *maybe* able to use it to arrest him. I doubted the charges would stick, but it might convince him to quit while he was ahead. I didn't want to consider the worst-case scenario.

"Where are they, Reba?"

"Don't know." Reba made a show of looking around. "Finn was holding court in the kitchen earlier, but I haven't

seen him in a while. Jarrett went upstairs twenty minutes ago,
I think."

Wanna see something cool?

"What're you gonna do, Virgil?"

I shrugged. "Whatever I have to."

Reba grabbed my hand as I turned to leave. "Be careful."

If Jarrett was upstairs, there was a good chance Finn was
with him. **Sometimes he gets drunk and we fool around. It doesn't
mean nothing to him.**

I climbed the stairs **turning and twisting like a Tetris piece
to fit around the bodies blocking the way.** I stopped on the
second-floor landing and turned down the hall. I peeked into
each room until I found Finn's bedroom. I could tell it was
his by the one-note musky odor permeating the air.

The light of the moon shining through the window cast
shadows across the walls. Finn's football jersey was flung over
the back of a chair, and other clothes lay in piles on the carpet. His bed was unmade. Movement from the side caught
my eye, and I turned to find a large terrarium on top of Finn's
dresser. Inside, a brown-striped snake watched me through
the glass.

Keeping an eye on the snake, I searched Finn's drawers,
but I didn't find anything. I dug around Finn's closet and in
his desk. The most interesting object I found was an old dog
collar with a tag that had the name MUSTARD etched on it. I

was about to give up and leave when I decided to check the pockets of the jeans on the floor. I felt like a weirdo rifling through Finn's discarded clothes, but the feeling vanished when I turned up a pill bottle. The label said it was lorazepam for Finn Duckett, to be taken every eight to twelve hours as needed.

I used my phone to search for the medication. I learned it was a benzo used to treat anxiety before my battery died.

"What're you doing in here?" a voice hissed.

I slipped the pill bottle into my pocket before turning around. "Sorry, I was looking for the bathroom, and—"

It was Jarrett. **He shuts the door and flings himself at me.** "Finn'll flip out if he finds you going through his room." **Jarrett's smiling when I catch his eye.**

"Did you know?"

Jarrett shook his head, confused. "Know what?"

"That Finn was drugging girls at his parties? That he drugged me?"

"I . . ." Jarrett's shoulders collapsed. His chin dipped toward his chest. "You should get outta here."

"Was it Finn at the show last night? Is Finn the monster that attacked me? Was it him who attacked you, too?"

Tears rimmed Jarrett's eyes. "Did the boys knock your brains around too hard during flag football, Virgil? Finn will kill you. He'll kill *me*."

I dug in my pocket for the pill bottle and held it up. "I've got proof now. I'll show this to Chief Duran. She should be able to use it to stop Finn."

"You can't stop him." Terror saturated Jarrett's words.

"What is he?" I moved toward Jarrett. "What am I turning into?"

A buzz from his pocket startled Jarrett. He pulled out his phone. "I can't. I gotta go."

"Is it him? Where is he?"

Jarrett had already turned toward the door, but he paused. "He knows it was Reba who told you what he was up to. He's gonna teach her to keep her mouth shut."

"Finn's got Reba?!" I rushed Jarrett, but he knocked me back so hard I stumbled and fell.

"Leave it alone, Virgil. Leave the party, leave Merritt. You don't belong here." Jarrett took off and shut the door behind him.

SIXTY-FOUR

I SCRAMBLED TO MY FEET AND RAN DOWNSTAIRS TO SEARCH for Reba. I spied Chuck in the living room and tackled him, shoving him against the wall before he could react.

"Where's Finn? Where's Reba?"

Chuck tried to break away, but I drew on a well of strength I didn't know I possessed to keep him pinned. "What the hell are you on?"

I bared my teeth and spoke from my chest. "Tell me where they are or I will break your fucking jaw."

People gathered around us, the anticipation of a fight drawing them like bugs to a zapper.

"I don't know! Jesus, Knox!" This time he managed to force me back. Barely.

"Whoa, Virgil." Astrid pulled me away from Chuck and

led me outside where it was quieter. "What's going on?"

My mind was racing. "It's Finn. He's the monster. I found a bottle of lorazepam that he's been using to drug people, and then Jarrett said Finn knew it was Reba who ratted on him and he needed to teach her a lesson and—"

Astrid remained calm. "Did you call Chief Duran?"

"My phone's dead."

"Okay. I'll do it." Astrid reached for her phone and swore. "It's in the car. Stay here. I'll be right back." She ducked inside and disappeared.

The bass from the music thumped inside my skull, making it difficult to think. It was Finn the entire time. He was a monster. He was *the* monster. And it hadn't been enough to hurt me, he'd kept me close so he could taunt me. He'd gotten off on watching me suffer. And now he had Reba.

A howl from the direction of the sprawl chilled my blood. I took off running without giving it a moment's thought. I knew where Finn had taken Reba. I was drawn to the clearing where I'd been attacked. It whispered my name. I couldn't have pointed to its location on a map, but I could smell it. I could've closed my eyes and let my feet carry me there. My scars were the map and the poison in my blood a compass.

I slowed when I reached the clearing. "Reba? Finn?"

Only the wind replied.

I cupped my hands to my mouth. "Reba!"

This time I heard a rustling to my left. I spotted a body leaning against a tree, hands and feet bound, head covered. I ran to it and knelt. I yanked off the pillowcase.

"Finn?"

Moonlight filtered through the trees to illuminate Finn's terror. A gag in his mouth prevented him from screaming, but he tried.

I tore the gag free. "Where's Reba, you psycho?"

Finn bucked and jerked, but he was bound tight. "What the hell're you on about? Did you do this to me? I'm gonna kill you—"

I grabbed Finn's hair and yanked his head back. "Look, I know you've been drugging girls—I know you drugged me too—and I've got proof. Chief Duran's on the way, so you better tell me what you did to Reba. Now."

Finn's lip curled. "I didn't drug no one, and I'd never hurt Reba. *Never.*"

I pulled the pill bottle from my pocket and held it in front of his face.

"Where'd you get those?" Finn squirmed again. When he realized he couldn't shake loose, he slumped in defeat. "I got anxiety, okay? Those help keep me from freaking out. If you tell anyone, I swear to God I'll make you pay."

I tried to find the seams in Finn's explanation but couldn't. After seeing how the town treated Tripp's father, I could understand why Finn would keep his anxiety a secret. But something wasn't adding up. "Reba said after what happened to Skylar Montrose, you drugged her, and when she woke up in your bed the next morning, you threatened her. Said it wasn't safe for her."

Sweat rolled down Finn's forehead and cheeks. "I didn't threaten her. I did find her out of her skull on whatever she'd taken, but I didn't give it to her. I put her in my room so no one would mess with her." He shut his eyes and clenched his jaw. "You don't understand. I love that girl."

"But you know she told me about the pills and that I told Chief Duran. That's why you had the boys use me for tackling practice during PE and why you ruined the show last night."

"I told the boys to rough you up because you sent the chief after me for shit I didn't do." He shook his head. "But I didn't have nothing to do with last night."

"But Jarrett said—"

Finn's eyes went white and wild. "Is he here? Untie me. We gotta go." He held out his bound hands.

"Where were you the night of the homecoming dance when I was tied to the fence?"

Finn shook his hands in my face again, trying to convince me to untie him. When I refused, he scowled. "You know it was Dylan who tied you up. You heard him confess!"

"Jarrett said you were together that night. He told me you liked to fool around when you got drunk."

Finn spit. "I ain't no faggot!"

The word, the hard T, hit me like a fist. This time, I hit back.

"What the hell, Virgil?" Finn rubbed his jaw.

I crouched down so I was at eye level with Finn. It took all my patience not to choke an answer from him, but nothing was making sense. Jarrett had said Finn was the monster, but I didn't see a monster in front of me. "If you weren't with Jarrett that night, then where were you?"

Finn's lower lip trembled. "I . . ."

Don't tell no one about this, all right?

"Whatever you say stays between us," I said. "I swear it on my life."

All at once, Finn's remaining composure collapsed. "I just do what Jarrett says. I have to or else. You don't know what he's like." Finn was blubbering, making him difficult to understand. "He said Dylan had to confess, so I made sure he did. And sometimes I give him a couple of my pills, but I swear I didn't know what he was using them for!" Finn was trembling. "You gotta untie me. If he catches us out here, he'll kill us."

A howl rose nearby.

"Please!" Finn pleaded.

I wasn't sure what was going on, but Finn seemed genuinely

scared of Jarrett, and if he was telling the truth, then that meant Jarrett had been behind everything. Me being drugged and blacking out, the harassment, the play being ruined. My attack.

Blink

Blink

Blink

It meant Jarrett was the monster.

"If I free you, will you tell Chief Duran everything you told me?"

Finn's laughter sounded demented. "It won't matter. You can't do nothing."

"Will you tell her or not?"

The howl sounded closer. The hair on the back of my neck rose.

"Fine! I'll do whatever you want!"

My fingers were damp with sweat, and I struggled to work the knot loose. Mosquitoes swarmed and strands of hair kept getting in my face. I had almost freed Finn's hands when I felt shadows gather behind me. Finn stiffened, and what little color he'd had in his cheeks fled.

"Now, why would you wanna go and free Finn when I went through so much trouble trussing him up for you?"

Slowly, I rose to my feet and turned around. Jarrett stood in the clearing with his hands in his pockets, flashing his shiny, white teeth.

"You said Reba was out here."

Jarrett brushed my accusation aside. "Nah. Reba's napping in her truck."

So much had happened, and I hadn't had enough time to sort truth from fiction, but I was beginning to see more clearly. "Tripp had it right. You act like Finn's the one in charge, but it's you. You're pulling the strings."

Jarrett and I circled each other. He motioned at Finn with his chin. "Finn ain't had an original idea in his whole life. But he *is* a bully. I just point him where I need him to go."

"You drugged me."

One beer shouldn't do much.

"Yup."

"Twice?"

Drink! Drink! Drink!

Jarrett nodded.

"So you could get me out to the sprawl and attack me?"

Ain't nothing good in the sprawl at night.

Jarrett scoffed. "Attack you? I didn't attack you, Virgil. I *chose* you. I made you stronger. I set you free."

It lowers itself onto my back.

The smug certainty in his voice stoked my anger. "You terrorized me! I stopped eating! I had to sleep in my closet because it was the only place I felt remotely safe! My life has been hell since you attacked me!"

"Because you keep fighting what you're meant to be."

You're a monster, baby. Be a monster.

"I'm not like you."

Jarrett grinned. "Oh, I think you are."

I kept one eye on Jarrett and the other on Finn, who was still trying to untie himself. He'd gotten his hands loose, but he couldn't undo the knot holding his ankles together.

"Why me?" I asked. "Why not Finn or Chuck?"

"Because no one would miss you. No one would care if you were gone." Jarrett might have been ten feet away, but he was still able to wound me.

"My dad would miss me."

"Or maybe he'd be grateful he don't have to look after you no more. He could right his sinking ship of a life without you dragging him down."

Maybe if I'd had thicker skin, I wouldn't have needed so many stitches.

Jarrett was right. My dad would probably be better off without me.

"Your so-called friends and your boyfriend figured out real quick they didn't need you." Jarrett shrugged. "Folks around here would've gotten along fine, too."

Snot ran from my nose. "What are you?"

Jarrett spread his hands and his smile deepened. "What I was meant to be. I was chosen, same as I chose you. What I gave you is a gift if you'd just quit whining and embrace it." He pointed at Finn. "Think of all the shit he put you through."

"That was you!" I shouted.

"I told you I only pointed him in the right direction. He's still a bully, and he enjoyed making you miserable."

I turned to Finn and caught his eye. "Is it true?"

Finn's mouth moved silently.

"I brought him out here for you. Consider him another gift. Take all that anger and fear you been keeping inside you and make *Finn* feel it."

What did it matter anymore? The poison was already inside me. It's not like Finn wasn't guilty. He might not have drugged anyone and he might not have attacked me, but he'd enjoyed tormenting Dylan. I'd seen it on his face. And even if harassing me hadn't been his idea, he'd run with it and had gotten off on doing it.

"Come on. You'll like it."

I would. I knew I would. I could hurt Finn, make him bleed, and I would love it.

"Hey, wanna see something cool?" Jarrett's knees bent backward. His bones cracked. He fell to all fours and his back arched as spikes erupted from his spine. A layer of coarse hair grew to cover his body. His jaw popped open and elongated to make room for rows of razor sharp fangs. I knew that monster. I recognized it. I'd seen it the night I was attacked, I'd seen it looming over me in the theater, and I saw it every time I looked in the mirror.

"You're a monster, Virgil. Be a monster."

My body exploded with pain. I felt like my bones had been pulverized. I was being flayed alive. The excruciating agony I'd felt when I cut away the scabs was nothing compared to what I felt in the clearing. I collapsed to the mud. I didn't scream.

I howled.

Finn was shrieking. I could hear everything now. His heartbeat, the blood pulsing through his veins. I could smell his sweat, the urine soaking his shorts, the blood where the rope had chafed his wrists. And when I unclenched my eyes, the world was new. I wasn't in the dark anymore. The whole of the sprawl was lit with life, and Jarrett was the sun.

"Hurt him like he hurt you." Jarrett's voice was low, more animal than person.

I turned to Finn. He scrabbled backward. I raised my arm, my claws gleamed in the moonlight. It wasn't even a question of whether I wanted to hurt Finn. I did. I wanted to hurt him until he begged me to stop.

"I'm sorry! I'm sorry!" Finn cried, but I didn't care. It's too easy to be sorry after the damage has been done. Sorry could never undo the pain he'd caused.

"Virgil, don't."

I turned.

Tripp stood at the edge of the clearing, his hands out in front of him.

"This is what you are," Jarrett said.

"No, it ain't." Tripp edged closer. "And you know I'm right."

"You're a monster, Virgil."

"I know what you been through, but being in pain don't give you the right to inflict it on others."

"Be a monster."

I hesitated. I looked back at Finn, cowering beneath me.

"What'll this accomplish?" Tripp stepped cautiously toward me. "You hurt him and then he hurts someone else and they keep doing it to the next person forever?"

"Shut up!" Jarrett snarled. "Don't be weak, Virgil. Not like you were with Dylan."

My teeth were long, my claws were sharp, and my skin was thick. Nothing could ever hurt me again. This was the gift Jarrett had given me. Except, he hadn't given me anything. He'd stolen something from me the night he'd attacked me, and I wasn't sure if I could ever get it back. Not even by stealing it from Finn.

I lowered my hand.

Jarrett roared. He leapt at Tripp. Without thinking, I rammed into Jarrett before he could reach Tripp. I sank my teeth into his flesh. I raked his skin with my claws. If Jarrett wanted me to be a monster, then I would be the monster *he* feared at night.

Jarrett kicked me back. I slammed into a tree, shaking dead

branches loose. I was on my feet again, my reflexes faster in this form. I howled as Jarrett ran toward me. I lowered my shoulders and went under him, lifting him into the air and hurling him down to the mud. Jarrett elbowed me in the throat and crawled out from under me. I stumbled backward, trying to breathe.

Jarrett rose to his full height and returned his attention to Tripp. He howled and howled as his muscles bunched and he prepared to attack. I was too far away. Jarrett was going to kill him, and there was nothing I could do to stop it from happening.

Tripp flinched, covering his head with his arms.

A shot rang out. Jarrett yelped as his body hit the ground. In the confusion, I flung myself at him, but he was faster than me and regained his feet quickly. He snarled. A second shot took him in the shoulder. He fell to all fours and fled.

Chief Duran aimed her rifle in the direction Jarrett had run. I expected her to turn the gun on me, but she lowered the barrel and called for an ambulance on her radio.

I collapsed to the ground. My bones shattered, my claws and teeth retracted. My skin was thin and fragile again. The pain of being human was excruciating. I thought it was more than I could bear.

Tripp held my hand. "You're okay, Virgil. I got you."

I didn't scream.

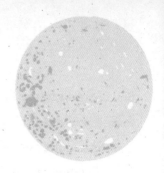

SIXTY-FIVE

I SAT IN TRIPP'S TRUCK IN THE PARKING LOT OF TASTY Cones. He'd given me a pair of sweatpants and an old shirt that had oil stains on it to wear. Chief Duran, seeing I wasn't hurt, had told Tripp to get me out of the sprawl while she took care of Finn. The only question Tripp had asked me since leaving was whether I wanted ice cream. I hadn't, but a brownie and some water sounded good, and Tripp had been happy to get them for me.

I'd turned on the radio to fill the silence while we sat in the parking lot, and I lost myself in a slow song I didn't recognize. My head was filled with thoughts about what happened, but I couldn't begin to parse them yet. I had a feeling I was going to be reckoning with everything that had occurred since I'd arrived in Merritt for a long time.

"Astrid says hey." Tripp dropped his phone into the cup holder and rested his hands on the wheel.

I'd forgotten about her, but she was the reason Tripp and Chief Duran had shown up and Finn was still alive. "Is she okay? How'd she get home?"

"Took the Jetta."

"But I have the keys."

Tripp laughed. "Apparently, she knows how to hot-wire a car."

"That figures."

"Yeah." Tripp was quiet again for a moment. Then he said, "Hey, you wouldn't mind if I asked your cousin out, would you?"

"I'm surprised you waited this long."

Tripp shrugged. "I didn't want to make things weird."

"Compared to what?"

"I guess you're right." Now that we'd started talking, Tripp didn't seem willing to stop. "Are you really leaving Merritt? Because I don't think you should. I made a list with a bunch of reasons why Merritt's better than Seattle—they're pretty much crap. Mostly, I just like having you around."

Everyone I love is here.

"I don't know. I thought I'd want to leave, but then I didn't, seeing as I had nothing to go back to. Now?" I shrugged. "How can I stay after what I did?"

It wasn't a question I meant for Tripp to answer, and thankfully he didn't try.

Chief Duran's squad car pulled into the space next to Tripp's truck, and Duran got out and knocked on the window.

"Heya, Chief," Tripp said.

Duran handed Tripp a folded twenty. "Mind getting me a diet soda? I gotta talk to Virgil."

Tripp nodded. "I'm keeping the change."

"Like hell you are."

I got out of the truck and met Duran around back. I expected her to throw cuffs on me and haul me to the station. Instead, she lowered the tailgate and motioned for me to sit.

"Finn Duckett's fine. A little bruised up, but nothing permanent."

Just because his bruises would fade didn't mean he wouldn't bear scars. "Did he say what happened?"

Duran chewed her lower lip. "Nothing that made sense. Astrid mentioned something about pills you found?"

I told Chief Duran about Finn's anxiety medication and how he claimed he'd given some to Jarrett. I told her about Dylan. I filled in the blanks, leaving out nothing. "What's going to happen to Finn?"

"Truthfully? Probably nothing. He had a prescription for the pills, and if it's like you say and he wasn't using them to drug other people, the most I can get him for is sharing them with Jarrett, and I can't even prove that."

Finn wasn't guilty of the crimes I'd suspected him of, but he was still a creep and a bully. "Did he, uh, say anything else?"

Duran shrugged. "Went on about a monster, but I doubt that story will make him any more popular around here than it made you."

"But you saw it. You shot it twice." I could still hear the sound of the monster's cry as the bullets tore into him.

"Well now," the chief said, "I fired my rifle at something. It was dark, so it's tough to say for sure. Might've been a bear."

"It was Jarrett Hart."

Duran frowned skeptically. "I don't know about that—"

"Jarrett was the monster. He was the one who attacked me." Saying it made it feel real.

"Well, when I find Mr. Hart, I'll ask him about it."

I folded my hands in my lap and looked down. "I'm like him now. I'm a monster, too."

Chief Duran brushed my concern aside. "You're nothing like him."

"I am! It's inside me! I almost killed Finn!"

Chief Duran lifted her left leg and hiked up the cuff of her pants. She had a nasty scar covering her calf. It looked like something had taken a huge bite out of the muscle. "Monster attacked me when I was fourteen. I was in the sprawl on a dare."

I couldn't believe it. "Why didn't you tell me? Everyone was saying I was crazy, but you knew the truth."

"Folks believe what they want. When I was attacked, everyone said it must've been a dog that bit me. Others said I shouldn't have been in the sprawl in the first place."

"You still could've told me."

Chief Duran at least had the sense to look a little guilty for keeping it from me. "Maybe it would've helped. Maybe it wouldn't. I did what I thought was right and tried to keep you safe."

I wondered if knowing would've changed anything. Probably not. "Wait, if you were attacked, then—"

Chief Duran let her pants leg fall. "You *could* turn into a monster, but you don't have to."

"But Jarrett—"

"Made a choice. You can make a different one."

Tripp returned with Chief Duran's soda and a cone with three scoops of chocolate ice cream for himself.

"You best get him home," Duran said to Tripp. "I got a feeling his daddy's anxious to have a word with him. Best not to make him wait."

"Yes, ma'am."

Tripp and I watched Chief Duran drive away. Tripp offered me his cone. I took it and worked on it for a while, enjoying the sweet, rich chocolate.

"Everything square with you and the chief?"

"Yeah. Finn's fine. She doesn't know what happened to Jarrett."

"She shot him good," Tripp said. "Maybe he's dead."

I doubted it, but I was sure we'd find out eventually. Something had been bugging me since we'd left the sprawl, and I finally worked up the courage to ask. "Hey, when you showed up in the sprawl, how'd you know it was me?"

Tripp furrowed his brow. "What do you mean?"

"I was a monster; Jarrett was a monster. How'd you know which was which?"

"There was a monster out there, all right, but that's how Jarrett's always looked."

"You didn't see a monster when you looked at me?"

Tripp shook his head. "Nope. I only saw you."

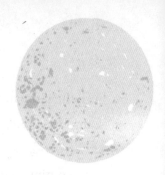

SIXTY-SIX

MR. HILLIKER THREW HIS HANDS IN THE AIR. "WILL SOMEONE please tell me why I do this to myself?"

Tripp looked up from where he was standing onstage reading his lines. "Because you love us and can't imagine a better way to spend your evenings?"

"Keep dreaming, Mr. Swafford. Also, if you're not off book by Monday, I'm giving your part to Virgil."

I held up my hands and backed away. "Don't look at me. I don't want Puck. I'm happy right where I am."

"Shakespeare's so hard, Hilly. Why's it gotta have all these words?" Tripp shook the script. "Why couldn't we have done something cool like *The Addams Family* musical for the spring show?"

Astrid, who was sitting on the stage beside Tripp, snorted.

"Because the football team needed new jerseys."

"Ding, ding, ding." Mr. Hilliker tapped his nose and then pointed at Astrid. "Ten points for Miss Knox."

Tripp continued to complain about the number of lines he had to memorize despite being given the best part in the show. If anyone was born to play the mischievous Puck, it was Tripp.

I still didn't know whether Mr. Hilliker or Tripp had convinced Astrid to audition, but she'd been cast as Helena, and she really was as talented as Hilliker had said.

The rest of the cast members were wary of me after I'd walked out on *Clue*, but Mr. Hilliker had cast me as Oberon and said all was forgiven. It wasn't forgotten, though. Not by me, at least. It took more effort than I wanted to admit to walk back onto the stage, but I did it, and it was a little less frightening each time.

When Mr. Hilliker cut us loose, I found Tripp and Astrid waiting for me by my bag. They had their heads together and were whispering. I wasn't sure if they were dating, but they spent a lot of time laughing at jokes I didn't understand.

Tripp looked up first. "Hey, we're gonna hang out at my house. Wanna come?"

"Tripp's dad found some old videos from when he was in high school. They put on a talent show—"

"Dad was in a country punk band called Young Bucks—"

I grimaced. "I didn't know country punk was an actual genre of music."

Tripp snorted. "It sure shouldn't be."

Astrid looked like she was going to explode. "That's not even the best part. He was in a talent show and apparently our dads were in it too, and they did this whole comedy routine."

"Wait, say that again?"

"Oh, you heard me. Our dads did a comedy show, and it was apparently so bad that Principal Dixon swore to never hold another talent show again, ending a fifty-year-old tradition."

I'd heard my dad's jokes before, so I had a good idea how bad it had been.

"Come on," Tripp said. "We'll stop for pizza on the way."

The thought of pizza made my stomach rumble. "I really want to, but I've got a meeting tonight."

Usually, when Tripp wanted me to do something, he'd keep at me, wearing me down until I agreed. But not this time.

"I'll tell you about it at lunch tomorrow," Astrid said.

Tripp clapped me on the back. "And it ain't like the tape's gonna self-destruct after we watch it."

I shouldered my backpack and started toward the exit. "I should get moving. Grandma's probably waiting."

Astrid laughed. "And we know how much Grandma hates to wait."

I waved goodbye to Mr. Hilliker on my way to the parking lot. Grandma was idling in the Jetta, and she got out to let me drive. I didn't bother asking when I'd be allowed to take my actual test—I'd turned sixteen two months earlier—because I knew Grandma would glare down her nose and ask me how long I thought I deserved to be punished for stealing the car. I'd accepted that I'd be ready when Grandma said I was.

"Seat belt," Grandma said.

"And check my mirrors."

A smile graced her lips. "Then get to it. I won't abide being tardy."

I pulled away from school and headed south. The community center wasn't far, but Grandma made me take a winding series of back roads so I could get more practice.

Grandma turned down the music. "Your dad's asked me to tell you not to make any plans this weekend."

"I don't know, Grandma. You know how full my social calendar is." I glanced at her and winked.

Grandma's frown was halfhearted. "He and your grandfather and Frankie have been putting up drywall at the house all week, and they're about done. He figures you should be able to start painting."

"They're really almost finished? And none of them have killed each other?"

"Working on the house has been good for those boys."

Grandma sounded happy with herself, seeing as it'd been her idea. Not buying the house—that'd been Dad—but saving money by having Grandpa and Frank help Dad renovate it. They'd gutted the old house. Torn it down to the frame and started over.

"I'll be there. So long as you help Dad pick out the paint. He's practically color-blind."

That made Grandma laugh. "Deal. And maybe next weekend we can talk about taking your driving test."

"Yes, ma'am."

I pulled up in front of the community center and switched places with Grandma.

She rolled down the window. "I'll be back in a couple hours."

"Thanks, Grandma."

It was going to take more than renovating a house to fix our family—Uncle Frank still drank too much, Grandpa still refused to talk about his feelings or anyone else's, and Dad still carried the weight of the world on his shoulders—but we were trying. Grandpa had started telling stories about when he was younger that he'd never spoken of before, Uncle Frank was trying out only drinking on the weekends, and Dad had come to a couple therapy sessions with me. It wasn't much, but if the tallest trees could grow from the smallest seeds, then maybe we could grow, too.

SIXTY-SEVEN

IN ONE OF THE MEETING ROOMS IN THE COMMUNITY CENTER,
chairs were arranged in a circle, but they were empty. Despite
Grandma worrying I'd be late, I had actually arrived ten minutes early. I stood at the folding table and poured myself a
plastic cup of soda and grabbed a chocolate cake doughnut. I
was reading a message from Deja filling me in on the gossip
in her life. I'd given her my new number and apologized for
being a dick. I hadn't reached out to Luca yet—I wasn't quite
ready for that—but Deja made sure, in her roundabout way,
that I knew he was okay. That maybe, one day, we would all
be okay.

"Don't hog the good ones." Chief Duran sidled up beside
me and tossed me a grin. She was wearing a pair of denim
shorts and a plaid shirt that hung loosely on her.

"Hey, Jodie."

Duran insisted I call her Jodie when we were in the community center. "Out there, I'm Merritt's chief of police," she'd said. "In here I'm just Jodie." The support group had been her idea. It was why she'd given me her card in the first place. She understood what I'd been through and thought I might benefit from being around others who'd been through it too. It would've been more helpful if she'd told me that outright, but better late than never.

"How's the play coming along?"

I swallowed a mouthful of doughnut. "It's not too bad."

"And your daddy?"

"You'd know better than me." I tried to hide my smirk.

Watching Duran's cheeks turn bright red was the highlight of my day. She coughed. "Well, it's not like we were out late. And it was only a movie." She stopped and frowned. "Your daddy and I are grown adults who don't have to explain ourselves to you."

"I know, but it's fun watching you squirm."

"Where's my Taser when I need it?"

The divorce was barely finalized, so it felt weird to think about my dad dating Chief Duran, but he seemed happier when she was around, so I kept my mouth shut.

Duran grabbed a doughnut and coffee, and we drifted toward a quieter corner.

"Any word on Jarrett?" I asked, keeping my voice low.

"Nothing."

It'd been over two months since that night in the sprawl. The scabby lesions had fallen off, leaving nothing but clear skin underneath. I still had the scars, though. Those would remain with me for the rest of my life.

"Mayor Hart's been hollering for my removal, but she ain't got the support of the council, so my job's safe for now."

"You mean people here actually like you?"

"Nah," Duran said. "They just dislike the mayor a skosh more."

When I finished laughing, I said, "Do you think he's still out there?"

"I don't know, Virgil. I went back to the sprawl, but I couldn't find a lick of blood."

For the first couple weeks I'd waited, terrified, for Jarrett to return. Every so often, I'd thought I'd heard a howl from the sprawl, but it was difficult to tell for sure. Eventually, I'd moved out of the closet and into my bed. I was still scared and I still had nightmares, but I'd survived. I refused to let my fear of Jarrett prevent me from living my life.

"Everyone's saying he ran away."

"He wouldn't be the first," Duran said.

Maybe she was right. Maybe he was still in the sprawl, prowling the swamp, trapped by the choices he'd made. Or maybe he wasn't trapped at all. Maybe Jarrett Hart was exactly where and *what* he wanted to be.

"Either way," Duran said. "We got warning signs posted around the sprawl now to keep folks from wandering where they shouldn't."

"I hope it's enough."

"Me too."

As more people filtered in, Duran and I found seats and joined the circle. I recognized some of the faces from previous meetings, but there were new ones, too.

"Mind if I sit here?" Finn Duckett motioned at the empty seat beside me.

That night in the sprawl had changed Finn. He'd quit the football team, he sat alone at lunch staring into space, his hair looked like he hadn't brushed it in weeks, and there were no more parties. I didn't know if the changes were permanent or if they were a temporary reaction to what he'd experienced. I suspected that the damage Jarrett had done to him went far deeper than anyone knew, and I could sympathize with Finn even if I didn't trust or like him.

Finn Duckett and I were never going to be friends. But I could still help him. I could tell him that I understood what he was going through. I could tell him that he wasn't to blame for what Jarrett did to him. I could tell him that trauma has gravity that will constantly try to tug you backward, but that if you keep moving forward, eventually its hold will weaken. Not completely. There remained moments when a noise triggered those memories and it was like I was in the sprawl again.

But I didn't have to be there alone, and, despite all Finn had done, neither did he.

I nodded. "Yeah, you can sit."

Finn settled in, his knees clasped together, his hands folded in his lap, and his shoulders bowed.

I didn't scream.

I looked around the room, smiled, and said, "Hey, my name's Virgil, and I was attacked by a monster."

ACKNOWLEDGMENTS

Howl is a deeply personal story, and I never would have had the courage to write it without an entire village of support. These last two years have been trying for the body and soul, and I'm so grateful to have these people in my life.

I am indebted to Katie Shea Boutillier for her unwavering support and enthusiasm, and to the entire team at Donald Maas, without whom I would be a mess.

To Liesa Abrams for letting me tell this story, and to Amanda Ramirez for helping me drag it across the finish line.

I am deeply grateful to every single person at Simon & Schuster for every little thing you do. It's you all who spin the straw into gold when no one is looking, and my books are infinitely better because of your hard work and dedication.

I would be lost without my friends and family to keep me anchored. Their love, and especially their patience, throughout the writing of *Howl* made it possible for me to tell this story.

Publishing books during this pandemic has been challenging, and I want to especially thank the librarians, teachers, and booksellers who keep finding inventive ways to get books into the hands of the readers who need them most.